# He wasn't meant for her.

He was meant for the throne. And the daemon king expected her to help him force Michael to accept it.

His lips were full and warm against hers. Lily didn't reject the intimacy of his moist, hot tongue. She opened for him. She eagerly met his tongue with flicks of her own. She pressed into his muscular body and his arms fell from her face to her back where they smoothed and molded her curves to fit him. She had been forced to take haven in hell, but she tasted heaven on Michael's lips. It was a paradise flavored with salty tears.

Her father had made a deal with the daemon king to protect her eighteen years ago and now Lily knew what price she would have to pay for his protection.

# BRIMSTONE
# PRINCE

## BARBARA J. HANCOCK

HarperCollins
PUBLISHERS
Since 1817

First Published in Great Britain 2017
By Mills & Boon, an imprint of HarperCollins*Publishers*
1 London Bridge Street, London, SE1 9GF

© 2017 Barbara J. Hancock

ISBN: 978-0-263-93022-1

89-1017

Our policy is to use papers that are natural, renewable and recyclable products and made from wood grown in sustainable forests. The logging and manufacturing processes conform to the legal environmental regulations of the country of origin.

Printed and bound in Spain
by CPI, Barcelona

**Barbara J. Hancock** lives in the foothills of the Blue Ridge Mountains where her daily walk takes her to the edge of the wilderness and back again. When Barbara isn't writing modern gothic romance that embraces the shadows with a unique blend of heat and heart, she can be found wrangling twin boys and spoiling her pets.

For Sam, Daisy, Brownie, Betsy and Punk. . .
the rescued dogs who have rescued me.

# Prologue

He was dying. The blade his former partner, Reynard, had plunged into his back had failed to kill him immediately, but the blow would be fatal all the same. Samuel Santiago could taste sulfur in the back of his parched throat. When he coughed up blood, it was tinged with black. He could feel the burn as the taint from the daemon blade Reynard had used spread its way through his veins.

Daemons weren't damned. But just like men, they could choose evil paths.

The cab dropped him at a familiar corner in Santa Fe. He was able to walk slowly but surely to the address of the apartment building where his young daughter would be sound asleep. He had a job to do. His Latin-scribed blade was wrapped in burlap and hidden beneath his coat. It and secrecy would be the gifts he'd leave Lily and her mother, Sophia. He'd been wise to forge a deal that would protect her and her mother from Reynard's treachery, even if he hadn't been able to protect himself.

It took forever for the elevator to respond to the summons of the glowing button that wavered in and out of focus as he waited. The Rogue daemons Reynard had sold his soul to were blackened by the desire to rule the hell dimension and then conquer heaven. They wanted to reclaim the paradise Lucifer had rebelliously left. Hell was embroiled in revolution. Loyalists against Rogues. But the Rogues couldn't be stopped by Lucifer's Army alone. At one time, Samuel had hunted all daemons, but he'd learned that Loyalists had no quarrel with humans. It was the Rogues who desired to enslave and destroy. The daemon king needed help from humans to defeat the Rogues. That fact might save Lily's life.

Rogues would hunt him down. He looked over his shoulder when a random noise from a nearby apartment made him feel as if they were already behind him preparing to pounce.

The hall was empty. Somewhere in the distance a small dog barked.

Samuel stumbled into the elevator. He jabbed at the button to close the door as if the hounds of hell snapped at his feet. In a way, they did. He didn't sigh in relief when the door closed. He leaned against the elevator's humming wall, tense and watchful, as it rose up to the tallest floor. It was almost midnight. They would be sleeping. He didn't have much time. He couldn't see them. He couldn't say goodbye. He couldn't risk staying longer than it would take to place the wrapped sword on the mantel.

Lily had his blood. For better or worse. He supposed that was a gift he would leave her, too, although it often seemed a curse. His affinity for daemons had led him to join with Reynard in hunting them. It was Reynard's joy in the hunt, his increased ruthlessness, that had led Samuel to question his gift. He was drawn to daemons and they were drawn to him, but in the end he had decided he was supposed to be the bridge between humanity and daemons, not their executioner.

That realization had come too late.

The Rogues were evil because they sought power and dominion over the entire universe. Loyalists only wanted to build an autonomous life for themselves. Lucifer didn't fall from heaven. He leaped. Others had followed him. His death at the hands of Rogues had begun the revolution.

Samuel quietly let himself into the apartment. He left his key and the sword on the mantel near the kachina dolls his wife had arranged above the fireplace. The colorful Hopi statues had caught his eye many years ago, even before he'd fallen in love with the woman who carved them. She'd been at a stall in a Native American market. He'd paused, drawn to a spiritual song from the dolls that only his affinity could hear. She would know when she found the sword that it was a farewell. They had only ever had stolen moments anyway. His life wasn't his own. He hadn't been free to settle down and live with the family he loved.

Maybe Sophia would understand the deal he'd had to make to protect Lily.

An indistinct murmur was his undoing. His resolve had been firm. Get in. Get out. But he heard a rustle and murmur and he was drawn to his daughter's bedroom. He didn't go in. He only peeked from the door. She had murmured in her sleep. He watched as his three-year-old child snuggled deeper into her pillow. The softest whimper reached his ears. Samuel had to reach for the doorframe to hold himself in place rather than go to her.

Was it a nightmare, or did she sense his presence and his pain? Her mother might understand the desperate measures he'd been driven to take, but would Lily?

He watched as soft moonlight from the window illuminated her hand. Her tiny fist opened to reveal a kachina doll that had been grasped in her fingers. A frisson of dread shivered down his spine when he saw it was the doll that had been carved in the shape of a warrior angel. The wings down its back had been painted black long ago by one of Sophia's Hopi ancestors. Unlike the other kachina dolls that were traditionally carved with indistinct features and masks with rough edges and curves, the warrior angel was like a Renaissance sculpture in miniature form, but crafted of wood instead of stone.

Had a Hopi priest seen his daughter's future in some prophetic dream long, long ago?

He forced himself to turn away. He spared only a glance for the bedroom a little farther down the hall. Sophia had been a softness to his otherwise jagged life. It had been weakness to love her. But it was strength to leave her now. The wound on his back screamed for surcease that would never come. He had to walk away. He was a deadly magnet on an ordinary day. Injured and weak, he was an irresistible lure to Rogues or anyone with Brimstone in their blood.

In time, Lily would be a magnet as well. That's why he'd been forced to ask for help.

This time as he made his way to the street, the building around him was utterly silent. No creature stirred. The simple operation of the elevator doors sounded like a shriek. Finally, he made it to the street where he remained on foot. He headed to the bus station. One dogged step after another. If anyone saw him, they would have assumed he was a drunken vagrant. He planned to get on a bus and ride as far away as he could from his precious family before he fell.

He could only hope and pray that the daemon deal he'd made would protect Lily once he was gone.

# Chapter 1

When the daemon stepped from the shadows, the darkness seemed to cling to his tall, lean form, separating from the black leather of his jacket and the faded denim of his jeans reluctantly. For long seconds, his angular face and muscled shoulders seemed to be draped in a dark wing-like mantle. Lily Santiago's breath caught in her lungs as familiarity punched her in the gut until he came forward another step.

She blinked as he moved, and she exhaled a long shaky breath as the shadows retreated to the corner of the kiva where they belonged. The daemon didn't have wings. *But he should*, her senses told her. *He should*. An impossible familiarity began to foment in her brain. *She'd seen this daemon before*.

The underground Hopi chamber was a circular room with a packed earthen floor and stacked stone walls. There was only one opening to the sky where an old wooden ladder would have leaned. She'd used a nylon climbing rope to descend the ten feet. The abandoned chamber would have been dark at midday—at midnight only her lantern and the occasional flash of the daemon's nightglow eyes as they refracted the low light held back the night. The firepit on the other side of the sipapu had been cold for a century or more. She rose slowly from her crouched position near the kachina dolls she had carefully placed for the ceremony she was about to invoke. She gripped a short silver flute in one clenched fist.

"Move away from the edge," the daemon ordered.

Lily had heard daemons speak before, yet none of their voices had been so deep and melodic. Her heart thrummed in response to the mellow drawl of his vowels and the low pitch of his husky tone. He wore a guitar on his back, she noted. The silver-studded strap crossed his broad chest and she could see the neck of the instrument behind his right shoulder.

If his voice caused gooseflesh to rise on her bare arms, it was the Brimstone of his blood that forged a deeper reaction. Her stomach coiled. Her muscles tightened. Her skin flushed and her breath, once caught, now came too quickly between parched, parted lips. She was used to being buffered against the Brimstone burn. She'd known she would have to be much stronger outside the palace walls.

Her affinity for daemons was her greatest strength and her greatest potential weakness. She could summon them, but she couldn't control them. Her control was limited to the elemental spirits that dwelled in the kachina dolls her mother had carved. Those she could summon *and* control.

But daemons were different.

No one could control Brimstone's burn, not even the daemon whose veins flowed with the lava of hell. Her affinity made her vulnerable, so she stood and waited for the inevitable fight.

"I promised my mother when she died that I would seal every sipapu in New Mexico with the skills she had taught me," Lily said. It was a warning. She wasn't here to fight, but neither would she be swayed from her mission.

The sipapu was a hole at the center of the kiva. It was thought by many to be a symbolic opening to the lower world. Hopi people believed that their ancestors had risen up from such places to become a part of this world. In most kivas, the hole was only a few inches deep. In this unexplored, undiscovered kiva she had found with the direction of her affinity and her mother's kachina dolls, the sipapu's floor was so deep that it wasn't revealed by her lantern's light, and a cool waft of air rose up to chill the whole chamber.

Lily set her teeth, hardened her jaw and dug her heels into the hard-packed desert earth that had been carved into a religious chamber hundreds of years ago. She needed to seal the portal to the lower world. Then she needed to pretend she had discovered the kiva and the surrounding ruin of a small unknown Hopi pueblo on an innocent hike so that archaeologists and Native historians could come in and excavate the site.

"A noble promise, but I bet you've met resistance along the way," the daemon replied.

He didn't hold a weapon. But he was obviously big and powerful. Not to mention the whole daemons-being-nearly-immortal thing. At five foot four inches, and one hundred ten pounds, she was in trouble. She had no one to rely on for protection but herself. Not anymore.

The daemon edged closer. The kiva chamber was a large circular room. She was separated from the approaching daemon by the fire pit and the sipapu, but the sipapu was only about a foot in diameter and he'd already made his way around the bigger indention of the pit that was still blackened by ancient fire.

"I have a sacred duty. I handle resistance as it comes. I've sealed every single sipapu I've discovered," Lily warned.

Her family tree could be traced to ancient Aztecs on one side and to Spanish settlers on the other, but it had always been rooted by one simple thing: standing against evil. There was irony in that, considering where she'd spent the last fifteen years, but she had no time to let that slow her down.

The daemon didn't flinch or falter when she refused to move away from the portal. He continued to approach. Slowly, carefully, as if he were giving her time to get used to his presence. The pleasure of his voice spread warmth to other places already warmed by his Brimstone burn. The whole chamber had gone from chilled to heated. Her gooseflesh was gone. Her flush had deepened. The perspiration had evaporated from her skin. She'd been warned to guard against daemon persuasiveness. Her powerful affinity wouldn't protect her from it. On the contrary, it made her more susceptible than most.

"The other daemons who tried to stop you were Rogues. They want as many pathways to the hell dimension as possible to remain open as they resist the rule of the rightful daemon king," the daemon said in a soft, reasonable voice, as if he was pacifying a madwoman.

Who was he and how did he know these things?

Considering her free hand had gone to the hilt of a hidden sword at her back, his tone was probably justified. She could feel the grimace that stretched her face taut as she prepared to battle. She was no warrior, but the small elemental spirit dolls at her feet weren't her only weapon. The flute and the dolls helped her channel her affinity to call on the elemental spirits. In days long past, she would have been deemed a priestess. Her mother had trained her in the old Hopi ways…*but the sword had come from her father.*

"My mother gave me a job to do and the sacred tools with which to do it. My father gave me this," Lily said. The rasp of steel against its leather scabbard sounded loud in the underground room.

Perhaps the daemon could see the Latin prayers scribed

into the blade even by lantern light, but if he could he didn't retreat. He came toward her one more step. Then two.

"And what makes you aware of the daemon king's wishes?" Lily asked as she brought her father's blade down in a practiced move that prepared for the daemon's attack.

The whole while she took in the daemon's appearance. The absence of wings didn't matter. Her mother had given her a gift along with her training and her tools. It was nestled in the backpack that had held all the kachina dolls that were now arranged near the sipapu. Hundreds of years ago one of her ancestors had carved an unusual kachina doll. It had been passed down for generations. From the time the daemon had stepped from the shadows, she'd recognized the sharp angle of his jaw and the full swell of his lips. She recognized the thickness of his wavy, shoulder-length hair swept by the desert winds. His broad shoulders, the set of his eyes and the patrician nose were all familiar.

The kachina doll had stiff wings that had been carved in a mantle down its back and painted black. This daemon had no wings. That initial illusion had only been created by shadows. But his fallen angel's voice made the idea of wings possible every time he spoke.

*He couldn't be her warrior angel.*

Her hand gripped the hilt of her sword to stop the trembling in her wrists and fingers. This couldn't be her family's kachina come to life. He was no nature spirit or ancestor who had come to help her. When he moved, she could see the glint of Brimstone glow in his eyes. She could feel the heat of his blood. She refused to let fire and familiarity influence her actions.

"The daemon king doesn't rely on sipapu portals. He has his own pathways he protects," the daemon explained. "But it isn't safe for a human to meddle in these matters."

He had paused, but it didn't feel like a reprieve. It felt like he was waiting for an opportunity to pounce.

"Are you his servant then? And you've come to help me?" Lily asked.

Likeness to her family's oldest treasure aside, she still held the sword at the ready. Over the long, hot months of the strangest summer job any runaway had ever taken on, she'd learned to guard against daemon deception. They couldn't be trusted. It wasn't her Hopi mother who had told her that the devil had a silver tongue. That bit of wisdom had come from her guardian himself.

"No. I'm not his servant. I'm his adopted grandson," the daemon said. "My name is Michael D'Arcy Turov."

Her sword didn't waver, but the air did catch in her lungs again in a hiccup of surprise. Her guardian's heir wasn't here to hurt her. She'd never been allowed to meet him, but she'd known about him from afar. The guitar on his back should have given his identity way, but her shock over his features had distracted her.

Michael Turov was a living replica of her warrior angel, but he was also the Brimstone prince. He was the talk of the hell dimension and had been since it had become common knowledge that he didn't want the throne.

The unusual kachina her Hopi family had once worshipped, then treasured for centuries, was the perfect likeness of a daemon prince. She wondered why her guardian, the daemon king, had never deemed it necessary to warn her. Lily was distracted by the revelation only long enough to blink in surprise, but that was long enough. The daemon leaped. His body slammed into hers and her planted feet slid backward with the force of his superior weight and strength. His momentum pushed her back from the portal's edge, and his hands over hers on the hilt of her sword kept her from using it in defense.

It didn't matter. She couldn't have attacked him anyway. Not even if she hadn't realized he was trying to protect her from the sipapu's edge. She'd always slept with the beautiful kachina beneath her pillow. When Michael Turov pressed her back against the chamber's earthen wall so that his body was between her and the open sipapu, the shock of his Brimstone heat didn't stop her from tracing the familiar features of his face with her gaze. It was almost too sharply cut to be traditionally handsome. There was something inhuman in the perfectly pronounced bone structure beneath his skin.

This daemon prince's face was the reason she'd been drawn to kachinas in the first place.

Face-to-face with a living replica of the unusual doll, her hand twitched against the hilt of the sword. Her mother had been a carver, but Lily suddenly ached to be an artist. Could she re-create the angles of his cheeks and jaw? Could she capture in wood the ferocity of his expression while still creating the slight softness of his lips? She noted his mouth seemed to tilt on one side as if he laughed at the world, or himself, or some unseen joy in the shadows that gamboled for his attention alone.

"Grim, we're about to have some unsavory visitors. You might want to come out here and give us a hand," Michael said. "Or a paw."

His gaze swept over her face as he spoke as if *he* was the sculptor who would try to capture the blend of Hopi and Spanish that came together to create her brown eyes, dramatic brows and dark hair. Her hair had loosened when she hit the wall. It had fallen around her face in a black waterfall of straight silky chunks.

"Your hair reflects the light," Michael said.

Maybe it was a daemon prince thing to say, but it wasn't a usual thing for her to hear. She'd been kept in isolation her whole life. The wonder in his tone and the admiration in his eyes gave her pause. For the first time, her grip loosened beneath his fingers on the hilt of her sword.

"Who is Grim?" Lily asked.

Michael turned his face toward the shadows where he'd appeared earlier and his move—when she dragged her gaze from the razor's edge of his lean jaw—allowed her to see a monstrous doglike beast swirl into being as ashy embers coalesced into a canine shape. A snarling maw of snow-white teeth was the first part to solidify, followed by a muscular form surrounded by shifting fur that seemed more smoke than hair at the ends.

Lily's nose twitched as the pleasant scent of wood smoke filled the air around them. It was a scent her body instinctively associated with hearth and home—because of the slight sulfuric burn, not in spite of it. She'd found a haven in hell with her mother as a child. They'd created a home in one wing of an immense Gothic palace others would have feared.

Her hands tightened again and she tried to pull from the daemon's grip, but he held fast. His hands were big and warm around hers. She glanced down. The indentations his guitar strings had caused in the tips of his fingers were slightly rough against her skin.

"Grim is a friend. And we're going to need his help," he warned.

She stilled and looked up into Michael Turov's gaze. In this position, the glint was gone and all she saw were sincere hazel irises rimmed with a darker chocolate as he met her gaze without blinking. But movement behind him kept her from becoming mesmerized. Smoke poured up from the hole in the ground. The sipapu now seemed like a slumbering volcano that had wakened. The wood smoke scent was suddenly tainted by a much stronger sulfuric stench.

"Let us take the lead," Michael said. "Rogues give no quarter and they have particular reason to want me dead."

"Oh, so you came to make it worse then?" Lily joked. "Don't let my hesitancy to lop off your head fool you. I don't need anyone to take the lead. Not a prince or a…" She failed to be able to label the creature across from them that snarled and snapped at the sulfuric smoke.

"Hellhound," Michael supplied. "Grim is my hellhound."

"Of course he is," Lily replied.

A fissure had begun to open up from the sipapu. She gasped, more concerned at the destruction of the kiva than she was over what the fissure signified…until daemons began to climb from the widening portal.

"Complete your ritual," Michael yelled over the grinding of crumbling earth.

But frankly, she was too busy deflecting the daemon blade that aimed for the back of Michael's neck. He fell back as her sword clashed, metal against metal, and sparks flew. Several Rogues had climbed from the sipapu, but several more had come from the shadows and the smoke. Half a dozen daemons attacked. Michael fought with his bare hands and his hellhound's crushing bite. She fought alongside them until she realized they didn't need her help. For now. The widening fissure was the threat if it allowed more of the Rogue daemons to join in the fray.

Her traditional kachinas were already in place. She raised the flute to her lips and called the spirits to life with the song her mother had taught her. It didn't matter that her mother had considered it nothing but tradition and a comfort during the difficult times following her father's death. Lily's affinity brought the old ways to life. The song came from her flute, but it also came from the affinity in her heart and the Hopi blood in her veins. She could feel Michael's gaze on her as she moved. She'd never done the ritual with an audience. For the first time, distraction threatened. She struggled to block the daemon prince from her mind, but hadn't he somehow always been there? The hidden kachina in her backpack was one of her earliest memories. It had fascinated her forever. While her mother's kachinas were masked and carved with blocked shapes, the one with wings had been rendered with meticulously lifelike features. She hadn't known how meticulously until moments ago when Michael Turov had walked into the kiva.

The earth calmed as she played. The fissure shrank, and then closed. The sipapu became filled in to the point of being a shallow, symbolic hole the size of a melon. There was a pause as the kachina spirits quieted and the universe accepted her interference. She'd run away from her refuge in hell in just this way by widening a sipapu portal with the kachinas' help. Even though it had been three months, she still couldn't believe that the daemon king hadn't retrieved her.

In the lantern's glow, motes of ancient desert dust hung in the air before they began to float and fall again.

Lily fell, too, her energy completely spent. But instead of the hard-packed soil she expected, her body was caught by strong, muscular arms.

Michael quickly carried his slight burden up out of the earth. Grim helped without being asked. Walking a short distance ahead, he led Michael and the woman he carried through pathways only he could find. Michael was used to walking through the chill of an otherworldly portal. He was used to dematerializing in one place and reappearing in another. He laid the woman on a smooth patch of ground and shrugged out of his jacket to roll it up and cushion her head. Then he forced himself away to start a fire beneath the rising moon and sleepy stars winking awake in the night sky. The desert sky wasn't black. It was a midnight blue so deep and lush it reminded him of velvet. But the night would grow cold and the young woman, no matter how ferociously she'd fought, didn't have Brimstone in her blood to keep her warm.

The fire kindled easily while she murmured in her sleep.

He approached her after the fire was built. She drew him with a powerful pull—like the moon to his sea—and damned if he didn't feel like waves crested and crashed inside of his chest with every heartbeat. She didn't seem hurt, only drained. Sleep was probably what she needed to recover. She was petite, but athletic, and obviously used to fighting daemons. He touched her face when a particularly loud whimper escaped from her rosy lips. It was a mistake. The scars that tracked along his arms flared to life with a red glow. The sudden ignition startled him into stumbling backwards to cradle his tingling fingers against his chest.

The tempest in his chest was shocked into stillness.

Her affinity was stronger than any he'd felt before. And it called the Brimstone in his blood to roaring life in spite of a lifetime of practice at tamping it down. After that touch, he took a seat well away from the young woman. He put the fire between them. Not because the flare had hurt him. It hadn't.

*It had been a pure pleasurable jolt of heat akin to desire.*

Where had this woman gotten an affinity so strong that it tempted him to loose his Brimstone burn? He had inherited affinity from his own mother, Victoria D'Arcy. Affinity for daemons had been passed to his grandmother, Elizabeth, by a monk named Samuel. She had passed it to her daughters and, in turn, it had come to him. But each passing had diluted the affinity's strength.

He was used to its almost musical call. He wasn't used to this. The woman's affinity was nearly pure and so powerful that he could feel it calling the Brimstone blood he'd inherited from his biological father even though he had a lifetime of experience guarding against it.

He hadn't trusted his daemon blood since it had almost killed him as a child.

He hunted daemons. He refused to accept that he was nearly one himself. But hunting Rogue daemons wasn't the only family business and the daemon king wasn't their only concern.

The Turov estate was one of the largest in Sonoma, California with thousands of acres of vines. His stepfather had established it right after the Russian Revolution when he'd brought his parents to America and he'd had many years to bring it to lush, thriving success.

Brimstone wasn't all bad. It had extended Adam Turov's life and allowed him to help Michael's mother after Michael's real father had died. Turov had helped Victoria defeat the Order of Samuel when they'd kidnapped Michael as a small child. Then, Turov had married Victoria and raised Michael as his own.

The Brimstone in Michael's blood had almost killed him when it had first flamed high during his rescue. He'd never trusted it since.

He reached for his guitar to keep himself from standing and going to the woman again. Her restless murmurs drew him as much as her affinity. She was distressed. What worried this amazing woman who had used her affinity and her dolls to call Fire, Water, Wind and Earth to defeat the Rogues that stalked her? Were more daemons on their way? He could see Grim silhouetted on a rise just outside of the fire's light. The hellhound was alert and watching for trouble, but Michael still felt every protective instinct he possessed on high alert as well.

The fire's glow was gentle in comparison to the glare that had come from his scars. It helped to filter the woman's murmurs and sounds through a soft haze of smoke. By all accounts, his grandmother had been a remarkable woman, too. She'd loved the daemon king before he was a king. He'd loved her as well. So much so that he'd "adopted" her human children after her death. Unfortunately, his devotion to the D'Arcy family shadowed Michael's future.

And now it would shadow this woman's future as well.

He was in the fight of his life against more than the Brimstone in his veins. He fought against the daemon king's expectations. Ezekiel had proclaimed Michael the heir to the throne of hell. But Michael's scars were a constant reminder why that could never happen. They didn't glow anymore. He'd succeeded in extinguishing the flare. He always would. He refused to acknowledge his daemon heritage, now or ever. He'd seen the harm his own blood could do. He'd grown up knowing that daemons couldn't be trusted. He refused to accept a position that might make it impossible for him to protect others from the power in his blood.

His guitar came to life in his hands as the elements had come to life for the woman. She'd used a flute and the dolls to channel her affinity. He used the guitar's strings. But he wasn't calling anything. He played to drown out her affinity's call. He played to control the Brimstone in his veins. If he also soothed her distress, so be it. He would give her peace before he shattered her peace completely.

Because in spite of needing to keep his distance from the woman who obviously tempted his burn, he needed her help to find the one thing his "grandfather" the daemon king wanted more than Michael—Lucifer's wings.

* * *

Guitar music woke her. Classical Spanish guitar expertly played and accompanied by flawless singing. It was a song about a desert flower she'd heard before, but for some reason the lyrics romanticizing a woman as a beautiful, hardy bloom made her flush. She hadn't told him her name. If he asked now she might say "Jane." Anything but allow him to see that the sound of her name from his lips as he sang caused a rush of response she'd never felt before.

"You have a powerful gift. I've never seen anything like that…and I've seen more than most." He stopped singing to speak, but he continued to play.

She had blinked open her eyes and lifted her torso from the ground. From her propped position, she could see his fingers deftly flying over the strings. The calluses she'd felt on each digit were explained by his swift, experienced manipulations. He wasn't a casual player. He played often and long, enough to cause permanent ridges. He plucked, strummed and slid his hand on the neck as easily as another man would breathe.

The guitar was a rockabilly beauty complete with inlaid turquoise and silver panels. The color was brilliant against his black t-shirt and faded denim.

Nearby, a tiny fire crackled. It had been built with the kind of foraging only an experienced desert camper could accomplish—brush, twigs, dung—all patiently scavenged from the barren landscape. The fire held back the night with a soft wavering circle of light, which only served to make the vast expanse of blue-black sky above them seem limitless and cold. There, bright diamond bits of stars twinkled while down below a daemon prince bent over his strings and the flash of glimmering polished maple. A vintage motorcycle was parked near the outer reaches of the light. Farther out still, her dusty SUV was exactly where she'd left it before night fell.

She didn't believe in coincidence. A ward of the daemon king learned early and well to notice every tweak, every manipulation to the universe around them. The daemon king hadn't retrieved her and now his grandson appeared. What trickery was this?

"The kachinas. I need to pack them properly," Lily said, suddenly appalled that she hadn't thought of the sacred dolls right away. She was light-headed, but she rose to her feet and made for the pack that had been placed near the fire.

"Easy does it. You went down hard," the daemon prince said. Michael. His name was Michael. She'd been sheltered in a secluded wing of the palace. Kept away from others because of her affinity. But she knew all the D'Arcy family by name. They were the daemon king's beloveds and Michael's sudden appearance in her life was cause for concern. He continued to play his guitar, but he'd tensed. He watched her as if she might faint into the fire.

"I'm fine. Summoning takes a lot of energy. Like a marathon. I could run ten more miles if I had to. Just need carbs and water," Lily said.

She rummaged through her bag for a protein bar and a bottle of water. As she ate and hydrated, she repacked the dolls in their burlap wraps. She was relieved to note that Michael had been careful with the kachinas. None were busted or broken. He'd also placed her flute back in its velveteen pouch. The special kachina that bore a remarkable likeness to the daemon prince was still wrapped and undisturbed.

Her relief lasted only as long as it took for her to realize her father's sword was missing. It hadn't been returned to the sheath that rested between her shoulder blades beneath her shirt and it wasn't in the specially altered side pocket of her backpack that ran the length of the bag. Only the top of the hilt showed when it was in her backpack, but she was used to the weight and balance of the bag when the sword was hidden within it. Her father's sword was gone.

Slowly, Lily stood. The pack dropped at her feet as she flexed her arms out at her sides. The daemon prince's fingers stilled on his strings. He watched her rise. He met her accusing gaze. The flickering fire made mysteries of his dark-rimmed eyes. She couldn't read them or guess what his intentions might be.

Daemons couldn't be trusted. Surely, a daemon prince least of all.

"I need your help. Normally, I rely on Grim to guide me to Rogues over pathways that aren't fully a part of this world. But he's a hellhound and he can't guide me to where I need to go this time," Michael said.

He shifted to place his guitar on the ground beside him and then rose so gracefully that he seemed to be standing before her between one blink and the next. His movements echoed with the grace of the rhythm and blues he played as did his voice. But there was another quality to his voice—a smokiness that hinted at pain. Lily swallowed because his grace and his pain were alluring. She had heard of him. Of course she had. She knew he was the heir to the throne of hell and she knew he wasn't happy about it. She was suddenly afraid that she knew why the daemon king had allowed her to run away. The music of this daemon prince was as seductive as the fire in his veins. Her affinity must have brought him to her. Had the daemon king planned it that way?

"I've been searching for a guide. Someone who can help me retrieve my grandfather's crown. It isn't an actual crown, but a symbol of his right to rule the hell dimension.

He sacrificed it years ago to save my father's life. It's my duty to get it—them—back," Michael said.

"Them?" Lily asked. It was extremely dangerous to have a conversation with a daemon, but she had no choice. She wasn't leaving without her father's sword. She firmed her spine as if he was coming at her with weapons instead of words. *Because daemons used words as weapons.*

He'd stepped closer and closer to her as he spoke. His face bathed in the light from the dancing flames was hypnotic in its familiarity and the startling newness of seeing it animated, alive, life-size and so achingly appealing.

"Lucifer's wings. When Rogues like the ones that just attacked us revolted, they cut them from his dead body and coated them in molten bronze. They hung above the Rogue Council until the council was defeated and driven from hell by my grandfather. He's the king now. The wings rightfully belong to him," Michael explained. "The only problem is that they're currently in heaven."

"Bronzed wings singed black by Brimstone," Lily whispered. She'd seen them once or twice or a million times as a child, but the daemon king, Ezekiel, looked nothing like her doll. A daemon who looked exactly like her kachina searching for black wings caused an eerie awareness of destiny to prickle along her skin.

"Yes. I must retrieve them from heaven and deliver them to my grandfather in hell. It's complicated…but doing so will complete a bargain between us," Michael said.

"Lucifer's wings are in heaven," Lily repeated. She could easily imagine the kachina doll in her pack with its dark wings and Michael's face.

"The elemental spirits you call might be able to guide us to find them," Michael said as if he was certain of her abilities. More certain than she. He had no idea how unpredictable spirits could be. And he had no idea that she had her own obligation to his grandfather.

"It's possible. It's also possible they'll refuse to help you. Sealing a portal to hell is one thing. Stealing from heaven another. Where is my sword?" Lily asked.

He had stopped very near her. The fire now backlit his features until they were entirely in shadow. Her chin lifted in response to his height and his nearness, but she could no better read his eyes in shadows than she could in firelight. In a way, she'd known him all her life, but in much more tangible ways he was mysterious, a threat to her and to her duty and possibly even her soul. He obviously denied his Brimstone blood. He refused to live in hell and his heat was tamped down so that someone without her level of affinity might not even detect it but his controlled burn seduced in ways that a more rampant fire never had. It was a distant intrigue to her senses. One she had to work to resist.

"I'll give you your sword and help you close the portals you promised your mother you would close. You'll lead me to Lucifer's wings," Michael proposed.

Gone was the almost lyrical quality to his speech. He had spoken in a loud, clear voice as if a proclamation had been made.

Lily's chest tightened. The air had gone thick and still around her. The dancing flames slowed. Her mother had warned her. Daemon deals were dangerous. They'd lived in hell for years because of a deal her father had forged with the daemon king before he died. But Lily couldn't turn away. She was held in place by the universe pausing around her as it waited for her to accept or reject this daemon prince's plea.

Because it was a plea. She could feel the tension in the man before her. He didn't touch her, but he stood so close

that his Brimstone heat caused her cheeks to flush. He'd
said that retrieving the wings would cement a bargain between him and the daemon king. In her bag, the kachina
doll had black wings that had been carved hundreds of
years ago by a Hopi ancestor she'd never known.

Michael D'Arcy Turov should have wings.

Lily knew it. The dolls in her bag were wrapped and
silent. She didn't summon any spirit for guidance. It was
her heart that whispered the truth.

"I'm Lily Santiago. Give me back my father's sword and
I'll guide you to Lucifer's wings," she agreed.

The flickering flames halted. Sparks above them hung
suspended in the air. Her lungs froze. Her heart paused, but
after a moment of panic everything resumed as it should.
The fire flickered. She breathed. Her heart pounded. And
Michael Turov, the daemon prince, turned away. But not
before she saw the flash of triumph in his suddenly illuminated eyes.

# Chapter 2

Hell had no stars. The sky above the palace was as thick and impenetrable as velvet. There was no moon. No planets. Only a nothingness of an atmospheric blanket that existed to separate a lower dimension from another. One had to rise up to the outer earth to see the stars, moon and sun. In hell, day was divided from night by the passage of time and by a slight violet haze that distinguished the coming of dawn and a deeper purple hue that signified the fall into dusk.

The hell dimension was beautiful—different, dark—but beautiful. Ezekiel often wondered that anyone could find it frightening or ugly.

Of course, the purple haze illuminating the carnage of battlefields was hideous. A sight he would never forget. And for a daemon king, "never" was a very long time.

He had been a warrior king during a time when war was inevitable. But it was time for a shift. Hell needed different leadership. Even a warrior king could dream of peace.

He stood on his own private balcony looking up at the velvet sky of hell's night and instead of thinking about war he thought about children, grandchildren and great-grandchildren. He thought about Samuel Santiago and the deal they'd made. For a human, Santiago had been surprisingly capable of planning for the future. Ezekiel had cared for them separately—Lily and Michael, but he'd watched them grow and he'd waited for the right time for them to meet. His grandson was almost twenty-one. It was time, but that didn't stop Ezekiel from worrying about his ward outside the palace walls for the first time. Her affinity had always taken his utmost ability to dampen in the palace, but he'd had to keep her presence mostly hidden until the time was right.

Rogues would be drawn to her. She was in terrible danger. Ezekiel fisted his hands and placed them on the cold stone rail in front of him. A daemon king had to take risks sometimes. Bold moves had to be braved. Even if it meant he risked losing them both. To Rogue daemons, to each other, or, worst of all, to a betrayal of all he held dear. Michael was only half daemon. Lily was human. Yet the fate of hell was in their hands.

Ezekiel stood for hours watching the black velvet sky lighten to purple. The passage of time was tricky in the hell dimension. They had yet to completely understand and master it. He had manipulated time to bring Lily and Michael together as peers. Time in the palace didn't stand still. It was only infinitesimally slowed. Lily had actually been born first, but she'd needed to wait for Michael. Now, they were together. Santiago and D'Arcy. Kindling waiting for a spark. Things would proceed quickly. Yet it seemed an eternity passed as he watched and waited.

Lily cleaned and polished the sword with the same reverence she'd shown the kachinas. Her entire world had been one wing of a dark Gothic palace for many years. There was plenty of time to devote to ritual and habit when your world was one of confinement. Her mother had filled their days with art and music as well as exercise and training. Lily continued the practice after her mother had died.

"There are prayers scribed on my sword…it didn't hurt you to touch them?" she asked.

Michael still stood near her after he'd given her back

her father's sword. She tried to ignore the intensity of his gaze, but it carried an almost tangible heat that flushed her cheeks.

"My mother was human. My father was a daemon. I'm only half-damned. Your sword is uncomfortable for me to touch, but not impossible," Michael said. "Your father was a daemon killer?"

"Yes," Lily responded. "Until he decided he wasn't a killer after all."

"But you decided you would kill in his stead?" Michael asked.

Lily noticed him take a step toward her, but she wasn't sure he noticed himself. There was nothing she could do about the affinity for daemons in her blood. The daemon king was the only being she knew who could dampen her call. It was a vulnerable feeling to be fully herself in the New Mexico desert, but it was liberating as well. She would deal, come what may.

But when Michael took another step toward her she couldn't help that her heartbeat quickened.

His Brimstone was a pleasant burn even if it shouldn't be.

"I defend myself and my work," she answered. Then she sheathed her father's sword at her back and rose slowly to meet his advance. Only at that point did he realize he'd moved toward her. He stopped. He blinked. His hands fisted at his sides.

"Is it your command of the elements that calls me? Your command of fire?" Michael asked.

"My kachinas are packed away," Lily reminded him.

"Then what? I have control over the Brimstone in my blood. I gained control as a child and I've never lost it. I've always credited the music for keeping it in check. My music soothes it. Or so I thought," Michael said. He'd taken two more steps. He was directly in front of her now. She had to lift her chin to look up into his eyes. They glittered in the firelight. He didn't have to tell her that his Brimstone was burning nearly out of control. She could feel it. The heat came off of him in waves and nothing could have stopped her from taking the last step between them.

Her affinity had blossomed up and out. Her body hummed with it. No song necessary at all. She took that step and Michael sucked in a deep breath in response as her breasts touched his chest.

"Daemons are drawn to me. It's something bequeathed by my father's blood," Lily confessed.

"Samuel's Kiss bequeathed an affinity to my mother and her sister through their mother. A dying man saved my grandmother. Gave her mouth-to-mouth resuscitation, but he gifted her something else with those life-saving breaths," Michael said. "She passed it to her children, and my mother passed it to me."

Lily hummed out loud when his hands came up to cup the sides of her face. Moisture filled her eyes. She'd never known her father was responsible for gifting the D'Arcys with affinity. Ezekiel had never told her. *Michael's human grandmother*. The passage of time in the hell dimension didn't match with the passage of time on earth.

"My father's name was Samuel," she breathed out.

"How is this possible? Samuel died before my mother was born," Michael said. His mouth was so close to hers that his warm breath caused her lips to tingle.

"I don't know," Lily lied just as Michael leaned to press his lips to hers.

The moisture in her eyes wasn't for the loss of her father. He'd already been gone a long time. She'd shed all the tears she could shed for him years ago. Her eyes filled because she knew in that instant that she'd been right about the daemon king's manipulations. Michael wasn't some random prince she'd met in the desert night. He was the reason she'd been allowed to leave the palace. And it didn't matter that his likeness was nestled with her kachina dolls in a dusty backpack on the sand.

He wasn't meant for her. Her destiny might be twined with his but not for reasons of the heart. He was meant for the throne. And the daemon king expected her to help him force Michael to accept it. His Brimstone blood made him vulnerable to her powerful affinity and that made him vulnerable to the daemon king's manipulations, if she didn't resist them herself.

His lips were full and warm against hers. She didn't reject the intimacy of his moist, hot tongue. She opened for him. She eagerly met his tongue with flicks of her own. She pressed into his muscular body and his arms fell from her face to her back, where they smoothed and molded the curves of her body to fit against him. She had been forced to find haven in hell, but she tasted heaven on Michael's lips. It was a paradise flavored with salty tears.

She would be damned if she did and damned if she didn't.

Her father had made a deal with the daemon king to protect her. For Lily, it had been fifteen years ago. On earth more time had passed. Enough for a Brimstone prince to be born and grow to his majority. And now Lily could guess what price she might have to pay for Ezekiel's protection.

The hellhound saved them. He leaped through the fire, scattering embers and sparks and coals in his wake as a ferocious growl erupted from his chest. They broke apart and he landed between them on stiff legs with his back hunched high.

"What the hell, Grim?" Michael protested.

"No. He's right. We can't burn so bright. It's time to go," Lily said. She was already finishing the job Grim had started, kicking apart the fire and burying the coals with desert sand.

"We don't know which direction to take yet," Michael protested.

"Away. First we go away and then I'll take the time to determine specifics," Lily said. "Rogues always find me. *You* found me. More will come. Especially if I don't tamp the affinity down." She stomped on the buried fire as if to physically illustrate her point. Then she stilled and closed her eyes. She actually knew when he took a step toward her. Lily raised her hands and held them up to ward him away.

He might have gone to her side anyway except Grim was staring out into the desert night growling at the darkness. Something was out there stalking them. Probably more than one thing.

"Right. Come on," Michael said.

It took only seconds to grab their things. His guitar. Her bag. Grim growled louder, deep in his chest, an obvious warning to whatever approached. Lily glanced one more time at her dented SUV, but it was too far away. Michael had climbed onto his motorcycle. It was a decision of the moment to hop on behind him and wrap her arms around his chest. He didn't seem surprised. The machine roared to life beneath them as daemons appeared from the shadows.

Michael wasted no more time. He pointed the motorcycle to the road and goosed the accelerator. Lily held on tight as they narrowly escaped dozens of daemons they couldn't have possibly defeated even with Grim's help. The hellhound must have been able to count. Lily saw him materialize on the road beside them, already running full speed, his legs a blur of shifting smoke.

They drove until dawn, which arrived in a burst of russet hues from umber to golden orange, but in the hours of road-eating travel Lily failed to figure out how she could break it to Michael Turov that he'd just rescued the woman who would be forced to seal his hellish fate.

# Chapter 3

Michael instinctively headed to the nearest redoubt he knew. Lily needed a protected place to perform her ritual and he would need to switch the motorcycle for a vehicle that could hold supplies for two. When he'd started touring the Southwest, he'd decided to travel light, but he'd also wanted safe places to crash in between gigs and inevitable clashes with Rogues. He'd found the perfect place already built by a wealthy survivalist with an environmentalist streak outside of Phoenix, Arizona.

He pulled the motorcycle into a drive that had been created with packed earth and crushed gravel as reddish brown as the surrounding sand. He felt Lily become more alert behind him after the mind-numbing miles they'd traveled. The sun was rising, but the earth-sheltered home built into the ground of the Sonoran Desert would be a cool respite. Especially if they went to separate rooms. A glittering expanse of glass greeted them, but between the layers of glass were blinds that automatically opened and closed when necessary to keep the temperature of the home consistent. The thick cement construction was hidden by earth and the roof was covered with desert grass with only strategically placed skylights to indicate the home beneath the ground.

Like an ordinary dog, his beloved Grim waited at the sliding glass front door. The hellhound could have morphed through in a swirl of smoky shadow. Instead, he watched and waited for them to climb off the motorcycle and walk to his side. Michael watched as Lily approached the massive, ugly creature carefully, but without trepidation. Hellhounds were rare. He wasn't surprised she'd never seen one. He only knew of one other in existence besides Grim. His cousin, Sam, had been given a hellhound puppy when he was a baby. There was much to admire in Lily's attitude toward the beast that was as tall as her chest. When she actually reached to place her hand lightly on the top of Grim's head as if a hell-spawned dog was nothing to fear, Michael stopped and stared.

She was petite. Her jeans were dusty and torn at the knee. Her pack had seen better days. But as the sun rose it glinted off her hair the way the lantern light had the night before. It created a halo effect that caused him to blink and look away.

He clenched his jaw against the burn in his blood. Samuel's daughter. Had the affinity in her blood been so powerful that it affected her aging the way Brimstone did with daemons? He'd heard of Samuel's Kiss his whole life. It had changed the course of his family's history. His mother never would have fallen in love with his daemon father if it hadn't been for the affinity Samuel had bequeathed to her. He had mixed feelings about that.

The door opened with a whoosh of displaced air. The passive solar home was always a perfect, comfortable temperature. It was his inner heat that caused perspiration to dot his upper lip.

"Make yourself comfortable. There should be food, drink, towels…anything you need," Michael offered. He was already retreating to the master bedroom, where hopefully a cold shower would help him regain control of the lava in his veins.

Lily showered and put on a fresh change of clothes from her backpack. She washed out the clothes she'd been wearing and hung them in the spare bathroom to dry. She found canned fruit in the kitchen and sat down to eat a bowl of peaches while water ran in a nearby room. She needed calories to deal with elemental spirits, and eating redirected some of the tension from resisting Michael's Brimstone pull.

Had the daemon king meant to throw them together? Would he spell out what he expected from her or was she supposed to play this by ear? The debt she owed him would have its price. She'd always known that.

Once the water had been turned off for a long while, Lily went in search of her host. She didn't want to set up her mother's kachinas and play her flute without warning the daemon prince to brace himself against her affinity's call.

She found him bare chested and tending several minor wounds in the master bedroom in front of a full-length mirror. He'd pulled on a pair of slim-cut jeans after his shower, but they rode loose and low on his hips. So loose and so low that she could see the muscular plane of his abdomen and the dusting of golden hair that disappeared into the waistband of his pants. He was lean, hard, beautiful…and scarred.

Lily stopped in the doorway with an inadvertent gasp on her lips.

His body was amazing. Muscular and obviously toned for something besides strumming the guitar. No wonder he'd been able to fight the Rogue daemons with his bare hands. His arms bulged and rippled as he moved to place a bandage on a cut on his side. But there were other ripples, too. Burn marks dimpled his skin on his chest and back. Similar marks lightly streaked his arms and his abdomen.

"From a time when I didn't know how to control the burn. It almost consumed me," Michael said. He answered a question she never would have asked. "My father was a daemon. I'm not. I never will be," he continued. "The Brimstone doesn't rule me."

"Daemons aren't inherently evil, you know. They're not human, but Brimstone doesn't actually signify damnation…" Lily began.

"I can fight my blood and I will," Michael interrupted.

Lily nodded as if she understood why he would reject his heritage. She had run away from hell herself. She should understand. But his burn was already such a part of the man she had just met that she couldn't believe he would be so deluded about who and what he was.

"Let me help you with that," she offered. She came into the room where he was trying to reach one last cut on his back with an antiseptic wipe.

"Be careful. Sometimes my blood can be dangerous," Michael warned.

"It seems fine right now. No smoke. No fire. Look. The bandages aren't turning to ash," Lily teased. She dabbed at the cut and listened to his very mortal hiss before reaching for the bandage he'd already taken from its wrapper.

"For now. I've got it under control," Michael said. She could hear the tension in his voice. He spoke with a tight jaw and narrowed eyes.

If so, he was doing better than she was. Her heartbeat had quickened. Her lungs had tightened. She was as close to him as it was possible to be without embarrassing herself and it wasn't close enough. She'd had several months of practice dampening her affinity, but that practice fell to dust with Michael. Her hands trembled as she placed the bandage over the cut on his back.

But worse than the tremble that betrayed his effect on her…she allowed her fingers to brush over the ripples of his scars. His chest expanded in a sudden gulp of air at her touch. She shivered. Her affinity tuned her in to the agony of his long-ago pain. No wonder he rejected the heat of his Brimstone blood. It had almost burned him alive from the inside out.

Their gazes met in the mirror and Lily's hand paused. She didn't jerk it away, even though his skin began to heat.

"You want the bandages to scorch?" Michael asked. His voice had gone deeper and more melodic than before.

If she'd been honest, she would have told him she was a full-on pyromaniac in that moment. She'd been sheltered from this burn her entire life even though she'd been raised in hell. The daemon king had buffered and dampened and kept her safe. She'd run away from that refuge. She'd run from the frying pan into the fire. And she wanted Michael to burn. Her father had used the last hours of his life to bargain for her safety, and now all she wanted was to step into this dangerous man's arms and throw away all thoughts of a safe haven.

Even so, alarm flared in her breast when Michael stepped forward, nudging her body toward the mirror with his. She didn't resist. She backed up until she was pressed between the cool glass and his hot chest. Her hand had fallen away from his back, but now she lifted both of them. She meant to press her palms against his shoulders to hold him back. But the move became another caress of sensitive fingers down the scars on his arms.

He trembled beneath her touch and she looked up to see that he'd closed his eyes.

"This won't be a refuge for long. We have to determine where we go from here," Michael said. His voice was only a rough whisper. It revealed what her touch made him feel, but he didn't lean to kiss her. She could feel the desire in his body. She could tell that he held himself in check even though he was pressed against her. The glass at her back no longer felt cool. His Brimstone heat had transferred to her. She wondered that the mirror didn't melt, because she felt as liquid as lava.

"I'm going to have to play the flute. My affinity will fill this place," Lily warned.

"I'll be outside. For as long as I can manage to resist," Michael said.

But he didn't immediately move. Their respiration synchronized. They breathed in and out together. Each slow, shaky inhalation was a confession. Each exhalation seemed to invite and encourage their lips to draw closer. Tingles of awareness charged her skin as he drew nearer. Their mouths were only slightly apart, their gazes locked, their breath coming faster and shallower when Michael finally moved away. The cool rush of space between them was harsh. They had stood together far longer than they should have. The pause hadn't been innocent. It had been a test of self-control—for both of them.

Lily shivered, suddenly chilled.

She watched as he pulled on a clean T-shirt and called for Grim. The hellhound rolled into being from the paws up as it moved toward the door. She'd been sheltered in the palace. She'd never seen one of the giant creatures until today, but he still reminded her of home. She touched the top of his head earlier because there was something familiar about the frightening beast who obviously loved his master. Touching Grim had soothed her. Touching Michael had left her completely undone. He was scarred from his own Brimstone, in and out.

She was already certain there was no way she would be able to fulfill her guardian's wishes if what he asked was for her to throw Michael into the flames he'd spent his whole life resisting.

# Chapter 4

Her bag was a trusty familiar tool she approached with more caution than she'd used before. Michael's presence and the daemon king's possible manipulations were added elements that caused her previous work with the elemental spirits to seem like child's play. A child who had no idea she had been playing with fire.

This time she dug deep into her pack to draw out the oldest kachina first. She'd never dared to use it in a ritual and she certainly wouldn't now that she'd met its living, breathing embodiment. But she couldn't resist unwrapping its familiar shape and tilting its face toward the light. Sun beamed into the room, softened by the tinted glass of the skylight above her. The kachina's carved features were barely illuminated. She'd memorized them long ago, but now she'd seen the sharp angles of cheek and jaw in real life. The tightening of anger and concern. The softening of humor…and desire.

She'd tasted Michael's lips. She'd craved the heat of his tongue. Lily had grown up in a palace in hell. She called on Earth, Wind, Fire and Water and they answered her call. But this tiny figure come to life had shaken the fabric of her reality until it seemed the very shadows whispered with secrets she could almost hear for the first time. The recessed skylight was framed by several feet of packed earth encased in adobe that had been painted rich, deep ocher. Desert grass moved in an outside breeze she couldn't feel and its swaying created a dance of shadows across the kachina's face.

A warrior angel. A daemon prince. Its black wings boldly arched over its muscular back. Lily closed her fist around the doll, feeling its weight and shape in her hand. Every curve, every angle fit perfectly into the soft crevices of her palm as if the lines and indentations had been made to hold it.

She had no time for this reverie.

Sunlight wavered, painted dark by grass shadows and passing clouds. She quickly rewrapped the kachina and vowed not to take him out again. Instead, she reached for the wrapped dolls that represented Earth, Wind and Water. She imagined she could feel heat rising from the wrapped form that represented Fire as her hand hovered over it. Her fingers were a hairsbreadth away when she fisted them and pulled them away.

She would leave Fire in her pack, unsummoned. She'd had enough heat for one day. Her lips still tingled and no amount of moistening kept her from feeling a parched ache for a forbidden sweetness she suspected only a daemon prince's kiss could satisfy.

Her flute was cool to her touch when she slid it from its pouch. The dolls were easily placed in position. Dancing shadows painted their blocky features with darkness and light. The earth-bermed home surrounded on the top and three sides by packed desert dirt was ideal for the ceremony she would initiate to call for the spirits' guidance. It wasn't a kiva, but the earth embraced it. Lily dropped her pack on the bed and sank down on a woven rug that was only the thinnest of barriers between her and the packed-earth floor.

This time she softly trilled an ironic measure of a classic tune about stairs to heaven. Spirits were playful. They wouldn't mind. And she needed to settle her nerves. Affinity took the tune from there, quickly morphing her wry beginning into a complexity of air and vibration that claimed her entire body from blood to breath to bone. She communed with the universe by sound. Her music was a prayer. She combined the teachings of her mother with the power gifted to her by her father to come to a deeper connection with the spirits than others had achieved before. Her ability was unique, but that meant it was a challenge to navigate. She felt her way through every possibility as she went along.

Hair began to move around her face, tossed by a breeze that was both as natural as could be and eerily impossible in the closed room. Beneath her the earthen floor trembled, and moisture began to coalesce in the air around her until her parched lips were dampened and her lashes sparkled with what felt like unshed tears.

Lily paused in her playing. She held her breath. The last note faded and she carefully lowered her flute from her lips.

"Lucifer's wings," she whispered into the silence that seemed heavy with humidity from an approaching storm. The complex challenges she faced made the words seem more curse than request. The wings had to be meant for Michael Turov. They wouldn't be a means of escape or a bargaining chip he could use to barter his way out of hell. They would seal his fate. Michael Turov's rejection of his daemon legacy was well-known in the hell dimension. He'd visited. He'd walked away. No one expected him to return for good…except the daemon king.

"L-L-Lucifer's wings," she said again. Her hair whipped around her cheeks now. It had grown damp and stung her eyes and skin like a thousand tiny lashes. The earth rumbled. A crackle of electricity charged the air as if lightning was seconds away. A wash of ozone rode the elemental breeze.

Her pack at the edge of the bed behind her tumbled to the floor and landed open beside her. The two dolls she'd tried to leave wrapped and hidden rolled out. The warrior angel figure stopped against her shoe, still wrapped, still unsummoned. But the doll that represented Fire was loosened. Its burlap wrap was scorched and blackened. Smoke curled from it into the air.

Lily grabbed for the smoking doll, but it was too late. She cried out and pulled back burned fingers as the wrappings burst into flame. More smoke than the fuel justified billowed upand rose into the spirit-tossed air, but Wind and Water didn't touch the rolling gray smoke. It had a life of its own and it was soon evident exactly what…or whom… the smoke would become.

Lily stumbled to her feet and backed away as rain began to fall. Her wind-whipped hair was plastered against her face, but she saw the smoke come together to form a familiar figure. The grumble of the earth seemed a herald of sorts, more powerful than a plague of angels' trumpets as the smoky form became solid walking toward her.

He moved like a king before he was any more than ashy smoke. As his muscular body solidified, he conquered the room by right and by the price he'd paid evidenced by every scar he bore—both seen and unseen. Lily knew Ezekiel's heart was as craggy as the battle-marked planes of his chest and cheeks.

She had summoned the daemon king. Or had she? She doubted if her guardian had to be called. He'd arrived at his own appointed time.

"Sir," Lily said. If her earlier "Lucifer's wings" had been a curse, this was a prayer. Because she dreaded the price of the protection he'd given her these last fifteen years.

"You are well. Your mother's request might have been lethal," Ezekiel said. His voice was deep and rich, warm with an interest that could be terrifying if you weren't braced for it. Lily had the practice of years behind her, but she still blanched. Her cheeks chilled and her head went light. Her mother had wanted to preserve the old Hopi sites from daemon destruction. But mostly Sophia had wanted to help Ezekiel against the Rogue threat. It had been a last gesture of unrequited love. Lily had agreed because she owed her guardian everything, even though Ezekiel's distant devotion was difficult to bear. Hadn't she seen her mother suffer for years because she had fallen in love with a "man" who merely cared for her as a means to an end?

"She wanted me to help you, but she also dreamed that one day I'd be free," Lily said.

Her guardian was fully formed now and his worn leather armor told much about his mood. He was perfectly capable of manifesting ordinary, everyday clothes. He didn't always dress like he sat on a medieval throne.

"The only way you will ever be free is to die. I've promised to prevent that for as long as I'm able," Ezekiel said. "But your affinity is your jailer. Not I." His scent was familiar. Wood smoke tinged with a hint of sulfur, ancient leather, and a metallic hint of blood. Yes, her childhood had been interesting. The daemon king smelled like home.

"So you haven't come to punish me for running away?" Lily half joked. She feared his devotion to the D'Arcy family he'd adopted because of his love for Elizabeth. Its ferocity. Its fire. She feared his expectations would consume her as she burned herself out trying to repay him. Never did she fear he would purposefully harm a single hair on her head. But he might inadvertently scorch her and everyone else on the earth to protect and promote those he truly loved.

"I would sooner slay an entire army of Rogues bent on my destruction," Ezekiel replied. "Alone. With my bare hands." He cared for her. Not in the way that he cared for the D'Arcys, but he did care. It had always been obvious that she and her mother were mere obligations. He'd disappeared for years at a time to watch over the D'Arcys while she and her mother stayed in the palace alone. She'd learned early on not to expect visits or attention. She hadn't learned not to be hurt by the neglect.

Lily could no longer hold herself back from the pull of the only familial affection she'd known since her parents' death. She threw herself into the daemon king's arms and he held her to his armored chest with a fierce grip just shy of being painfully ferocious. It was startling. He'd never been demonstrative with her in the past. She'd expected him to stiffen and hold her at arm's length.

"I worried," he said into her drying hair. The earth had quieted. The air was still. None of the spirits dared to make a peep in Ezekiel's presence.

"And yet you let me go," Lily said.

"Never trust a daemon," they both whispered together.

And then he set her from him, maintaining only one of her hands in both of his.

He was a daemon. He was the daemon king. He could care for her as a guardian more deeply than any mortal father and still he would use her to order the universe to his liking. Daemons were chess players with an eye for the long game—centuries long—and the game Ezekiel played held the balance of worlds in its outcome.

"You will help him retrieve Lucifer's wings with no reservation, no equivocation. But you already knew I would ask this of you," Ezekiel said.

She pulled her hand from his and turned away. Unfortunately, the tiny bedroom gave her no place to flee.

Even if she'd had the whole palace at her disposal or the entire desert, there was no place she could go to escape the obligation to the daemon king. He'd saved them. He'd shielded them. Her mother had fallen madly in love with Ezekiel, and he'd never hurt Sophia even though he hadn't loved her in the same way. Daemons loved long, and Ezekiel had loved Elizabeth D'Arcy and only her. Forever.

Elizabeth had been Michael's human grandmother. Ezekiel's love for her lived on in her children and grandchildren.

Yet the daemon king had been tender toward Sophia Santiago. The mighty warrior had treated her like a queen all the days of her life and he'd held her hand when she died. She'd known he didn't return her love, but the pain of that had been softened by his protective care for her daughter.

Lily loved him for that even though she feared him for his devotion to the D'Arcys. She knew her place in the scheme of things. She'd always known. She was the daemon king's ward, an obligation, no more, no less. It didn't negate her debt. Her father had made a deal with the devil and now she would pay the price.

"I will," Lily agreed.

Any freedom she'd contemplated turned to ash in Ezekiel's presence. He was her guardian. He was the only father she'd known for a very long time. Her affection and her affinity bound her to him as surely if not more so than her real father's daemon deal.

She would never be free. But it wasn't stalking rogues that damned her. Or a deal struck between Samuel and Ezekiel years ago. It was Ezekiel's scarred heart and the D'Arcys' claim on it. She wasn't immortal, but she was afraid she would strive to earn her place in his affections every day of her short life.

"It is done," he said, and no throne was necessary to make his words a royal decree.

His legs began to dissipate as he turned to walk away. Lily fought the tears that filled her eyes. Not because she didn't want him to see her cry, but because she couldn't stand to see him untouched by her tears.

"And then I'll come home," Lily promised.

The daemon king was already nothing but smoke and yet he replied, "Of course. The palace was built for you eons ago, after all."

After Ezekiel vanished—literally going up in smoke—Lily washed her face in the master bathroom sink and reset the ritual, this time with deadly seriousness. This time the elemental spirits cooperated immediately with no stormy hijinks. No doubt the spirits were as cowed as she was by the daemon king's visitation.

Wind and Earth created a recognizable channel in the floor of the bedroom and water rose up to flow along its curves. Words came from Lily's mouth, placed there by her ancestors' ancient knowledge of heaven and earth.

"The Colorado River," Lily whispered, but her voice was unfamiliar, colored by the spirits of all who had come before her. The path was revealed with no reservation, no equivocation. Her short-lived taste of freedom was over. She would never be free from the terrible weight of expectations from the only father she'd ever known. No matter what deals were struck and fulfilled, she was bound by her unrequited love for the daemon king. And to defy him more than she already had might mean losing him forever.

# Chapter 5

Spirit summoning made Grim nervous. The great ugly hellhound Michael loved stood stiff-legged and quivering as he stared at the adobe home for almost an hour while his master played.

Only the music kept Michael from responding a couple of times when he felt Lily's call all the way to the boiling marrow in his bones. He played obsessively until sweat ran down his cheeks and his body trembled against the pull he resisted.

"You aren't helping, you damned mutt," he ground out between his teeth.

Grim whined, but only came to lie at his feet when Michael thought his hellhound might never turn toward him again. Only then did Michael allow his fingers to still on the strings. The sun had set. The nocturnal activity of the desert came to life around him. Scurryings and scrapings, scufflings and squeaks began to fill the air with soft sound.

"She's done, isn't she?" he asked. Grim chuffed and collapsed as if he'd run a million miles with the intensity of his watch. Michael understood. His muscles ached from tension when he uncurled from around his guitar and stood.

The sliding glass door opened and Lily stepped out into the deepening night. Lanterns at either side of the entrance illuminated the beautiful young woman, and Michael slowly lowered his instrument to the ground as he stared.

She was soaked. Her hair and clothes plastered to her petite body. Steam began to rise from her as the cool night air hit her curves. But it was her haunted gaze that captured his attention. Her eyes were dark in the lantern light. Their brown irises deepened to a dusky midnight. And they were rimmed with red as if the water on her face was…tears.

He didn't think. He didn't hold himself back. As Grim bristled and let out a sound that was half growl, half whine, Michael strode forward to meet Lily and he was there to catch her when she stumbled forward into his arms.

"My God, woman. That wasn't a marathon. It must have been a crucible," he said. The sound of his own voice shook him as much as her appearance. He was hoarse. All the tension of the day spilling from his lips.

She was pale and clammy against him and her body shivered.

"I might need more than a protein bar this time," she said. Her teeth clicked together as she spoke.

Lily didn't resist when he gathered her up in his arms. She was limp. What had he done? Was his freedom worth hurting an innocent woman? The Brimstone in his blood burned him with shame. He'd done this to the daughter of a veritable saint with his selfish demands. Maybe he deserved to sit on the throne of hell. He was no better than his grandfather. Ezekiel's attention could focus on a goal with no consideration for those he burned out in the process. His mother had warned him about that since he was a small boy.

"Come on, Grim. I've got a job for you," Michael said.

She'd sipped a cup of soup before she was fully conscious enough to realize it. She came awake to a full stomach and the fiery heat of a massive hellhound snuggled against her side. When her eyes opened, Grim's glowing red irises blinked at her as if to say, "I'm a useful monster, aren't I? By the way, I know your secrets even if my master doesn't."

Then she noticed she was bundled in a clean, dry sheet and nothing else.

"Um. Little help?" she asked, muffled beneath sulfuric fur.

"Grim, that's good. You don't have to smother her with your devilish charm," Michael said.

The hellhound heating pad slowly got up, stretched and moved away. Lily blinked against the sudden light that glared from the fireplace once the hellhound wasn't shielding her from its glow. Michael sat on the hearth. He sipped dark wine from a glass. She noticed the sip first. The slow, savoring movement of his mouth on the rim of the crystal and the glistening moisture of the crushed fruit on his lips. The flick of his tongue. The intimacy of his throat as he swallowed.

Then she noticed the tape on his fingers. Every pad was bandaged, and the white of the bandages was stained with blood.

"Your hands," Lily said. She gripped the sheet around herself and rose to her knees. She and the hellhound had been lying in front of the fire so the move brought her to Michael's legs.

He didn't move away. He simply placed his glass to the side and waited to see what she would do. Lily held the sheet across her chest with one arm and reached for one of his hands with the other. He didn't resist. She looked from his taped fingers up to his shuttered eyes.

"I played to drown out your call," Michael said.

Her hair had dried in a riot of waterfall waves around her face and shoulders. She didn't have enough hands to hold her sheet and his hand and push back her hair. As if he noticed her quandary, he reached up with his free hand to softly brush waves back from her face. But he paused in the middle of the move when his hand glanced against her cheek. He released her hair to cup her jaw as if he couldn't merely perform a practical move when he was distracted by touching her instead.

"I don't want you to hurt yourself. Not for Lucifer's wings. Not for me. Ever again," Michael said.

"You hurt yourself for me," Lily reminded him. The hand on her face was bandaged, too. She couldn't imagine the intensity of his playing if it had hurt the hand that held the neck of his guitar.

"Purely selfish. I was protecting myself," he said.

She didn't have the heart to tell him that it was probably only the daemon king's presence that had dampened the Brimstone pull and the affinity's call between them so that he could resist. She didn't want to mention Ezekiel. Not while Michael's hand was on her face. Not while his warm gaze searched hers. It was the daemon king's manifestation that had drained her to the point of collapse. Summoning the devil himself took a lot out of a girl. Especially a girl with an affinity for Brimstone already strained by kisses from the future Prince of Darkness.

"Where are my clothes?" she asked instead.

"On the chair behind you. They were cold and damp," Michael explained.

"I'm warm now," Lily said. She was on her knees between his jean-clad legs. Warm was an understatement. The fire behind him was meaningless. The fire in his blood called to her and the daemon king was long gone.

Heat rose in her cheeks and spread down to her chest. His gaze tracked the movement as her skin flushed. Or did the track of his gaze cause the flush with its intensity? The sheet was a pristine contrast to the way her skin revealed her way-less-than-pristine thoughts.

His hand slid from her jaw to the nape of her neck beneath her hair. When the move tilted her face up, she didn't fight it. She should have. She should have pulled away. Stood. Put distance between them. There was no buffer here. Allowing the heat to build between them was suicide.

Her affinity was a beacon for Rogue daemons.

She both feared immolation and craved it. Feared it from Rogues. Craved it from Michael. When he leaned down to give her the burn she wordlessly begged for, on her knees and as supplicant as she could allow herself to be, the thought of Rogues was scorched away.

*For the first time in her life she was free.*

His lips were hot from Brimstone and dusky sweet from exquisite wine. They were also perfect. Full and masculine and so familiar she could close her eyes and explore with impunity. He gasped when she boldly traced their carved curves and swells with the tip of her tongue. Then he urged her closer until her stomach was pressed to the intimate swell of the erection between his legs. He curled down to deepen the kiss.

Suddenly, he was the royal. He would claim her. He would take control. She might be caught in a devil's bargain that would lead him all the way to hell, but in this—kissing, touching, claiming—he had the upper hand.

Lily held tight to his muscled legs, but his heat called and she allowed her palms to press and slide. Closer and closer along his thighs to find him, and measure the length of his penis caught and contained away from her by his jeans.

He growled against her mouth and moved his hands to her shoulders to urge her back. She went with his urgings. She made room for him to leave the hearth and join her, on his knees. Now they were both supplicant. Both begging. Distantly, Lily heard Grim whine, but she could only focus on getting closer to Michael's heat. All rational strategy was forgotten. Her vision of the Colorado River boiled away to nothing. The daemon king's manipulations paled in comparison to the demands of her and Michael's bodies.

Her sheet had fallen away.

She was naked for her Brimstone prince and when his lips left hers to trail down and claim her breasts with his mouth and hot, wet suction, she thought she would die. Her heart raced. Her lungs hitched. Her body burned.

Lily reached for him and even through his clothes his rising body heat transferred to her fingers. When she stroked her palms down from his shoulders to his bare arms, his skin was feverish to her touch. Impossibly hot. She brushed down the slightly roughened skin of his scars anyway. Learning, exploring and burning all the while.

But Grim's whine erupted into growls and Michael pulled away before she had even begun to know him as well as her affinity drove her to. He rose and went toward the hellhound.

Once their bodies were separated, she could feel the Brimstone burn of the intruders that were causing Grim such concern. Rogues. Here. No doubt called by her affinity that sang with an almost audible hum in her body when Michael touched her.

"We've got trouble," Michael said. He'd moved to the front window to place his hand on Grim's head and look outside.

"More than you can possibly know," Lily replied. She was already shrugging into her clothes, which were stiff and warm from drying by the fire. The fire's heat paled in comparison to Michael's Brimstone burn. She shivered at the loss of his touch in spite of the warmed clothes. Her fingers fumbled on the buttons while Michael turned from the window where he'd shrugged into his jacket to grab up his guitar. She hadn't noticed it leaning by the hearth. It was such a part of him. Like a shadow that moved when he moved and stilled when he stilled. He placed his arm through the tooled leather strap and settled the instrument against his back, where it fit perfectly as if made to match his planes and curves.

"How many?" she continued. Her own pack settled against her back with a weight that had become familiar over the past few months. Her affinity didn't tell her the odds. It was only a magnet that drew her toward daemons and their Brimstone blood. In the past, her father's affinity had been used to hunt and destroy daemons until he'd decided to fight the violence and hate. He'd split with the hunters. And his decision had led to his death at their hands.

"Too many to fight. Too many to face. We'll have to take the back way out," Michael said.

As if Grim understood his master's words, he turned from the window and ran toward the back of the earth-bermed home.

"I thought we were surrounded by dirt on three sides?" Lily said.

"I grew up on a vineyard estate. Playing in wine caves. Other kids had tree houses. I had tunnels and cellars. A maze of them beneath the vines. And I played hide-and-seek with a hellhound for fun," Michael explained. "Hidden exits are a family tradition. I had this one installed shortly after I began using this place."

He took her hand, and she let him pull her after Grim toward what seemed like a dead end at the back of the house where even the skylights failed to illuminate the shadows with moonlight. The fire still crackled and burned in the front room, but they stepped into chilled darkness that smelled of earth. She pulled her hand from Michael's when they paused. Touching him caused her affinity to flare. There was no logic in being any more of a beacon for the Rogues than she already was.

Loud thumps came from the front of the house. Rogues were at the door. Maybe they had seen Grim at the window and they were reluctant to break through the glass where he might be waiting.

Michael pushed aside a large cloth that hung on the earthen wall. She'd thought it was a Navajo blanket, but up close, even in the shadows she could see it was a woven tapestry of European origin. She reached up to touch the figure of a bird created with bright crimson plumage at the center of the piece.

"It's a Russian firebird," Michael explained. "That folktale has special significance to the Turov family." But he was already disappearing into the gaping hole he'd uncovered behind the tapestry. Lily followed as the sound of breaking glass came from the bedroom behind them. The skylight. One of the Rogues had decided to come through the roof.

She followed the prince through murky subterranean shadows. Grim had stopped in front of them. Michael pushed past his hellhound and she went with him. She couldn't be sure in the dark, but she thought the large creature was guarding their retreat.

The tunnel narrowed and dropped, taking them deeper underground. Her hands rose instinctively as they hurried along. She could barely see. She had to feel her way. Her fingers trailed across packed earth. Claustrophobia threatened. She tried to breathe normally but her respiration was hurried. In and out with every quickened step.

"Only a little farther," Michael said. His deep voice was

contained by the small space around them. The weight of the earth trapped the sound, making his melodious accent muffled and strange.

"What about Grim?" she asked. And suddenly her voice echoed as they exited the tunnel into a more cavernous space.

"Grim doesn't need a car to escape," Michael said.

And that's when Lily saw the gleam of chrome and glass and steel.

The vintage muscle car was black, or she might have seen it right away. Once her eyes had adjusted to the difference in the quality of light between the tunnel and the cavern, the car's striking curves and angles reproved her inability to see and appreciate right away. Rogues were only a few hundred feet behind them. A hellhound prepared to defend their retreat. But Lily still paused as Michael opened the driver-side door and tossed his guitar in the back seat.

Beside the car, Michael was also all striking curves and angles. The leather of his jacket gleamed. His teeth flashed in a quick, savage smile at her surprise.

"Run with me?" he asked.

She didn't need to be urged twice. There was no time to contemplate daemon deals, guilt or loyalty. In seconds she had ripped open the passenger door and tossed her pack in the back beside his guitar. They both sank into the buttery cream upholstery at the same time. Before she could close her door, growls and screams erupted from the tunnel. Lily almost got out of the car. Grim was in trouble. Michael reached to stop her.

"He's got this," he said. He had already closed his door. Now he reached across her body to pull the passenger-side door closed with a decisive thud. "He's much older and wiser than we are. He knows what to do." Even with the doors closed, the ferocious sounds of fighting penetrated the confines of the vehicle. "He's just buying us time."

Lily wasn't so certain. She'd never heard such horrible screams and she'd grown up in hell. If the ugly beast died at the hands of the Rogues she had lured with her affinity, she would never forgive herself.

"Buckle up and hang on," Michael said.

The car roared to life beneath them and Lily did as she was told. She'd never ridden in a sports car before, much less one that looked as deadly as this one.

"Also a Firebird, by the way. 1968. My father says it was a very good year," Michael said. He shifted the car into Reverse and they roared backward with no further explanation.

Lily yelped and grabbed for the dashboard. She expected to hear the crunch and slam of destruction as the car rammed into the solid earth wall behind them. But instead they whooshed from zero to sixty along another tunnel. This time the tunnel rose up instead of down. She was glad she forced her eyes open when they flew out into the night, because for long seconds the vehicle seemed suspended in starlight surrounded by the endless midnight blue of the desert sky.

When they slammed down into a road carved into the sand, adrenaline soothed the jarring of her body and soul. Sure, she bit her lip and tasted blood, but it was worth the moments of flight.

"Grim?" Lily shouted above the engine's roar.

"He's with us. Look," Michael said.

Lily looked out the window to see a blur of smoke and ember eyes running alongside the car.

He would have had her in front of the fire. The flickering flames reflected in the warm brown of her eyes had only matched the flames beneath his skin. She wasn't frightened by his heat. And that gave him permission to burn.

The flavor of familiar wine had changed against her tongue. It had become sweeter, richer and more intoxicating. Especially when she had explored his mouth with sensual, darting flicks that sent desire hotter than Brimstone straight to his...

They were running for their lives and he was lost in the physical sensations of what might have been if they could have continued to indulge.

He'd been careful to take no liberties when he'd stripped off her wet clothes. Oh, he'd noticed her lush beauty. He wasn't blind. But his primary drive had been to help and protect her. When she'd knelt between his legs, his drive had shifted.

She'd welcomed his touch. She'd welcomed his mouth on her perfect breasts. He held himself as still as possible as the memory rocked him with shudders behind the wheel.

His control hadn't been shaken. It had been boldly thrown aside. Worse than that, if he were free to pull the car over right here, right now, he'd continue where they'd left off.

Her lips had opened so hungrily. Her hands had eagerly reached for his erection. They were running for their lives, but he couldn't focus on the road because of the woman beside him. He could no longer pretend that he didn't want to burn with her again. He wanted to taste her and touch her. He wanted to bring her to trembling pleasure again and again.

But only by choice. Not driven mindlessly by his Brimstone burn. Never that. He was a man, not a monster. If he couldn't pleasure Lily as a man, then he wouldn't touch her at all.

# Chapter 6

The sun rose until heat waves hovered above the ground, causing it to shimmer in the distance as if this world was only a too-bright illusion, one that would disappear if she blinked or shielded her gaze. She played the game of not blinking until her eyes burned with unshed tears.

*Run with me.*

She would hear those words forever.

They would haunt her. As would the flash of mischievousness that had lit his eyes for a split second when she'd jumped into the car.

Grim was fully materialized now except for the blurred movement of his giant legs as they churned up dust beside the highway.

"How did he get away?" she asked when the world seemed real enough to risk speech once more.

"Hellhounds can travel between worlds. Between time and space and Lord knows where else. They use pathways we can't see. He and I often travel that way," Michael explained.

"So why did we have to run for the car?" Lily asked. "He couldn't take me, too?"

Michael downshifted on a rise. He glanced sideways at her, but only for a second before his attention was back on the road as he accelerated once more.

"Grim could take you. But he won't. Hellhounds are… unpredictable. He's led entire armies through those pathways," Michael said. Through the tinted windows, sunbeams glinted on streaks of hair that had been naturally highlighted by his time on a motorcycle without a helmet. Lily narrowed her eyes, but she still fought the constant need to blink. She had lived her life in darkness. She might never acclimate to the desert sun.

"He *wouldn't* take me," she said.

How cruel to be pained by both sunlight and the rejection of a monstrous creature of shadowy darkness.

She belonged to no world and no one.

Grim knew. Her obligation to Ezekiel might be a secret from his master, but the hellhound knew she had divided loyalties. From what she'd seen of Michael's hellish companion, the beast would brook no shades of gray. He might be an ugly monster spawned in the depths of hell, but he was pure of heart. More pure than Lily Santiago, the daemon king's ward who would die trying to earn a place for herself. Here. There. Anywhere. Her life was one long, ritualized sacrifice. If she played, summoned, served with all her heart perhaps one day she'd get love in return.

"He's always been temperamental," Michael said. Her silence was heavy in the car. She couldn't hide her dismay. "I blame it on the whole 'bred in the fires of hell' thing."

The vintage Firebird he drove as beautifully as he played and sang rolled to a stop. Lily was startled by the sudden cessation of movement and her game of not blinking was lost. Thankfully the moisture in her eyes had dried and no tears fell to betray her feelings. She could blame her sudden blinking on the sun. She looked around. Michael had pulled into a shabby gas station with two pumps and a peeled and cracked fiberglass statue of a man holding a wrench.

"He doesn't trust me," Lily said, softly. She didn't turn back to Michael. She spoke as if to the hazy reflection of herself in the tinted glass. Her voice was as cracked by circumstances and expectations as the fiberglass statue of the mechanic was worn by time and desert wind.

Not to mention tension.

She was drawn to Michael. And the daemon king had known she would be. It wasn't only her affinity for the Brimstone in his blood. The man was as appealing as his daemon heat.

"Lucifer's Army he trusts. But he's leery of a petite woman with a flute and a bag of dolls," Michael said. "Maybe it's because you're way too young to be Samuel's daughter. There are things about you that don't add up." She glanced at him. His hands were still on the steering wheel. He looked easy in the driver's seat as if there was no place he'd rather be. Yet she knew he belonged on stage, playing and singing for an adoring crowd. Of course, the whole world was Michael D'Arcy Turov's stage. She knew that even though she'd known him for only a short while.

"I'm going to freshen up," Lily said. What else could she do or say? She couldn't tell him she'd grown up in hell where time had flowed differently. She pushed open the car door and escaped only to find herself cornered by the very creature who seemed to know her secrets. Grim had solid legs again. He padded up to the car, panting lightly like a German shepherd who'd taken a quick morning jog.

"The daemon king is your rightful master, too, you know," she muttered to the suspicious beast.

Grim licked his lips and sat back on his haunches. His fiery eyes were toned down so that any humans in the vicinity would think him hideous but not hellish. How the attempt worked she'd never know. He was obviously supernatural, and even acting casual his whole demeanor was more Big Bad Wolf than ordinary puppy.

Michael got out of the car to pump gas. He watched her skirt the giant hell beast and make her way inside the gas station. She walked as normally as she could with two sets of eyes setting her back on fire.

The less-than-shiny restroom had only one working sink. She managed to get a small trickle of water to flow and she splashed it on her flushed face. It didn't do much to cool or calm her.

Rogues were drawn to her. They had been since she'd run away from the palace. There was no buffer for her on earth. Worse, Michael seemed to function as the opposite of a buffer. He enhanced her affinity's call. He was half daemon. His biological father had been an Ancient One. He'd chosen to fall in order to rule with Lucifer in the hell dimension. They'd given up their places in heaven for autonomy in hell. Rogues were younger daemons. They resented the Ancient Ones' choice. They wanted to take over the hell dimension, but their desire to rule hell was only a stepping-stone toward claiming heaven. Rogues had killed Lucifer. Lucifer's Army wanted autonomy. Rogues wanted dominion.

Ezekiel was an Ancient One who needed a Loyalist heir to keep Rogues from power.

No. A little gas station sink water wasn't going to absolve her sins. Both Michael and Ezekiel wanted her to help find Lucifer's wings. But Michael didn't want to wear them. He wanted to deliver them. He'd never made any secret of his distaste for the throne.

*Run with me.*

He hadn't meant it in the way her soul had heard it. There was no "away" far enough for her to run from Ezekiel's expectations or Rogues' hunger. But Michael was a powerful lure and her soul ached to answer his call. He was a what-if she wasn't free to explore. There was no future for her that included a man, a car and a hellhound's devotion.

Grim was right not to trust her. She looked into the

smudged and cracked glass as water swirled down the gur-
gling drain. She would fulfill her bargain. She would pay
the price Ezekiel asked for his years of protection. Then
she would go back to the cold, dark palace alone.

Her guardian's heart had always been out of her reach.
He had been a distant figure always too busy to provide
the time and attention she craved, but she owed him her
life and her mother's life. It didn't matter that his time had
always gone to the D'Arcys. She couldn't refuse him. Not
when his request was to help him save the one place she'd
ever called home.

Michael had pulled the car away from the pump and
parked it to the side. Lily walked toward it slowly, squint-
ing her eyes against the sun, but soaking up the heat. She'd
been cold since the Rogues had interrupted her and Michael by the fire. It was possible now that her body had
tasted his Brimstone burn she'd never be warm without
him again.

He was propped against the hood of the vintage car.
He wasn't playing his guitar. His arms were folded over
his chest. His boots were crossed at the ankles. His jeans
matched his boots. Worn and scuffed. They spoke of the
dust of miles traveled. He was waiting for her.

*Run with me.*

If she were free to run there was no way she could resist him.

"So we haven't had a chance to talk about your ritual…
How did your summoning turn out?" Michael asked.

Lily stopped in her tracks. She held on to the straps of
her pack. The wrapped dolls were dormant. Silent. All
her secrets hidden. For now. The daemon king was supposedly back in hell where he belonged. She was standing in the sun. She wanted to belong, but didn't. Not here.

And not there. She was as in-between as the pathways Grim traveled.

Grim knew shadows.

He came around the bumper of the Firebird with his nose in the air, sniffing out the hint of sulfur on her skin she could never quite wash away.

"The Colorado River will lead us. The clerk had a map. I can show you," Lily offered. She pulled the map she'd gotten from the service station counter from her back pocket. She forced herself to approach the car as she unfolded the map with each step. Michael pushed away from the fender with his hip and stood up straight to meet her. Grim paced a few steps away. His eyes were watchful.

Lily spread the map on the hood of the car. She was careful to keep some distance from Michael. He had tamped down his Brimstone heat and his affinity, too. His guitar was in the back seat. It sat there like a special passenger. Its seductive song silenced…for now. She was pretty sure it was unnatural for him to leave it there, neglected and unplayed.

It didn't matter.

All the self-control in the world—hers and his—didn't stop her body from humming in his presence.

She focused as much attention as possible on the map. It would have meant nothing to her without the spirits' guidance. Geography of his world wasn't her strong suit. It hadn't been her home for a very long time. Thanks to her elemental guides she was able to point out the exact route she'd seen traced in the dirt of Michael's bedroom floor.

"The Grand Canyon leads to heaven?" Michael asked.

"The river leads. The canyon is incidental. The carving of it a side effect of the river's flow." Lily shrugged off one of the wonders of the mortal world.

"And you couldn't follow *that* path to lead me to Lucifer's wings?" Michael asked Grim.

The hellhound tilted his head, but arrogantly. He was a creature of hell. What did he care about pathways he was forbidden to take?

Without being conscious of her actions, Lily had shrugged out of her backpack and placed it on the hood to hold down one corner of the map. Michael called her attention to the bag and its contents when he suddenly placed one hand over the lumps that showed beneath the worn canvas.

"If I hadn't seen you summoning with my own eyes, I would think you were going to lead me on a superstitious version of a wild-goose chase," Michael said. Every inch of her body tensed and Lily held her breath. His hand was directly over one of the larger lumps that indicated dolls other than the tiny carved representation of himself. She had no idea how her treasured warrior angel would react to Michael's touch. It had never reacted to hers. Unlike the other dolls, it seemed to have no powers whatsoever. Part of her fascination came from its silence.

She hurriedly grabbed for the backpack, more out of embarrassment than fear. She had no idea what Michael would think of the likeness, but she'd prefer he never see himself in a tiny doll she'd treasured for so many years. She was too hurried. Her rushing made her clumsy. Her whole body brushed against his and her hand tangled with his fingers. Had she actually wondered if this world was real all morning? Because it was suddenly ferociously real… Her skin flushed, her breath caught, every muscle tightened. There was no breeze—the air stood still—and yet she felt a rush of response lift her hair.

At first she thought her sudden movement had caused Grim to growl low in his chest. That maybe the contact of her against his master had worried him. The hellhound was up and pacing. Grim's hackles had risen and turned to something more like smoke swirling on his back. Michael narrowed his eyes, but his focus wasn't on the bag she had pulled away from his hand to clutch to her chest. Rather he looked back down the highway the way they'd come.

"It's time to go," he said.

The map resisted being folded correctly when she grabbed it off the hood of the car. She was breathing again, but her respiration was rushed and her fingers were clumsy. Grim was all swirl now. He hadn't disappeared, but he looked like nothing but smoke and ember eyes.

"Keep an eye on them," Michael ordered. Grim had vanished before his master finished speaking.

"It's getting worse. I don't think we'll be able to shake them as long as we're together," Lily said. She sounded winded. She *was* winded. That slight contact between them had left her oxygen-deprived. Michael had already opened the passenger-side door for her. A prince to her princess. His consideration was salt in the scratch of her reaction to him. She wasn't sure if she would have been able to operate the door handle herself.

"We have to be very careful. When we touch, the affinity is amplified," Michael warned. It was the understatement of the century. Did his body still vibrate as if it was an instrument's string? She wondered that hers wasn't quivering for the world to see, still reacting from the slight brush of her body against his.

As he crossed around to the driver's side, Lily swallowed. The distance between them was still negligible. Because it wasn't from the earth to the moon. She didn't have the guts to tell him actual touching might not be necessary at all. She still felt amplified. Every cell in her body seemed tuned to the possibility of the future touch and taste of him, but even if those touches never happened, the memory of previous ones might well keep her affinity vibrating forever.

There was a time she'd felt safe, if a little trapped, behind the palace's walls. She wasn't sure if she'd ever feel that way again. She'd flown with Michael, silhouetted against the desert sky. His burn and the adrenaline of that moment might be with her forever after.

Deep down she thought this new fear was a small price to pay for the exhilaration of that flight.

## Chapter 7

Peter could taste the wild, sweet affinity on the back of his tongue every time it was unleashed. He'd traveled across the world to this godforsaken desert before Samuel's daughter had even met the half-daemon prince. Her blood alone had lured with a purity of call he'd never sensed from others.

She'd been sheltered from detection for years. Hidden. Kept by Ezekiel. They had never suspected. Samuel, once the mightiest daemon hunter, had allied himself with the heir to Lucifer's throne. Such an alliance had been unexpected, as the Order of Samuel was already dismantled. Scattered to the winds. So few brothers were left to carry on Reynard's work. That great man had been murdered by D'Arcys and Loyalists. As had most of his followers.

Peter himself had been close to giving up. But he'd remained faithful. He'd survived by selling his soul to Rogues. In that he'd also followed in Reynard's footsteps.

And now he had hope again for the first time in years.

He traveled in a fleet of gleaming black vehicles with a group of Rogues more ruthless than any he'd known. They'd been on the trail of Samuel Santiago's daughter for months before Michael Turov had found her for them. The second he'd touched her they had pinpointed her exact location. Together they burned with the heat of a thousand suns. Residual desire coursed through Peter with the memory of that burn. The Rogues were like a pack of hounds on her scent and he, too, panted. But the Brimstone his deal had accepted into his blood was for the Order of Samuel. With Samuel's daughter he could rebuild what they had lost. Perhaps, in time, he could turn on the Rogue allies and purify the earth of the daemon scourge once and for all.

The Rogues could have heaven. What did he care of that far-off realm? He would rule a new order on earth. He wanted to bathe in Samuel's daughter's affinity, and when he no longer needed her, maybe he would bathe in her blood. All the years of powerless fury he'd suffered would be soothed.

They were close. So close. And other Rogues were close to a different prize they'd sought. Lucifer's wings were almost within their grasp. Ezekiel would be brought to his knees. But he wouldn't be bowing before Rogues. He would be bowing before a new order of saints. One led by Peter himself.

He hadn't had the flame nightmare in a very long time. When it visited him with a vengeance, as if to make up for years of leaving him in peace, the vivid memory of pain seared along the tracks of his scars and woke him with the sound of his own screams. Grim was there before the sound died down and the hulking beast almost smothered him with his concern. He pressed his great hairy body against Michael's arms as if he were putting out actual flames and not the memory of a first Brimstone burn that had almost annihilated a toddler too young to control it.

One of Michael's first lucid memories was of his mother's soothing song and touch. She'd held him in spite of the danger. She'd risked being burned alive in order to bring him back from the brink of combustion. Rogues had taken him to get to her and the daemon king. Adam Turov had helped

Michael and his mother defeat the Rogues that had also tortured him as a child.

His stepfather also had scars from his time with the Order of Samuel. But the beautiful opera singer, Victoria D'Arcy, had helped the daemon hunter to heal. They had raised Michael together even though his biological father had been a daemon. He'd had love, stability…and the looming threat of a grandfather who wanted to bequeath him the throne of hell on his twenty-first birthday.

Thankfully he'd been sleeping outside the roadside hotel to keep watch and to keep his distance from Lily Santiago when he woke screaming. The night air helped to cool his skin, and no one saw the glow along the tracks of his scars caused by the Brimstone in his blood rising to the surface.

Lily didn't have to touch him. Ever again. Keeping his distance did nothing. The memory of her touch was enough. He'd fallen to sleep hotter than he'd been in a very long time. Thus the dream. Thus the burn. He rose and went for his guitar for comfort. The music and the affinity his mother had bequeathed him held the Brimstone burn at bay.

Of course, the music did nothing to erase the memory of Lily's taste on his tongue.

Sometime after midnight, Lily woke suddenly with her heart pounding. Her fists were clenched, but the only intruder in her room was a stray shaft of moonlight beaming through the slim opening between the heavy motel drapes. It wasn't the first time she'd woken afraid from a sound sleep since she'd left the protected confines of the daemon king's palace. She'd been hunted from the start. Rogues craved her ability to lure and hunt daemons because of the power it would give them over Loyalist enemies. But their desire to use her was at war with their more personal desire to claim her affinity for their own pleasure.

Reason to run, for sure.

But running with a half-daemon prince wasn't exactly salvation, especially when she found herself uncomfortably close to having those same thoughts to covet and claim. She was no greedy Rogue daemon, but Michael's Brimstone was alluring.

*Michael would have been alluring if his blood was cold as ice.*

Lily rose from tangled sheets that spoke of her restless dreams and tiptoed to the window. She twitched the curtain just enough to look down on the Firebird gleaming in the pale moonlight. She hadn't expected to see Michael leaning against the hood in a familiar pose, his legs crossed at the ankle. She eased back, but he wasn't looking up at the window where she stood. He was concentrating on the guitar in his hands.

She couldn't hear his song. Not with her ears. But she suspected she'd woken with his playing, attuned to him in ways she couldn't understand. He played to quiet the Brimstone in his blood. To soothe away the burn. Knowing he was as restless as she was didn't help. He was used to controlling his burn. She was less practiced at pretending. Especially when she wasn't at all sure the attraction between them was something they could fight.

That's when she saw Grim. She'd been too distracted by the striking figure of a daemon prince curled around his guitar at midnight. At first she hadn't seen the giant shadow of his constant hellhound companion. But, unlike his master, the hellhound had seen her. His snout was pointed toward the window and for a second the burning coals of Grim's eyes met hers. He had been sitting at Michael's feet. He rose and walked several stiff-legged paces toward the hotel. Lily heeded the warning. Her fingers slid from the curtains and she turned away from the beautiful prince playing by the light of the moon.

Her backpack was only a few steps away. She kept it close at all times. In addition to the kachinas, her father's sword was stowed in a side pocket that served as a sheath. Only the top of its hilt protruded, but it was within easy reach should she need it. It was probably a mistake to pick up the pack and bring it with her when she climbed back into bed. She did it anyway. It wasn't safe to stare at Michael. But there was an alternative. She'd been staring at his kachina-doll likeness her whole life.

So why did the beat of her heart kick up again when she pulled out the tiny burlap bundle to unwind it? Why did every slow revolution of the doll as she freed it feel like a risk she couldn't afford to take?

The room was dark, illuminated only by the moon on one side and the soft glow of emergency lighting from the interior corridor on the opposite side.

She saw the doll with the pads of her fingers more than her eyes.

It was still a treasure, but it was no longer as compelling as it had been before. Now she'd seen the real warrior angel in action. She'd heard his song. She'd felt his burn. She'd tasted his perfect lips. But more than that, she'd felt his scars. The tiny carving hadn't revealed those scars to her. She'd had to see them on the real man in real life. Something deep in his changeable eyes told her there was much like the scars about him. Things the kachina doll had never revealed in spite of her familiarity with it.

She had to obey the daemon king.

But as she held the doll in her hands the smooth statue suddenly grew cool in her fingers and she trembled. The chill was unexpected. The real man could warm her if it wasn't forbidden in so many ways. The hellhound knew her secret. But Michael was the true mystery. A daemon prince determined to run away from the throne of hell. He was scarred by his past. He fought his future. Yet he'd had the kind of familial love she'd never known.

The doll was too cold to comfortably hold and she rewrapped it, puzzled by the sudden change. What could it mean?

Ezekiel had a plan, and she was entangled in his scheme because love and gratitude bound her. She'd run away only to find that her guardian wouldn't set her free. Whether Grim approved or not, one of her ancestors had seen the daemon prince in her future. Was he her destiny or would she be his damnation? Was the sudden chill from the doll meant as a warning?

She wanted to warn Michael. It wasn't the Brimstone in his blood he should fear. It was her place in Ezekiel's plan and the power she might have to overcome his resistance.

# Chapter 8

It wasn't safe for her to travel alone. She couldn't fight off an army of Rogues with her father's blade. She wasn't sure how much sleep they'd managed between them, but they were up before dawn to meet at the car as they'd planned. Grim had disappeared. She blinked at shadows to determine if the hellhound was lurking near his master, but couldn't decide if her gooseflesh was in response to the cool morning air or the beast's stare.

"We should separate and meet at the river, but I don't want to leave you on your own and Grim won't cooperate," Michael said.

Lily wouldn't have been keen to travel alone with the hellhound anyway.

"I'll think cold thoughts," she promised, knowing it was a lie.

"Will you?" Michael challenged. He had placed his guitar in the back seat and he braced his hands against the top of the car on the driver's side. Lily stood in the open door of the passenger side and met his gaze over the dusty roof. Something in his narrowed eyes spoke of tension and she dropped her eyes, but that only led her to look at his white-knuckled grip.

"Maybe you're the one that needs to chill?" Lily suggested.

"I'm working on it. Trust me," Michael said. He pushed away from the car and got behind the wheel in one fast, fluid motion. Lily swallowed. If this was him working on tamping down his Brimstone burn, she couldn't imagine him letting go. Couldn't, but did for several long moments as she tried to remember how to get into the car like a woman who wasn't lost in thoughts that could get her killed.

Only the sudden thought that the daemon king had known exactly what he was doing when he'd thrown them together spurred her to take a deep breath and get into the car. He wanted them harried and hounded by Rogues. He wanted them drawn together. He wanted them to crave the forbidden fruit while they went for the wings.

*A* mantle *fit for a future king.*

She'd wondered what Ezekiel's entire scheme entailed and maybe she was beginning to have an inkling of an answer. It was in the flush on her skin as she sat too close to Michael in the enclosed space. It was in the deep breath she took as she buckled her seat belt, already craving the scent of his skin, warmed from the outside by sun and from the inside by his fire.

Ezekiel was an Ancient One. He'd fallen from heaven to rule in hell. He'd battled Rogues for centuries. But he was a complex being with many facets all tilted toward strengthening his kingdom.

Michael's reluctance as the prince and heir of the throne was well-known, but Ezekiel was determined that he would be a king. Ezekiel had ruled alone for too long. He might want more for his beloved Elizabeth's grandson.

The idea of her royal guardian as a nearly immortal and unpredictable matchmaker caused panic to rise up in her chest.

"Hang on," Michael said. "The sooner we get to the wings the better."

Her body was pressed against the buttery leather by their momentum as the Firebird sped from the hotel parking lot. Her head grew light and her palms pressed against her hollow belly as her stomach dropped. Michael drove down the Arizona highway with a hound of hell literally at his bumper urging him on.

But would her task be over once they retrieved Lucifer's wings? She was afraid that leading Michael to heaven was only the beginning of her torment.

Ezekiel had said the palace had been built for her. She was used to the temporal tricks and treats of the hell dimension, where time was amorphous and seemingly unrelated to time on earth. The palace had seemed ancient and always. Built long before she'd been born.

Just as the kachina doll had been carved before Michael was born.

Ezekiel was older than the palace. And too knowing by far.

Had he forged the deal with her father to procure her as a future queen for his reluctant heir?

Michael tried to focus on the physicality of driving the vintage sports car down the long, desert highway. It was usually a pleasure. Collecting vintage cars throughout his prolonged life had been one of Adam Turov's hobbies. Michael had learned to love them at his stepfather's side, just as he'd learned to help with the running of Nightingale Vineyards.

It was more convenient to travel with Grim's ability. But driving wasn't about convenience. It was about controlling his own momentum and direction. He liked the feel of the steering wheel in hands.

While he'd learned about the vines and his stepfather's cars, he'd also been learning to control his Brimstone. It could be deadly. His scars proved how closely his own blood had come to taking his life.

Sitting beside Lily in the Firebird brought back memories of that first Burn. That's why he'd had the nightmare the night before.

But he couldn't deny there was a seductive, pleasurable edge to the heat when it rose in response to Lily's affinity. It was a new edge. One he hadn't had to deal with before. One that urged him to burn in spite of all the years he'd spent controlling the fire.

He looked down at the skin that showed below the cuffs of his jacket again and again. The scars were faint there, covered slightly by a fine dusting of golden brown hair, but he knew them. He had memorized their patterns for years as a meditation against losing control.

He didn't want to lose control of his Brimstone blood ever again. But he did desire the woman beside him. As he'd never desired another woman before. It wasn't only her affinity. Yes. That pull was powerful. His grip on the steering wheel was far tighter than it would have to be to keep the car on the road. And, yet, her affinity was only a small part of her allure.

She was determined and powerful and strong, but she was also in trouble. The instinct to protect her from hungry Rogues burned in him in ways that took him by surprise.

He needed her help to find the wings, but she needed his help to survive the Rogues who would never rest in hunting her down. He didn't burn for Lily only because of his Brimstone blood. He burned for her because he had heard about that ceaseless hunt from his mother and aunt his whole life, but actually seeing a woman hounded and harried by Rogues set him on fire in ways that had nothing to do with his daemon blood.

He wanted to help her escape her tormentors, but he also wanted her to know he would never be one of them. He wasn't a slave to his blood or the hunger for affinity it could cause in him if he lost control. He could sense her attraction to him. As the highway rolled by beneath them, she focused on the view outside the window, but he noticed the rise and fall of her chest, the flush on her cheeks, the fidgeting of her restless fingers. He didn't know if it was the same for her. If it was only his Brimstone blood that called to her or the hint of affinity he'd inherited from his mother, but whatever her reasons for desiring him…if and when they came together…it would be a conscious decision on his part. He wouldn't lose control.

He turned to look at her when he came to that decision and she tilted her head to meet his gaze at the same moment. The connection was there. No doubt. Her affinity stoked his burn. But there were other connections as well. Her determination and strength. Her humor in the face of danger. The glint of sun on her hair, the grace in her fight, the warmth in her brown eyes. He would want her if she weren't Samuel's daughter. Of that he was certain. He just wasn't sure if she'd ever believe it. She'd probably had to run and hide from hungry Rogues her whole life. But he was determined whatever they had wouldn't be ruled by Brimstone.

They saw the black sedans parked to block the highway long before there was no turning back. Like a wavering mirage of oily obstruction, the Rogue blockade shimmered in the noonday heat.

Nevertheless, Michael didn't turn around. He didn't veer off into the desert sand. Her real life warrior angel gripped the gearshift and Lily made the decision to place her hand over his as he shifted down to reduce the Firebird's speed.

He glanced from her face down to their hands.

The Rogues were following them, and others blocked their path. A touch no longer seemed to matter and yet it mattered so much she couldn't resist. His hand was tense and warm beneath her fingers. He had freshened the tape over the pads his constant playing wouldn't allow to heal. The vibrations of the car transferred through the gearshift and his palm to the back of his hand, then to her. The Firebird growled, its motor protesting the reduction of speed.

"We can't fight so many," Lily said. Dozens of daemons had exited the cars at their approach. In the rearview mirror more black vehicles came into view. Long black SUVs looking mean and lethal even with the tinted windows that hid their hungry occupants. The convoy behind them drove side-by-side three across, paying no heed to traffic laws or markings on the highway.

They were trapped. They had been from the start.

"Watch me. Fighting is as much a part of my heritage as wine and song," Michael said.

"And Brimstone blood," Lily whispered.

He didn't agree. He didn't have to. The heat rising from his body gave him away. The car slowed to a stop. They were a hundred yards from the blockade. The SUVs were closing in from behind.

"Stay in the car," Michael ordered. He sounded like a future king.

Grim had materialized. He stood by the car waiting for his master.

"I'm not safe in the car. Nowhere is safe for me," Lily said. *Except maybe Ezekiel's palace*, but she kept that thought to herself. She opened the door and got out before Michael could try to stop her. She wasn't hiding anymore.

Her sword came easily from its place in her pack. She quickly drew it and shrugged the backpack over her shoulders. She didn't bother to close the car door. Michael had also left his door open. The Firebird sat in the middle of the highway with its "wings" ineffectually spread. She might never get the chance to "fly" in it again. But at least she had. She had flown. Refuge wasn't everything. Home, for her, had always been elusive. A lie.

She was a tool. That's all she'd ever been. She could fight that or accept it. Her chest swelled as she gulped a big breath of bracing air. Ezekiel might want her to marry his heir. And she might never fulfill that wish. But she could be the best ward she could possibly be.

Her mother had wanted Lily to stop the Rogues for the daemon king. Sophia hadn't intended her daughter to do it with arm-to-arm combat. Sometimes the best intentions dissolved into necessity. Her father had prepared her for that. His sword felt balanced and deadly in her hands.

"I've resisted your call because I had to, not because I wanted to," Michael said as they turned to face in opposite directions. The SUVs had stopped and more Rogues than she'd thought could fit in the vehicles exited. Slowly. They were obviously savoring their triumph. "I've always hated the Brimstone in my blood. You make it very hard not to celebrate it."

Lily froze. She didn't look at him. But her whole body stilled in response to his declaration. He wanted her. What's more, he wanted to want her. They prepared for death, but she suddenly felt more alive than she'd ever been.

"These bastards want your affinity. They want Ezekiel's throne. I just want you. I need you to know it isn't affinity or my Brimstone. I've resisted its burn my whole life," Michael said. "I don't want to resist you."

"Now you tell me," Lily replied.

But she didn't believe him. She'd been a prisoner of her affinity her entire life because others couldn't or wouldn't control its effect on them. She wanted to believe that Michael was different, but that want was a weakness she couldn't afford.

Grim whined and shifted from Michael's side to hers in a swirl of disembodied smoke. He stood between her and the closest approaching daemon. The protective act caused tears to fill her eyes. He might not trust her, but he placed his intimidating body in harm's way for her after his master's declaration. The ferocity of his love for Michael caused her heart to ache in an echo of the same emotion. Even if they survived, she couldn't allow herself to love her warrior angel. Not when he would surely hate her once he knew Ezekiel planned to use her to tempt Michael to the throne.

"I'll show you when this is over. Count on it," Michael said.

She had no time to respond. Not to argue or throw herself in his arms. Suddenly, Michael and Grim exploded into action and she was left holding her sword and standing alone. Grim fought in an ever-widening circle around her. His terrible jaw crunched again and again and the air was filled with Rogue screams. But while he protected her, Michael was left to fight alone. Lily watched him bleed as daemon blades bit into him again and again. She was trapped by the smoky vapor of Grim's wake and the bodies and blood that fell all around. Before she could escape the circle a wall of fallen Rogue bodies prevented her from reaching Michael's side.

Once again she was enclosed and protected while others died.

Lily dropped to her knees. But she wasn't giving up. She allowed her father's sword to clank to the ground so that she could take the pack from her back. Her fingers fumbled with the wrappings, but long hours of practice saved her.

This time she unwrapped them all.

Earth, Wind, Fire, Water…and the tiny black-winged angel.

She placed them in position and wasn't surprised when the warrior angel claimed a place in the center of them all. Her flute came from its velvet pouch and she brought it to her lips in a move that seemed to take an eternity. Grim had howled in pain multiple times now. Many daemons had fallen, but there were too many for one hellhound to fight alone.

Michael was nowhere to be seen beyond the smoke. It wasn't only smoke from Grim's rapid materializations. His wounds smoked, and the bodies of fallen daemons smoked as well. The burned smell of wounded flesh and Brimstone filled the air. Her affinity had been shocked into paralysis, but the second her shaky breath brought forth the first note from the flute against her lips, the rush of it filled her body from the heart out. Blood pumped and the affinity rode it as well as her song until she vibrated with a music that daemons could hear above all else, even their own screams.

She thought she heard her name. She played on. She didn't pause. She summoned the elemental spirits that she'd been able to hear since she was born. To many they were only tradition. To her they were real.

Wind whipped her hair and her clothes and whirled smoke and sand into her eyes. She didn't close them. She tried to squint through the sulfuric smoke to find Michael. A storm coalesced around her and droplets of moisture fell. The earth trembled beneath her knees.

But it was Fire that saved them.

The ring of Rogue bodies piled around her burst into flames. Grim leaped over the ring of fire and disappeared. She knew he would reappear to fight by Michael's side. But would it be too late? The daemon king would never forgive her if she allowed his heir to die. Her heart thumped a more tragic reason to fear his death.

She would never be his queen. Not through manipulation. Not when he'd told her that he wanted to want her in spite of the Brimstone and not because of it. But she needed him to live for reasons other than Ezekiel's throne. Rivulets of water ran down her face, cooling the heat of the fire that consumed the Rogue daemons around her. The warrior angel kachina stood silently. Her flute didn't call it to life.

Lily wasn't sure if offering her as a bride was part of Ezekiel's plan, but she would give Michael up before she'd force him to…

The tiny kachina doll in the center of her elemental spirits toppled over and Lily gasped. Her song was broken just as her lungs had begun to be scorched from acrid smoke.

A howl like none before it rent the air. Lily's head went light and her stomach clenched in fear. There had been too many daemons. Michael had been right. Even with the power of her elemental spirit's fire amplified by Brimstone, they had lost.

# *Chapter 9*

Lily stood. Steam rose from her wet clothes and hair, threading upward to join the smoke of the burning dead. She couldn't see beyond a small circle of space left around her. She could only stumble in the direction of the howl that had trailed off to nothing. But not before the grief it conveyed chilled her to the bone.

She almost tripped over her father's sword and she paused long enough to pick it up. If Michael had fallen, it would do her no good. She couldn't stand against the daemons alone, and she doubted Grim would stay to help her if his master was dead.

The thought of Michael gone caused her chill to deepen, as if her very marrow had turned to ice in spite of the flow of burning Brimstone on the ground. She stepped over and around, weaving among the carnage until sulfuric ash coated her skin. Her lungs hitched in protest with every breath against the thick air.

Far beyond the ring of bodies Grim had created with his horrible jaws, there were other bodies strewn in a more haphazard way. Michael had commandeered a daemon blade. That one man could fight so many and win sent frissons of shock down her frozen spine. She looked away from the bodies to try to avoid imagining what they had done to her warrior angel before they'd fallen. But not before she saw that they burned. They *all* burned. Flames licked away at their flesh where the blades had parted their skin and Brimstone had escaped.

The elemental Fire she'd called had reached farther than she'd thought possible. Her desperation had strengthened the spirit's ability. The Brimstone Michael had released had been all the fuel it needed. Her elemental spirit had taken it from there.

But Michael must have been cut as well. There was no way he could have fought with so many Rogues and escaped injury. Lily stopped. With that thought, her heart froze, too. She couldn't go on. What if her ability had caused Michael to relive his worst nightmare and what if this time he hadn't been able to stop the burn?

A whining growl thawed her with a stab of fear that shocked her into motion. She forced herself to move toward the hellhound's terrible sounds. Tears streaked from her eyes. She blinked, cursing the hateful ash and smoke and horror that caused them.

Finally, she saw movement. She gripped her blade, but her fingers were numb. All the water had evaporated from her clothes and her body. It had saved her from being scorched, but it was fear that had kept her cold in the heat. If Michael was gone, she'd never be warm again. She knew it. Her body protested his loss even as her mind tried to deal.

She jerked to a halt again, her feet shuffling awkwardly, when she made out the hulking form of Grim and his fallen master. Smoke had cleared around them. It dissipated upward in spidery threads as if driven away by the hellhound's despair.

"No," Lily said. The syllable choked out from a throat raw from the thick, superheated air she'd breathed.

Grim raised his head. He growled low in his chest, but unlike the smoke she wouldn't be driven away. Michael wasn't dead. He couldn't be. She had worried about betraying him. This was so much worse.

Grim continued to growl, but she hurried forward. Michael's clothes smoked, but there was no flame. His face and hands were covered with blackened blood. A daemon blade was clutched in each fist. He had taken out dozens of Rogues and disarmed at least two of them. Alone. Before he'd been wounded so badly that he couldn't go on.

Lily dropped to her knees beside Michael's smoking body. Much of the blood wasn't his. He had soaked in the blood of his enemies. But only a second of relief came from that observation. He was injured. His leather jacket was shredded. She reached with her free hand to uncover his chest before she lost the nerve. Her sword arm was limp by her side between her and Grim. She didn't need to raise it against the mourning beast. She wouldn't. But she was glad when he allowed her to check his master's injuries.

A daemon blade had bitten him deeply. She closed her eyes against the sight but quickly forced them open again. The whole world seemed to pause as she held her breath to see if his chest still rose and fell. She started and released pent-up oxygen when he stirred and a soft moan came from between his slightly parted lips.

"They retreated to regroup. They'll be back," Michael struggled to say. "Go. Now. Grim, take her away."

"We won't leave you," Lily said. She glanced into Grim's eyes to be sure the monster agreed. He blinked in acknowledgment, then looked back at Michael.

"You didn't burn," Lily said. She said the words out loud to reassure herself and claim the miracle. She wasn't sure Michael heard.

"You're wrong. I always burn," Michael said. "But that was…intense."

Lily touched his face and he opened his eyes. The hazel of his irises was impossibly light and bright against his grimy skin. A rush of relief flooded through her, thawing, warming, but it was immediately chilled away by the truth. He had fought her element of Fire and won, but he was badly hurt and she didn't know what to do to save him.

Michael's eyes had widened as he took in her appearance, but he closed them again as if seeing her covered in ash and Brimstone blood was an added pain he couldn't bear.

"Leave me," he ordered.

The hellhound beside her shuffled and whined.

"No," Lily said again. More firmly than before. This time she raised the blade between her and Grim. She intended it to be a warning in case the hellhound thought she should listen to Michael. She wasn't prepared for the giant beast to throw himself against her sword. She released it but her reaction was too late to prevent the blade from slicing through Grim's smoky hair and into the flesh of his barrel chest.

"Grim," she shouted. Michael's eyes opened once more. The bloody sword clanked to the pavement and the hellhound slumped against his master's body. Lily reached for him, but she wasn't fast enough to help him before he fell over Michael's chest.

"Damn it, mutt. Don't die for me," Michael groaned. Then he cried out as the hellhound's pure Brimstone blood mingled with his, coating the ugly chest wound with its pure Brimstone flow.

Lily reached for Michael's arm and he released his death grip on the daemon blades. He grasped her hand as his face contorted in pain. She didn't try to pull Grim away from his master. The hellhound knew what to do. She leaned closer to Michael instead. Desperate to soothe his torment. She placed her lips against his. In that instant she shared his pain, burning and brutal and inexorably linked to a time when he'd almost died as a child.

She kissed him. Through the pain. She tasted ash, but she thought of wine. She faced immeasurable darkness, but she thought of the sun. And music. Her flute had been abandoned back in the circle with her kachina dolls. She hummed low in her throat instead. He was in agony, but her affinity reached out to engulf him in a nearly invisible aura that shimmered in the air around him to join with the waves of heat rising from the Brimstone blood that cauterized his wound.

She continued to hum against his lips until he went limp beneath her mouth. The extreme pain had caused him to pass out. Lily reluctantly pulled back. She had soothed him. It had been torturous, but without their connection it would have been worse.

Grim stirred and rose. Lily swallowed and wiped sweat from her brow. Her tears had dried. Or they had evaporated away. The hellhound dragged himself from Michael's body. The burn of their mingled blood had sealed his master's wound, but Grim still bled. He moved weakly away and collapsed nearby.

"You would gladly kill yourself to save him," Lily whispered. He blinked at her and whined.

She stood, but it was an unsteady process that took longer than usual. She'd nearly used herself up to perform the extreme summoning that had saved them. Sharing Michael's pain had almost been more than her body could handle. She could barely move now. Adrenaline had drained away, leaving her numb.

"I guess we would both kill ourselves for him," Lily said. The hellhound's head had slumped to the side and he breathed heavily as his body tried to recover. If he acknowledged their common cause, he couldn't show it. "I'm going for the car. We do need to get out of here and I don't think you're in any shape to take us anywhere."

She headed back to retrieve the Firebird. This time she walked through piles of ash that were beginning to blow away in the desert breeze. There would be nothing left but abandoned vehicles soon. It was hard to believe a battle had raged less than an hour ago. Only their bodies told the tale. She was no longer numb, but the aches and pains that had woken with her return to feeling made it hard to move. Only the knowledge that the surviving Rogues would be back made her hurry.

Michael and Grim needed time to heal. She needed to refuel. And there was something else even more important that she needed to do.

She sank behind the wheel of Michael's car. The seat had conformed to the muscular curves of his body, and it embraced her. She breathed deeply of the car's pleasant scent. She gripped the wheel. It reminded her of Michael, strong and uninjured, before he met her. Of the music he'd made and scars he'd managed to survive.

She would get him and Grim to safety and then she would seek out the answers she needed from the daemon king. She deserved to know all of his plans. Michael might be bound to the throne of hell, but she could never be part of the bargain that held him there. She wouldn't be used to sweeten the deal. He shouldn't be forced or beguiled onto the throne. She'd had enough of obligation, daemon deals and forced devotion. She would give up her haven in hell rather than marry someone who longed to be free.

# *Chapter 10*

Peter limped back for a car when he was certain Samuel's daughter and her half-daemon escort—and the hellhound—were gone. One of Peter's legs had been shredded almost to the bone by the hellhound's teeth. He'd been so close to his prize, but he'd retreated then. Thank Reynard. Because the Brimstone that tainted his blood might save him from the injury, but it would have killed him if it had ignited from what came after.

He'd heard the flute—deceptively beautiful and haunting, so delicate that it seemed to ride on a light desert wind. But the wind had whipped faster and harder and the music had become thunderous. He'd only been able to save himself from the fire the bitch had brought forth from her ridiculous dolls by crawling into a ditch and burrowing in sand when it had come to consume him. If he'd been a daemon, he'd be dead. They all were. Or dying. Too burned for their Brimstone blood to heal them.

He didn't pause when he'd crawled past the remains of his suffering companions. He had no blood to spare.

Peter's blood held only the taint of damnation from selling his soul to the Rogues. He'd endured hideous pain, but he hadn't burned from the inside out the way the daemons had.

If he survived the hellhound's bite, he'd live to fight another day.

His clothes were nothing but burned rags coated in sticky black blood. His leg screamed until he would have hacked it off if he'd had the strength or nerve. When he finally reached a sedan and crawled inside, his ruined hands shook on the steering wheel. Blisters had risen in response to the heat inside him even before his clothes had burst into flames. He'd been forced to smack the flames down on his arms and legs. The blisters had burst and their edges had charred. Now they peeled painfully, deep and raw.

He'd seen what had happened to the Rogues. Nothing was left of them but ash. He accepted his pain. Eventually, he gloried in it. The Brimstone would heal him. Hadn't it already gifted him with extended life and strength? As he headed toward the other group of Rogues, he blessed Reynard for the example he had set for the Order. Being used by the Rogues allowed them to use the Rogues in turn. If the other Rogues had been successful in carrying out their plans to steal Lucifer's wings from heaven, all wasn't lost. The Order would still eventually claim the girl.

Peter planned to make it to the wings and heal as he waited for Lily Santiago to come to him. He passed the time and distracted himself from the pain by imagining the torture he would use on the girl to make her comply with the Order's wishes. To his wishes. After he'd divested her of her flute and destroyed her dolls, of course. With those amplifying her affinity, she was far more dangerous than they'd thought.

She drove several hours with Michael slumped in the front seat and Grim taking up the entire back seat before she found an abandoned diner. The dilapidated building was ramshackle enough to be a doubtful retreat for a half-daemon prince. Only the tall steel post of its sign remained and she'd almost missed that in the glare of the desert sun. The building was off the road and below a rise. With the setting of the sun, it would be a hidden retreat for the night.

Or so she hoped.

She pulled the Firebird around to the back. She parked under a leaning canopy that had once held drive-in stalls for diners who wanted to eat in their cars. When she turned the engine off, Michael didn't stir. But when she opened the rear door, Grim jumped down, albeit gingerly, before he went to sniff around the premises.

He paused to sniff her first. She held still as he placed his great snout in her hand. She blinked, glad no one was around to see her eyes fill with tears. An injured Grim, no longer standoffish and suspicious, was nearly her undoing. She didn't deserve his trust, but she would need to use it tonight to do what she intended to do.

In the trunk of the car she found an emergency kit with a blanket, water and a few other meager supplies. She would forever think of this as the protein bar summer. If she survived. Michael regained consciousness enough to get his legs under him and help when she moved him to a makeshift cot she made out of a blanket and a mouse-eaten vinyl booth seat with most of its stuffing intact.

"The palace has beds nicer than this. Much nicer. Just so you know," Lily murmured. Her words were safe. He was already lost again in a deep amd hopefully healing sleep.

Before she left him, she smoothed his hair back from his face. She left water and a couple of bars within reach. He murmured beneath her touch, but he didn't wake again. If this was goodbye, he'd never know how close he came to being forced into an arranged marriage as well as a throne.

Outside, the moon had risen and the stars were sharp bits of light in an expanse of midnight blue only the wide desert horizon could display. Grim sat guarding the path back to the road. He whined when she approached and she bit her lip. She was afraid he was too weak to help her. She'd left her father's blade with Michael. He deserved better weapons than those he'd taken from the damned. Those she had thrown far into the desert. On her back, the pack she carried had only her flute and the kachina dolls inside.

All save the warrior angel that was clasped in her fist.

Stupid. Sentimental. But if she got lost on those pathways between that Michael had spoken of she didn't want to wander them alone.

"Grim. I need to speak to the daemon king," Lily began. The hellhound sat back on his haunches and his eyes began to glow. "I know you're weak. It might be too much to ask, but it's for Michael. Sort of. I need to know the truth. I can't make it to the palace without you. There are no sipapus nearby."

Grim's eyes were twin flames in the dark. His body was nothing but shadow. Suddenly she was compelled to be completely honest with the loyal beast. He deserved no less.

"He wouldn't want me to go. In the end, he'll hate me for what I have to do. But that's why I need to speak to Ezekiel. If I help him force Michael to accept the throne, I can never be his queen. He deserves better than that and… I deserve better, too. I've settled for less than love for too long," Lily said. By then, she'd approached the shadow of Grim and sunk down to hold the beast in her arms. His hair was soft and silky in her fists. Very unlike his forbidding appearance in daylight. She sensed when he relaxed beneath her touch. She pressed her face into his lionlike ruff in relief.

"I couldn't survive being only an obligation to Michael. Not him," Lily confessed. "I've been nothing but an obligation for too long. I have bargains to fulfill, but my heart can't be bargained with. Not anymore."

Grim pulled back. His eyes were so bright they illuminated the area around them like lanterns. The rest of the world had gone even darker.

"I want you to take me to the palace and return right away. You'll need to watch over him until he's well. Come what may. And if you're too weak to get me there…leave me between. Do you understand? Leave me and come back to him," Lily said.

Grim chuffed and growled. Then he turned to walk away. His shadow dissipated with every stride. Lily stumbled to her feet to follow before he left her behind.

She'd never felt anything like it. She'd left hell through an established earthen portal with the power of her elemental guides. This was entirely different. Her body probably disappeared like Grim as she ran after him, but to her senses she remained whole. The air changed. The ground changed. Grim paused and let her grip his ruff for guidance, but other than not being able to see or hear clearly, it seemed nothing but an endless stroll before she suddenly knew they were within the familiar palace walls.

True to their agreement, Grim went back the way they'd come no sooner than she found herself home. She was alone in her cozy quarters as if she'd never left.

*There was no shame in being afraid of his grandfather. His parents were brave and strong. His stepfather had saved hundreds of men, women and children from the Order of Samuel during his supernaturally extended life. And his mother had saved his stepfather. She'd saved Michael when he was a newborn, from the flames of a burning opera house and from the ignition of his first Burn when his half-daemon blood had nearly consumed him as a toddler.*

*They were both scared of Ezekiel. Michael was sixteen and he could tell when people stiffened and their smiles went tight. When those smiles didn't reach their eyes. He'd seen his stepfather, a former daemon hunter, tense and check the hollow between his shoulder blades where the hilt of his sword had hidden, ready, for a hundred years whenever Ezekiel visited the winery. He'd seen his mother send the daemon king away time and time again before she'd finally agreed on this visit.*

*She had to fulfill a bargain she'd struck. You never outran a daemon deal.*

*So even with Grim as an escort, Michael's entire body was tight and his blood was as cold as he could make it when he arrived at the daemon king's palace.*

*He didn't have a sword on his back. He had a guitar. And even though music was powerful, the instrument that was as much a part of him as his hands and heart didn't feel like much to count on when he entered Ezekiel's home. A deafening din had engulfed him and Grim when they'd materialized in the throne room. But the crowd had hushed and drawn in breath as if they were one monster, watching and waiting for him to trip up.*

*The red carpet leading to the throne wasn't infinite, but it seemed to go on forever. The room was filled with Loyalist daemons who'd come to see the heir to Lucifer's throne. He was sixteen. He just wanted to sing. He wanted to find his own way in a world that had been revealed as dark and deadly to him—yet also strangely wonderful—from his earliest memories.*

*His mother said he could choose. His stepfather said Ezekiel couldn't be trusted to honor that choice. They were both right. When he and Grim halted at the base of the dais that held the throne, Michael knew he was in for a fight if he tried to reject it. He'd never seen Ezekiel on the throne. He seemed more royal and impossible to rebel against. The daemon king had been his real father's commander. His real father, a daemon also named Michael, had died right after Michael was born.*

*Rogues had killed him.*

*"Ezekiel," Michael said. His voice was eaten by the great reaches of the room. It sounded small. Young. But there was strength in refusing to call the daemon king his grandfather. It was a title the king had assumed. It wasn't rightfully his. Michael might be prepared to stand against Rogues and the Order of Samuel for as long as he lived— and regardless of whether he ignored the Brimstone in his blood or not he would live a long, long time—but that didn't mean he had to fall in line with all of the daemon king's plans for him.*

*He looked away from Ezekiel's expectations. Beside the throne was an enormous suit of armor that loomed in the shadows. He only realized it was empty when he noticed that the helmet was open and hollow. It stared at him with blank visor slits. The stare was intimidating, but not as intimidating as the huge broadsword the suit seemed to "hold" with empty gloves. He wasn't used to seeing medieval-style swords outside of video games. His stepfather had recently begun training him with smaller, more graceful blades. How much would that broadsword weigh?*

*"Michael D'Arcy... Turov," Ezekiel announced. As always, he left a long pause between his mother's last name and his stepfather's, as if he added the last reluctantly. Ezekiel had loved his human grandmother. His mother's mother. A woman Michael had never known. She had died to protect Ezekiel from Rogues even though she was married to another man. Her offspring had been sired by a man who belonged to the Order of Samuel. She'd been forced to marry him in spite of her rebellious love for one of the daemons the Order stalked.*

*Ezekiel hadn't been able to be with Elizabeth D'Arcy or to save her, but he pledged himself to her children and her children's children in spite of the fact that she'd been*

*forced to marry a mortal man by the Order of Samuel. Her
descendants were tied to Ezekiel by his immortal devotion, one Michael couldn't begin to understand. He didn't
acknowledge the daemon blood that had come from his
biological father. Even though one day it might make him
prone to such a fierce emotion. It didn't matter that his
mother had loved a daemon and that their love had resulted in his birth. He'd refused to burn for a very long
time, and so far even his adolescent years hadn't challenged that.*

*He had his song. He had Grim. He had his parents. One
day he would figure out what else he needed and who he
was meant to be, but he didn't need Ezekiel or his throne.
Especially if accepting the throne meant giving up control
of his Brimstone blood.*

*"I'm here to fulfill my mother's bargain,"* Michael said.
*His mother had agreed he would visit Ezekiel in Hell when
he was old enough for the journey. It had been a stalling
tactic to keep the daemon king for pressing for a larger
part in their lives. His words were a formal declaration
he had practiced with his mother. He'd been schooled on
what to say and what not to say. He'd been warned against
making any other deals. Daemons were notorious manipu-
lators of the universe. They bargained as they breathed—
naturally and without effort. The cleverest human would
never be able to outwit a daemon king.*

*"You may stay as long as you like and come as often
as you please. This is your home. I pledge it to you now
in front of this company,"* Ezekiel proclaimed.

*The air went thick around Michael. He struggled to
inhale and exhale. Grim whined and pressed against
him, sensing his distress. Torches that lit the chamber
high above the crowd seemed to slow in their flickering.
The amber light around him no longer danced. The dae-*

mon guests had been quiet. Now they were still as death. Their pale faces merged into a blur that seemed to press in against him on all sides.

Ezekiel had wasted no time and Michael hadn't been prepared. No wonder his mother had put off the inevitable for as long as she could. They were a boy and his dog thrown among wolves. But he did have untapped resources. He was only half human. And his companion had been bred in the fires of hell itself.

"I have until my twenty-first birthday to choose. That's the agreement you made with my mother. Now it's an agreement between us. On that day you'll have my answer and you'll abide by it. Yes or no. Fire or song," Michael said into the void that came when the universe paused to wait for a daemon deal to be struck. He had to force the words out, but after, just when he thought he would pass out from lack of oxygen, the air normalized around him. The crowd shifted into life and relaxed, murmuring and laughing. The torches danced. Michael's chest expanded as he tried to breathe without gasping.

"I will protect the throne for you until that day," Ezekiel said.

Michael had stayed among the throng of Loyalists only for as long as he had to stay. He held Grim's great woolly ruff with one hand and wandered the room, but he was glad when Ezekiel sent a man in a suit to guide him away. He'd been led to a set of rooms in the east wing where he found a wonderland of tech and toys waiting. Every game system known to man. Some vintage ones were especially interesting. He discovered an amazing sound system and a recording studio that even rivaled his mother's. Michael's parents were wealthy, but Ezekiel's resources were obviously not limited by any idea that excess was wrong or might go to Michael's head.

*Even as he explored through all the rooms and what they held, Michael knew bribery when he saw it. He was sixteen. He wasn't stupid. He also suspected the daemon king was trying to make up for not saving his grandmother. The stuff was cool. He couldn't deny it. And it would make the time pass faster until he could go back home.*

*But it also made him twitchy. Like a mouse lured into a trap that hadn't snapped on its neck yet.*

*When Grim grew restless and paced to the door, Michael tossed down a video game controller and followed the hellhound out into the corridor. It was dark. Hours had passed since midnight and the crowds were gone. The hallways and passages were deserted. Michael followed Grim when he headed off as if he had somewhere to go. They passed room after room with gleaming marble floors and ceilings so full of faces and figures he couldn't tell where one ended and another began. The chaos of the carvings made the silence eerie. As if there should be cries and howls and laughter and shouts to match the art on the walls.*

*"What is it, Grim?" Michael asked. The hellhound was leading and he was following. They kept to the middle of the rooms and hallways and Michael was glad. Something about the art jogged his memories. Far above, he thought he saw a hint of movement again and again, but when he looked up and tried to focus, torchlight and shadows and hundreds of frozen faces met his eyes. "Not exactly a fairy-tale castle, is it?" he said. Grim paused for only a second to look at him. The hellhound seemed to wink at him as one of his eyes closed slower than the other.*

*They continued and finally the beast led him into the throne room from a back antechamber that was hidden behind the intimidating seat. The great room was empty. Most of the torches had been extinguished. Only a few provided a soft distant glow. Grim stopped and sat down as if the throne room had been his destination all along.*

*"Really? I walked away from vintage* Battle Tank *for this?" Michael said.*

*But he had to admit it was cool to visit the room when he wasn't being watching by a thousand eyes. The thought made him look around at the walls and ceiling. Okay. Not by a thousand living eyes. He allowed himself to step forward and slowly mount the steps of the dais. He climbed up to Lucifer's throne, which would have been creepier if he hadn't been raised to know that human myths about angels and demons were nowhere close to the truth.*

*To the right of the throne and slightly behind was the large suit of armor he'd noticed earlier in the evening. It distracted Michael from the throne itself. Though it was in shadows, the large broadsword held in front of the suit by two leather gauntlets caught the light. It shimmered and gleamed as if something dark lived and moved up and down its blade. The gleam called to Michael and he stepped to stand in front of the armor. It had obviously been worn by a tall, muscular man. He wouldn't fill it right now by half with his gawky teen body.*

*He wondered if he would even be able to lift the sword.*

*Suddenly, the need to try filled him, warming his heart and urging him to reach for the elaborately scrolled hilt. He brushed the gloves out of the way to reveal the sword was actually held by an iron stand not the empty suit of armor. The stand made him feel less intimidated by the armor. Whoever had worn it was gone. The armor was old and dusty. No one had disturbed it for years. The dust was probably as old as or older than Michael himself.*

*The hilt was too big for his hand to circumvent. He had to use both hands to pull the broadsword from the stand's hooked top. It came free only after he'd tugged with his whole weight several times. The clatter of its tip scraping the floor rang out in the empty room and echoed high and long off the cathedral ceiling above him.*

*Michael suddenly felt small.*

*The sword was far too heavy for him to brandish. The best he could do was place it carefully back in its stand. At least no one had seen him. Whoever had worn the armor had been one righteous badass. Respect.*

*He shouldn't have disturbed the dust on the sword. It was some kind of tribute to a fallen warrior. Like a memorial or something. But the sword wasn't why he'd come to the throne room. There was something here that was meant for him. He was supposed to be the heir to the throne.*

*He turned away from the armor and stepped back to what had brought him here in the first place.*

*Then, he sat.*

*It wasn't a choice or a statement. He just wanted to see what it was like. "Hard" and "cold" were his first thoughts.*

*"Off with their heads," he said, but the joke seemed lame even with no one around.*

*The stone leeched all his body heat until even his Brimstone, which required constant subconscious vigilance to tamp down, was out cold. He shivered. It should be nice to have a break, but his insides felt hollow, as if a part of him was gone. Tamping it down and completely losing it were two different things.*

*Grim watched him. His eyes ignited by the fires inside him. Michael rose and pretended he was only interested in looking closer at the carvings on the nearest wall rather than admit that he couldn't handle the throne.*

*He came face-to-face with a life-size carving of a man whose face was contorted in an angry scream. His eyes were closed. His mouth open wide. Michael forced him-*

*self closer, again pulled by a vague memory even as he was repelled by the expression on the carving's face. He stopped when his nose was a hairsbreadth away from the stone nose of the carved man. Far above, the torches that still burned barely illuminated where he stood. He wasn't sure if an undetected breeze suddenly caused the flames to leap and cast a great dark shadow over the wall, but he was completely certain of the movement when the carved man opened his eyes.*

*Michael jumped back, too startled to play it cool. The carving's stone irises were exposed and now he stared at Michael with a blank gaze that chilled him to the bone.*

*"They are the Rogues who weren't claimed by heaven or Oblivion when they fell. And the humans who helped Rogues to plot against heaven." A voice broke into his shock and he backed up several more steps from the wall.*

*An older daemon woman had come into the room without him noticing. She came closer to him and suddenly he knew "older" didn't begin to estimate her age. She was easily as old as or older than the daemon king. And she was familiar.*

*"It's been too long, Grim. You rarely come to see me anymore. I suppose this young man keeps you busy," she said. "I thought I'd find you here. Do you remember me? I'm Sybil. I took care of you when you were a child."*

*He remembered. Her great sewing kit he wasn't allowed to touch. Needles. Fabrics. Scissors and thread. Her smile. Long since he'd heard his mother refer to it as a "Mona Lisa smile."*

*"You watched me sew your mother's wedding dress. And your aunt's. I've dressed Adam and John a time or two as well. But Ezekiel keeps me busy these days and has for half a dozen years," Sybil said. "I'm still sewing. And I*

*find it easier to avoid the mortal realm. There comes a time when even a daemon's heart becomes full and finished."*

"The damned," Michael said. He looked back at the man in the wall. At all the men and women and children on the walls and ceiling high above them.

Dark memories had flooded back to join the pleasant memories of his former nanny. His daemon father had been trapped in a prison like this. The Rogue Council had imprisoned all the Loyalists they'd captured in a frieze on the walls of l'Opéra Severne. They'd been freed when the opera house burned to the ground, but some—like his true father—had sacrificed themselves to drag Reynard into Oblivion.

"A king who rules here must rule in darkness. But is it actually darker than the world you know or is it only different? Here darkness is displayed for all to see. There is beauty in justice. A king must mete it out. Especially a king of the damned," Sybil said. She had reached for Grim and he had come to her hand, snuffling like a puppy.

"My mother says different, not damned," Michael said. For some reason Sybil's smile and her words caused his heart to pound painfully in his chest. She was ancient. And she seemed so...resigned. Full and finished. It hurt him. His remembered affection for her felt heavy in his heart.

"Well, it's a choice for all of us to decide which, isn't it? And daemons must make choices often in their long lives," she said. Grim didn't mind her gloomy words. He snuggled against her, no doubt remembering her love from long ago and far away.

"You're wrong. And this is wrong. I don't think this is justice. This is revenge. There's a difference," Michael said. "If this is what comes of Brimstone blood then I'll pass."

Michael looked away from Sybil's soft smile. He stared

*at the man in the wall once more. These Rogues might deserve to suffer the same fate they'd chosen to inflict on others, but every soul deserved an impartial judge, and he knew his grandfather was far from that. There was corruption in this. A deep wrongness that offended the sense of true justice he'd inherited from his heroic stepfather. This was horror, and their suffering reminded him that this is what his daemon father had endured... Michael's heart still pounded but now it also burned.*

*His Brimstone flared in response to his distress.*

*It wouldn't hurt him. Not anymore. He was older and wiser. The scars on his arms and legs and chest were only reminders of how vulnerable he'd been as a half-human baby with no practice in controlling his Brimstone blood. But even though the only ones who might be harmed in the room were an ancient daemon woman and a hellhound spawned in the pits of hell, he exercised the control he'd begun to learn when he was a smaller child.*

*He tamped down the panic. He fisted his hands. Grim left Sybil and came to press against his side, absorbing some of his master's heat. The Rogues in the walls and ceiling writhed in response to his suddenly revealed presence. He'd been almost invisible when he was cold. His human half in control. Now he gleamed brighter than the torches to their dulled senses. They roiled and cried and gnashed their teeth. Michael backed away.*

*"I'll never be king of this place," he said. He set his jaw against the sulfuric burn in the back of his throat. He swallowed the heat back down to his core even though it burned as if he'd swallowed one of the torches that flickered on the walls.*

*Sybil looked from the wall to her former charge.*

"*Never is a very long time for a person with Brimstone blood,*" she warned. She continued to smile, but her smile was one of the tragic ones that didn't reach her eyes.

# *Chapter 11*

Ezekiel was a hardened warrior king, but he was a being who had walked on the golden streets of heaven itself. Lily couldn't go to him in rags covered in ash and hope for a favorable audience. Not now when her reception would be trickier than ever because of Michael's close call with death.

She had almost killed Ezekiel's beloved D'Arcy heir.

Quickly and quietly, she worked to improve her appearance without calling maids for help. She was loath to disturb the strange heavy silence that reverberated out in the palace corridors. Truthfully, she and her mother had always lived simply in their wing as if she wasn't the ward of a king.

Lily drew a bath and washed away the remnants of the battle. She didn't take the time to dry her thick hair. She plaited the wet strands into a long braid. Then she dressed in clothes very unlike the worn jeans and tees that had been her desert staples for months. The dress she chose was a simple silk shift, long and white. Her matching slippers felt insubstantial after weeks in sturdy boots and practical sneakers.

She was here. She'd always been here. She wanted Ezekiel to know she accepted her position. This wasn't about rebellion. All she asked was that she be left a heart when all was said and done.

Leaving the sanctuary of her rooms was difficult. Sophia had brought in comfortable furnishings and Southwestern fabrics and textiles to create a haven for them. On shelves throughout the room sat all of the kachinas she'd spent a lifetime carving. They had been like family and friends to a girl who'd had to grow up without real siblings. Lily had placed the warrior angel on her nightstand where a small faded spot indicated its usual position. After she dressed, she put it in the pocket of her dress. She placed her flute in the other pocket. She was unarmed, but she wasn't entirely alone. She held her head high, but her heart pounded.

She stepped into the hallway and immediately she was dwarfed by the immense width and height and depth of the palace around her. The building was an architectural masterpiece of supernatural size and scope. Its dark baroque beauty was complex, constructed with carvings and details no one human being could ever explore. Crafted of the deepest black marble, the walls and floors shone in perpetual candlelight and the purple haze of an atmosphere mortals would find strangely gloaming-like in the day or night.

Lily headed to the throne room. She'd been quiet. Her arrival hadn't been heralded. Ezekiel would still be waiting. His grandson had almost died for her. Because of her. She'd almost killed Elizabeth's grandson. It wasn't until she was nearly there that she caught a glimpse of her reflection in gigantic mirrors that rimmed the outer chamber. She was only a tiny figure in the lower corners, furtively flitting from one glass to another, but the brilliant white of her dress shone like a star. She'd meant the dress to serve as a parley flag. Not one of surrender, but one of peace and compromise. Now she saw it as a pristine rebellion against her life trapped in shadows. It was a strategic mistake she'd have to overcome. It was too late to turn back.

\* \* \*

Michael woke to the soft cool kiss of the night breeze on his face. He hurt. It had been a hell of a fight. Literally. But he could already feel the Brimstone burning steadily beneath his skin knitting and healing his injuries more speedily than any wholly human person could expect. For once, the reminder of his half-daemon blood didn't bother him. He would have died without the Brimstone. He would have been useless to Lily against the Rogues.

Lily?

His senses lasered into focus on the woman he'd last seen covered in ash and blood. He rose with a gasp and a groan as his worst injury was jarred. He would have a new scar by the looks of it when his stomach healed. Grim's Brimstone had cauterized the wound and saved his life. He remembered that too even as he squinted to look around him.

Grim?

He wasn't just alone. He was all alone. And Grim would never have left his side while he was injured unless the circumstances had been extreme.

As soon as he saw her father's sword, the bottles of water and protein bars left readily beside him, Michael knew Lily was gone. Where and why wasn't as readily apparent. He reached for the water. He forced himself to take the time to open and drain it before he picked up the sword and tried to walk even though his heart had begun to pound. Every moment that passed strengthened him, but when he saw the Firebird nearby, Lily's absence went from a concern to alarm bells clanging in his head. She couldn't have gotten far on foot. If she'd gone for supplies she would have taken the car and she would have known that seeking medical help for him was useless.

Had Rogues attacked again while he was unconscious?

Had Lily and Grim been taken? Michael staggered out from under the leaning metal canopy of the deserted drive-in where Lily had parked the car. The defunct restaurant was off of the main road and below a rise. There was nothing left of its sign but a rusty pole. She'd managed to get them this far, but what had happened once she'd left him on the makeshift bed? His protective instincts didn't care that he wasn't operating at one hundred percent or that his Brimstone was busy healing his body. They flared and he groaned against the fury and concern burning in his gut.

Then Grim materialized from the starlit darkness of the desert night.

Michael stood in stunned silence as the hideous hellhound stalked toward him surrounded by the smoky haze of his solidifying fur...but also by the scent of pure Brimstone that could have only come from one place.

The hell dimension.

His loyal hellhound had been to hell while he was sleeping and he'd come back with the glow of flames flickering in his eyes.

"Where's Lily?" Michael asked. He straightened. He dropped his free hand from the wound on his stomach. His pain hadn't stopped, but he ignored it now. He knew Grim. Though the hellhound couldn't speak his walk, his stance, his smoky hackles all told Michael what he dreaded to hear.

Lily had gone to hell.

He'd been afraid that Rogues would hurt her by their endless hungry hunt, but he hadn't been worried about the greatest threat of all...his grandfather. There was no one hungrier than the daemon king. And for some reason Lily Santiago had gone to face his grandfather alone.

Doors swung open on either side of an intimidating statue of the long-dead Lucifer that graced the cathedral-like antechamber outside the throne room. She paused at its feet. White, trembling, determined to burn in her own way in her own time. She looked up, way up, at the wings. They stretched out from both of his mighty shoulders. The tips of the wings created the frame for the massive entry doors. Large enough to welcome an army or a plague of angels. They waited for one petite ward to stand her ground.

"He'll wear those wings. They're meant to be his. But he'll also have the sun and his song," Lily pledged. "I won't be used to keep him in darkness."

No one heard. The chamber was too large for her voice to echo against its impossible reaches. It didn't matter. She heard and she meant every word.

Lily braced her spine and placed her hands in her pockets. The flute and the kachina were cold comfort. Ezekiel was angry. She could feel a hint of his Brimstone unbuffered and that had rarely happened before. Their bargain was for her to help Michael retrieve Lucifer's wings. She'd almost boiled his blood instead. She had to face Ezekiel's fury before she could even begin to bargain for her heart.

She'd immolated an army of Rogue daemons, but she was afraid to face the daemon king. Her love for him was a horrible, unrequited weight on her chest. She could barely draw breath against it.

The throne room was empty as the whole palace had been save for the lone figure of the daemon king on Lucifer's throne. She was accustomed to the empty suit of armor that stood "guard" to the right of the throne so she wasn't fooled. The armor had always been empty. No one spoke of the daemon who had once worn it as Guardian of the king. Torches replaced candles here. They flickered with dancing light in Gothic sconces that lined the walls high above her head. Their light created an ambient pathway that glowed along a length of scarlet carpet, the only color that softened an otherwise gray-and-black room. Only the stone frieze that lined the walls and columns and even the ceiling far above created any other relief from the marble floor's flat obsidian shine. Torchlight illuminated the carved faces and figures and caused movement to appear where there could be none save leaping shadows caused by flame.

Lily didn't hesitate or wait for a gesture of welcome. There would be none. She moved forward on feet forced to be steady and sure by nothing but an iron will. Hadn't she always been a tiny figure tossed into a black sea on a life raft of a king's whim? The carpet was more solid beneath her feet than her position in the palace had ever been.

She did pause when Ezekiel stood. She paused and then stutter-stepped to movement again, refusing to be afraid. He would never harm her. Not physically. Never. But he would never love her enough, and that was harm in and of itself.

"I didn't mean to hurt him. I had no choice," Lily said. The daemon king headed toward her slowly and surely. Her speech didn't stop him. He gave no indication that he'd heard her at all. "I acted instinctively. I didn't know they would…burn."

The carpet was no longer the only color in the room. Ezekiel's eyes glowed with dancing crimson flames that rivaled the torches with their light. Had she been wrong? Would the only father she'd ever known punish her for her mistake?

She wasn't prepared for the daemon king's embrace when it came. She braced for fury. She wasn't braced for the move that swept her off her feet and into his fierce arms. Her breath left her body, shocked and squeezed from her lungs.

"They almost had you," he said against her ear. His

voice filled the room even as a whisper. "It happened so suddenly. Your affinity went from a compelling whisper to a scream. I didn't expect it to happen so fast."

"But you knew my affinity would call to Michael. You knew it would be amplified once we were together," Lily said. She didn't pull herself from his arms. Not right away.

"Yes. I knew. This was my fault. Entirely. I never should have let you go alone," Ezekiel said.

He wasn't angry with her. He was angry with himself. That's why his eyes glowed and his Brimstone burn wasn't as hidden from her affinity as usual. For a second she allowed his arms to warm her. She hugged him back. But her warmth and relief was short-lived.

"I might have ruined all our plans with my carelessness," Ezekiel said.

*Our plans.* He hadn't been concerned about her. He'd been concerned his throne would be vacant and his kingdom left for Rogue decimation.

"Elizabeth's grandson deserves better than a burning death in the desert," he continued.

Lily pushed back from his broad chest and the daemon king let her go. Now she noticed he was dressed in an impeccably tailored suit minus only the tie. No armor. No royal accoutrements.

"He's alive. I think he's going to be okay. Thanks to Grim," Lily said. She placed her hands back in her pockets. The flute and kachina doll were still there. "I'll still be able to help him retrieve Lucifer's wings. And maybe that means he'll wind up on your throne."

She moved back from her guardian. The glow in his eyes had dimmed, but his Brimstone was still burning bright. She needed to distance herself from him before she asked.

"He's agreed to attend a celebration at the palace on his

twenty-first birthday. His whole family will be here. All the D'Arcys," Ezekiel said. She could see a glint of blue in his irises now. The flames had died down. The reprieve wouldn't last.

"I won't be his queen, Ezekiel. I'll never be his queen," Lily said. She could no longer wait for the right moment to defy him. That moment would never come.

She'd been wrong that his Brimstone would flare. Cold abruptly filled the entire room instead. The air became so chilled that she shivered against it. Ezekiel had damped down his fire so completely that he'd sucked all the residual heat from the room, and her own body heat had been drained.

"You intend to defy me in this?" he said softly. He placed his hands behind his hips and clasped his fingers together. It was his usual pose when he was displeased. Casual, but tense. This time his tension was even more obvious in the stiffness of his shoulders and arms. She wasn't fooled by his tone or the chill. He was furious. It was in his nature to control it. She should be thankful. If he'd been a lesser daemon she might have been scorched away whether he meant to hurt her or not.

"So I was right. That's your grand scheme. To use my affinity to secure your chosen heir," Lily said. "I've never defied you. I owe you everything," If she'd been stronger, her flute and her warrior angel would be nothing but dust left in her clenched fists. She drifted farther away from Ezekiel. But this time he followed. Only a few gracefully casual steps, but she wasn't mistaken to feel stalked.

He wasn't a man. He was an Ancient One. And he'd never cared for her beyond his intention that she should wed his heir. She knew that now.

"I've loved you for as long as I can remember. My mother loved you, too. We received protection, but our love wasn't enough in return. You ask for more. I understand. I promised you Lucifer's wings. That is the bargain between us," Lily said. "But that is all. Our bargain ends there." He couldn't force her to do more without another deal, but he was a master of manipulation. It would take every ounce of her wit and will to outmaneuver his wishes. She was playing chess with a nearly immortal being. She might check him, but a checkmate would be nearly impossible.

She held the kachina. She held the flute. She met Ezekiel's cold gaze. Midnight blue without any stars. In her hand, the kachina grew icy. It didn't matter. She was already chilled to the bone. She didn't flinch when Ezekiel reached to smooth a tendril of hair that had dried and escaped her braid. He was always unknowable. But she did know his heart belonged to the D'Arcys. She knew it was a hard and scarred heart that couldn't expand to include her. How could she settle for less than love from anyone else?

Sometimes the impossible happened. If you refused to give in.

"You're afraid the wings won't be enough. You want my affinity to seal the deal. But I'm not just a lure. I'm not a prize," Lily said. "If I force him to accept the throne, he'll hate me."

"He'll never hate you, Lily. You're wrong. No one with Brimstone blood could hate you. Your affinity will see to that," Ezekiel said.

Suddenly, Lily felt the flames of Brimstone in her own heart. Or an emotion that mimicked them perfectly. She hadn't wanted to anger Ezekiel. And he knew it. He wasn't afraid of her anger at all.

He should have been.

"I'll leave before I risk tying him to me with affinity rather than affection," she warned.

"This is your home," Ezekiel said. His hand fell away from her face.

"Yes, I know. It was built for me. Daemon deals and plans and schemes before I was even born. I'm done with them all. I came to tell you that I owe you for the protection you promised my father, but I no longer need it. I don't want to be safe anymore," Lily said. She turned away from the hard look that settled onto his craggy features. "I love you, but I've lived in the shadows of your affections for the D'Arcys for too long. Meeting Michael has clarified for me how cold my life in hell has been," Lily said. She wanted more. If she couldn't have more, she'd at least have freedom.

"You'll be here for the celebration," Ezekiel said.

All the D'Arcys would be in the palace for Michael's birthday. After that, he'd be a king on the throne and forever out of her reach. Lily had never been so cold.

"I almost burned an entire army with nothing but a flute. Don't underestimate my determination," Lily said.

"For *him*. You almost burned the world for Michael. To save him," Ezekiel said. His voice had never sounded so sophisticated and otherworldly. As if he knew her better than she knew herself.

"I'll help retrieve the wings. I'll be here for the celebration. But then I'll leave," Lily said. "Whether or not he accepts the throne will be entirely up to him. My affinity won't be part of the bargain."

Ezekiel didn't protest when she spun away and hurried from the room. It was a mistake to agree to remain for Michael's birthday. Every second in his company was another chance for her to succumb to the temptation to settle for less. Especially because she imagined that less with Michael would be more than she had ever had before. It would be hard to leave the only home she'd ever known.

But even harder to leave the one man who had filled her heart with a quarter of what she suspected he had to give.

She'd never defied Ezekiel. She'd never stood her ground. It felt like flying through the starlit air in a Firebird at midnight. The hushed shadows of the palace fell away from her as she went back to her rooms. The gloom seemed to be afraid of the starlight she'd found in her soul.

"Grim, what have you done?" Lily asked the absent hellhound when the figure of Michael on her bed met her as she entered her room. She closed the door behind her and hesitantly moved toward the prone man she'd thought she left behind in the desert. He was awake. His hazel gaze tracked her as she crossed the room.

She noted the absence of ash on his features. The blood had been washed away. His body was bare save for low-riding jeans that looked fresher than the ones he'd worn before. There was an angry livid slash across his chest and numerous other scrapes and bruises blackened from the Brimstone cauterization that would leave more scars to join with the faded scars of his long-ago brush with death. But he looked surprisingly well.

"You can't walk away from a daemon deal," Michael said.

He probably spoke of the deal she'd made with him. But her cheeks flamed. She'd just walked away from a deal Ezekiel thought went hand in hand with the one she'd made with him. Michael could never know. Even once he realized she'd taken him to the wings because of Ezekiel's wishes.

"You had water. And Grim. I was going to come back," Lily said.

She had taken her hands from her pockets. Thank goodness the warrior angel hadn't been on her nightstand. It was hidden in her pocket, but it was a bulge in the clinging sheath he could easily see.

Michael propped himself up on his elbows. His muscles rippled and he didn't groan.

"Were you?" he asked. "We have an agreement, but now I wonder if it takes a back seat to other bargains you may have made."

He left the bed more fluidly than she thought possible after his near brush with death. He wasn't recovering. He was recovered.

"I was worried. I thought you might have been taken here against your will," Michael continued. "But then Grim brought me to this apartment and I find a room that obviously belongs to you." He stalked toward her on steady, strong legs, gesturing at the shelves of Kachina dolls her mother had made. She had almost burned the world with her flute…from a distance. She had been sheltered and protected for years. He had destroyed daemon after daemon in hand-to-hand combat. That potential for violence showed in the coil and release of every muscle as he moved. She backed away from his advance, but then she came up against the bedroom wall. She had nowhere else to retreat.

"Lily, what have you done?" Michael asked, repeating her earlier accusation. But his words and the intimidating movement of his body toward her didn't match the glow in his eyes. They searched her with more hunger than accusation. A rush of blood roared in her ears as her heartbeat increased. Fear. Yes. But tinged with a thrill of anticipation.

"He's my guardian. I've lived here since my father died," Lily confessed.

"So it isn't the affinity that influenced your age. It was growing up in the hell dimension. This palace has been your home," Michael said. His lids had lowered so she couldn't read his eyes. His hands rested lightly on her bare upper arms. They belied the tension she could see in his body. "Why doesn't he force the throne on you then?" Michael asked, coming uncomfortably close to what Ezekiel wanted.

"I'm not a D'Arcy. And I never will be," Lily said. She met his gaze. She was Samuel Santiago's daughter. Only Ezekiel would find that lacking.

"Never?" Michael asked. His movement resumed until his body was pressed lightly to hers. Not an imposition. An invitation. One her and her affinity wanted to accept. "Never..." he repeated, and this time his breath teased across her lips when he spoke because he'd tilted his head down until their mouths were almost touching. "It seems never is a very long time for us both. I should be angrier, but I find myself too damn glad that you're whole and here and not hurt in any way."

Lily closed her eyes and held herself very still to keep from claiming the kiss he seemed to offer. Her affinity was less controlled. His heat caused it to rise up and engulf their bodies in an aura of power. She trembled against it. He must have felt her shaking because his hands tightened slightly. He stroked her skin with his thumbs. Meant to reassure or to inflame? Whatever his intentions, the later was the result.

Her nipples peaked against the silk of her gown. She opened her eyes and glanced down. Against the white of her dress, her flush was embarrassingly obvious. He followed her gaze. He lightened his touch when he saw that his grip dimpled her skin.

But he didn't let her go.

Instead he stroked one hand up to the strap of her gown and then teased several digits lightly over her collarbone and down to the vee of silk between her breasts. He'd shifted his body back—barely an inch, but an inch was enough to see her reaction to his touch through the smooth material of her dress. She didn't have a curvy figure, but her pleasure in his touch and his perusal made her breasts seem siren-worthy.

Suddenly, she didn't want to hide her flush or her pebbled nipples. She wanted him to look. She wanted him to know. Her gaze rose up to meet his, instinctively seeking to gauge his reaction to her obvious signs of arousal. She caught her breath when she saw twin flames deep in his hazel eyes, darkening them and brightening them at the same time.

"Why didn't you tell me that you were the daemon king's ward?" Michael asked.

"The two of you aren't on the best of terms. You promised to help me fulfill my mother's request," Lily replied, softly. "I thought it best to keep my past to myself." She didn't tell him about the precious kachina doll in her pocket. About how much a part of her past he was.

"Ezekiel raised you? I'm beginning to understand why Grim didn't trust you," Michael said. But his hand skimmed up to cup the nape of her neck. He didn't step away. She was caught and seduced at the same time. The fires in his eyes flickered softly. He had widened the space between them to caress her, but he still leaned close when he spoke. She closed her eyes again against the dizzy swoop of desire that flowed from his fingers to her stomach and lower. She swallowed. Then she opened her eyes, afraid the swooning blink had been too long. She couldn't afford to miss one second of his reaction to her deception.

"Ezekiel is a master of manipulation. He's a daemon. That's what daemons do. When you found me in the desert and revealed your identity, I thought it couldn't be a coincidence," Lily confessed. "I thought I'd run away from the palace to fulfill my mother's wishes. But he let me go."

"He knew I'd fail to find the wings alone. And he wanted to keep tabs on my progress," Michael guessed. But did he guess there was more to Ezekiel's plan? She felt like a medieval princess offered up as a bride with no thought to her own desires.

"Yes. He used me. The affinity makes me useful. Just as it made my father useful," Lily said. Her eyes filled, but she didn't let the moisture fall. She had never been anything but a means to an end to Ezekiel. She knew that now. She'd risked her life to help him by sealing the sipapu portals that had worried her mother. She'd done it because she loved her mother. But her love for her guardian had been a factor, too.

"And just as my mother was useful and her mother before her," Michael said. He let go of her arm and lifted his hand to brush the loosening strands of hair back from her face. Again, she closed her eyes against her reaction to his touch and then opened them so she wouldn't miss what might come next. He toyed with strands of hair as he observed her. The quickened rise and fall of her chest. The tip of her tongue moistening her lips. He was as watchful as she was. They both explored the truth and the possibilities held in the next moment and the next.

Because one truth that went unspoken was suffusing them in an almost visible glow. Lily licked her lips. They'd gone dry from Michael's Brimstone heat. He was barely tamping it down; in the palace they were buffered from Rogue detection.

"I understand daemon games, Lily. Even if I usually refuse to acknowledge that half of my heritage," Michael said.

He was looking at her lips again. His attention drawn by the movement of her tongue.

"Usually?" Lily asked.

"I'm standing in hell. I'm holding you. My blood is on fire. There's no way I can ignore who I am when I'm with you in this way," Michael confessed. This time he closed his eyes. For a long time he stood with his chin tilted up and his lips pursed in thought. Someone without affinity might have thought he was fighting the burn or working up the self-control to back away.

A cool flood of adrenaline rushed up Lily's spine. Gooseflesh rose on her skin. She gasped and then wondered that the adrenaline didn't cause steam when it met with Michael's burn.

*Because he was savoring, not resisting.*

He was fully enjoying the call of her affinity and his Brimstone response, here, where they were sheltered and fully free to burn.

When his eyes opened, the hazel was consumed. Fire had claimed his pupils as it had claimed his body. Lily reached for his arms because her knees had gone weak. She was surprised when blisters didn't rise on her fingers. The heat from Michael's skin was glorious. Her affinity wouldn't allow her to be afraid. She was as drawn to him as he was to her.

"I'm sorry if you're caught in the webs Ezekiel weaves. I've spent my life caught as well. But when you and I are together this aura burns everything else away. I don't care about heaven or hell," Michael said. He pressed his body fully against hers, and the wall helped to hold her for the kiss that came seconds later. She was able to let go of his arms and bury her fingers in the waves of his mussed hair. She fisted handfuls and he groaned against her lips in response.

Michael would never need to mourn the loss of the sun. He was the sun. Fiery and blazing bright. She'd spent a lifetime in a purple haze of darkness, but the man who devoured her mouth burned those memories away. His sculpted lips were a pure sensory pleasure to trace with her tongue. His gasps of reaction were as delicious as his salty skin. And when their tongues met and twined, the rough, slick slide made her melt in intimate ways her imagination understood even though her experience was lacking.

He moved his hands from her face and neck down to her waist. He molded her against him, and the thin silk of her dress was hardly a barrier to the muscled expanse of his bare chest, hard abs and even harder arousal that pressed against her stomach. A wild aching hollow seemed to open in response to his erection. One that demanded to be filled.

Lily allowed her hands to fall from his hair to his shoulders. She wrapped her arms around him and he responded by dropping his hands to her hips and lifting her up. Her skirt was hiked by his movements and her legs were slightly freed. Enough to wrap around his lean waist and settle her heat against him. She rode his erection now. Its pulsating length, though contained in his jeans, was cupped by the hollow between her legs.

His head fell back and their mouths parted. They were both breathing heavily and oxygen was necessary, but Lily still moaned in protest.

"Damned if I can bring myself to care where you come from or who raised you," Michael said.

Hell was filled with the damned. The palace walls and ceilings were carved with hundreds upon hundreds of faces and figures—men, women, human and Rogue—who were trapped because they weren't welcome in heaven or into Oblivion. Only Lily's rooms were free of the damned.

Or they had been until now.

Only giving in to this burn didn't feel like damnation. That would come later when they were forced to part.

She and Michael might both regret succumbing to the

fires that raged between them. Because they were going to succumb. There was no turning back now.

Michael held her and slowly walked toward the bed he'd been lying on before. She leaned down, but didn't kiss him. She met his gaze instead. She searched the flames and saw a reflection of herself in their depths.

"Ezekiel doesn't matter. This is for us. Whatever pleasure. Whatever pain. It's ours to fan and face," Lily whispered. Then she leaned to brush her lips against his. Once, twice, before he fell back on the bed, taking her with him.

# Chapter 12

Although she landed on top of Michael, she wasn't fooled. His body hummed with power and potential. And the few feet she'd fallen as he'd lain back on the bed had been as exhilarating as their midnight escape in the vintage sports car when they'd flown through the twinkling night sky. Michael was the Firebird and the driver. She was only along for the ride.

She held his shoulders to prop herself up as she strad-dled his bare stomach. The muscles beneath her fingers were taut. The Brimstone burning beneath his skin was high-octane fuel. When his hands urged her hips lower and she settled on his swollen erection, he tilted his head back in pleasure and his eyes closed. He groaned through open lips and his chest rose and fell as if he'd suddenly gone winded and weak.

Lily moved against him. Her name sighed from his lips in a plea. For what? Maybe she was the driver after all. She was still flying. Her stomach was light and her heartbeat fluttered as if there were still hundreds of feet left to fall. But Michael's heat buoyed her. She ran her hands from his shoulders down his scarred arms. Every slight ridge only seemed to define the beauty of his masculine curves. He enjoyed her touch. Hadn't she wanted to touch him this way when to do so would have meant certain detection by Rogues? She wouldn't resist now even though there were reasons she should.

She explored all of his exposed skin while he held himself still beneath her. He breathed heavily but his only other movement was the quivering of his skin beneath her fingers. She trailed them across his chest. She circled his pecs. She was careful around his recently healed injury, but he didn't push her hand away. He seemed to wait and watch while his excitement built. She placed her palms on either side of his flat stomach, and all the while the undulation of her hips was automatic. She was finally rewarded with the soft, low sound of her name from his lips again and again.

She was a virgin and inexperienced to the extreme. She'd been sheltered her whole life. Michael's had been her first kiss. His had been the first male hands to touch her in a sensual way. Though she felt like she was flying without reliable wings, the thrill was glorious. He burned beneath her hands. His trembling had increased until he shuddered beneath her. He allowed her this control. He'd given her the keys. Slowly, she leaned down to place her face close to his. His eyes were slightly open now. He watched her come closer and closer.

"I should warn you I'm approaching my limit," Michael said in a hoarse whisper.

"I'm not cold anymore. I never realized how cold I'd become," Lily said. "How much colder it was after I touched you, then was forced to let go."

"Don't let go, Lily. It's going to get hotter. Much hotter. Don't let go," Michael said.

His lips were parched. Heat waves shimmered in the air around them. Lily's affinity protected her even as it caused their temperatures to rise higher. She wasn't afraid of the heat. But the lightness in her stomach wasn't the pure flight of adrenaline. She was afraid of falling. Michael took her too high. He lifted her from the depths of hell, and hell was the only thing she'd ever known.

Her pause roused him from his pleasured reverie and

Michael's eyes opened fully to search her face. Whatever he saw there stilled his shudders. He lifted his hands to gently cup her cheeks. His fingers were steady against her skin.

"I've got you," he said. It wasn't a daemon deal; it was a masculine promise. One she believed. Her fear eased. He urged her the last millimeters to bring their lips together. His lips were rough, but she'd quickly become addicted to their sculptured perfection. She traced their familiar curves with her tongue, desperate to absorb the heat, shape and taste before circumstances separated them forever. "We've got this respite. For now. Let's enjoy it," he continued.

Michael rose up and rolled Lily over to the side. He allowed their lips to part only for the seconds necessary to change position. Then he was the driver once more. Slowly and hungrily he devoured her mouth and plundered its depths with his tongue. Her dress was scrunched to her waist. It seemed a relief when he drew back to pull the white silk up and over her head. He tossed it to the floor. The soft thump of the treasures in its pockets barely penetrated her senses. Her breasts were bare. The only covering left on her body was a tiny scrap of white low on her hips and moist between her legs. The kachina was forgotten in the arms of the actual Brimstone prince. The flute wasn't necessary to call forth the affinity they shared.

"You're too perfect. Look at your skin. Smoother than the silk you wore," Michael said. The ridges on his fingertips trailed over the skin he praised and Lily shivered beneath the calluses caused by his guitar strings. This time her shiver wasn't caused by fear. And her adrenaline was all desire. She looked down to see his hand's roughness against the pink flush of her areolae and distended nipples. He teased her nipple until it grew harder and then he cupped the globe of her breast to offer it to his lips. He bent to suck and she continued to watch his fingers and lips on her skin. Her hips ground into the mattress. Heat and electricity arced straight from the nipple he tasted to the aching flesh between her legs.

"You're one to complain of perfection," Lily breathlessly teased. She touched the curve of his cheek and jaw. Scars or not. Daemon or human. The sharply cut angles of his face were beloved and perfect to her. She'd longed for him before she'd met him.

"No complaints. Only humbled. You bring me to my knees with a glance, a touch, your song," Michael said against the breast he'd made tender and damp. The moisture from his tongue dissipated quickly in the heated air. He appreciated her reaction to the temperature change when she released the breath she'd held in a long sigh. He slid his hand from under her breast to her stomach. Feeling the rise and fall of her quickened respiration. "I'm going to touch you, Lily."

She wasn't sure if it was a considerate warning or a sensual promise. Her breath caught again. Her attention flew from his hand on her stomach to his face. Their gazes locked. He had drawn back to watch her reactions. He pressed his hand firmly to the quivers his words caused deep in her abdomen.

Then he lightened his touch and gently continued the downward journey of his fingers to trail along the band of her low-riding panties. She followed the direction of his gaze when he dropped it from hers and a sigh rose, shakily turning into a groan as his rough fingers teased beneath the silk to find the light dusting of hair between her legs.

*Fire.* Brimstone or not. Affinity or not. Fire from his fingers to the bud he had sought. Lily cried out. She reached to hold on, but ended up stilling his hand with hers gripped around his arm. Afraid once more. Too hot. Too much. She would be alone again. This couldn't be always between them. And once she'd flown with Michael how could she survive the cold, lonely ground again?

"Shhhh. Let me warm you. Forget about everything else. Just feel," Michael urged. His voice was a deep, sensual vibration against her side. He met her eyes again. Fire flickered in his, deep and dark. All hazel consumed by its glow. Lily's fingers loosened and she slid her hands from his arm to his shoulders.

He dipped to take her lips as his fingers continued their movement. Lily gasped into his mouth. Her tongue desperately twined with his. So hungry. So hot. Heat waves and the glow of affinity surrounded and embraced them.

The Firebird escape had seemed like flight, but when his dexterous touch played her as expertly as he played any instrument he touched, Lily cried out in a long release of all tension and control. Every cell in her body was thrummed and warmed, touched and thawed.

She wasn't ashamed of the moisture that flowed down her face because it evaporated as it tracked down her hot skin. She looked up at the man above her. Her warrior angel. Her daemon prince. Hers always, come what may. He watched her, intensely. He might detect the tears before they disappeared. He might see the spiky droplets on her lashes. But he didn't speak. He only watched her as he tore the cloth from her hips. He watched her breast rise and fall as he impatiently ripped his zipper down.

His erection was thick and intimidating, but Lily was too hungry to care. She still had a hollow that only he could fill. Whether it was caused by her affinity or by her cold heart, she couldn't be sure. She no longer cared. He moved away just long enough to remove his jeans and to remove a foil packet from the wallet in his pocket. When he settled between her legs after a brief pause to sheath his erection, she spread to welcome his weight. She wrapped her legs and her arms around him.

There was fumbling as he used his hands to fit them together, but then nothing but movement and fullness and a friction she'd never known could be so right. She was slick, but there was still pain as he worked his hips to fit his swollen length inside. Then there was only pleasure, sharp at times, but pure pleasure more intense for the sharpness as he rocked, burying himself in secret depths no one had ever plumbed.

Lily cried out his name. Behind tightly clenched lids she saw the handsome kachina doll but its features fogged and in their place was Michael. All Michael. She opened her lids to watch him. The beautiful, familiar face clenched intently as he began to shudder with his release. Her orgasm followed in response to the spasms of his erection inside her.

"Together," she managed to say, softly, as he collapsed in her arms.

Michael fell asleep. She watched him beside her for a long time before she slipped from bed to the shower in the next room. Even the hottest water was cool against her skin. She lathered up, more aware of her skin than she'd ever been. There were some tender aches and pains, but mostly there was a sensitized physical memory of everywhere he'd touched and tasted on her body. Her fingers followed the paths he'd taken. Remembering. Recalling. Reexperiencing every moment of the time they'd stolen together.

Because it was stolen.

They had to leave the palace once more. They had to go back out into the world to retrieve the wings. And once they were found, Lily would have to face Michael's reaction to Ezekiel's scheme. She'd have to walk away. She might never experience his touch again.

His heat still seemed such a part of her. Maybe it would warm her forever even after they were apart.

Towels were a poor substitute for the warmth of Michael's touch, but she dried the water from her skin and dressed quickly before she gave in to the temptation of seeking him out again. If they didn't leave the palace soon, Ezekiel might come to urge them on with their quest. Lily wasn't ready to face the daemon king and the Brimstone prince at the same time. Not now. The birthday celebration would be soon enough to handle the fallout from the daemon deals as they converged.

Not to mention the D'Arcys.

Lily pulled on boots and laced them tightly. Paired with jeans, a button-up shirt and a black leather jacket, the boots helped her to feel serious and back on track when she left the bathroom to wake Michael.

But her warrior angel was already awake.

In seconds she took in the scene and guessed what had happened. He'd risen from the bed to join her in the bathroom, but he'd stepped on the dress she'd forgotten on the ground. He'd felt the hard lump of the kachina doll beneath his foot and he'd retrieved it from the pocket. She should have removed it to a safer hiding place herself before Michael woke up. But she'd been lost in the heated reverie of her time in his arms. She hoped those memories would stay with her to soften the look she saw on his face right now.

Shock. Anger. Disbelief. And all the flame gone from his eyes. They were as pale as she'd ever seen them. Pure hazel and cold as ice.

"What is this?" Michael asked. He held the kachina doll toward her in a fist that was white-knuckled and trembling.

"A gift from my mother. And her mother before her.

It was carved by one of our Aztec ancestors many years ago," Lily explained.

"I'm supposed to believe that one of your ancestors knew my face this well before I was even born?" Michael asked. His voice dripped with an acidic sacrilege that burned worse than fire.

"My beliefs aren't dimmed by your disbelief. Kachinas represent the spirit world. They give us wisdom and messages from our ancestors. They connect us to the unseen. I've treasured that warrior angel since I was child," Lily said. She stepped toward his towering figure. One measured tread at a time.

"So you didn't carve it to summon me the way you summon your elemental spirits? You haven't used it against me?" Michael said.

Lily wouldn't change his mind. It had been made up in an instant when he'd seen his face carved in wood and placed in her pocket. Still, she would promote whatever truth she was free to promote between them. Her embarrassment had kept the kachina doll hidden for too long.

"I'm not a sculptor, Michael. Look at the doll. It was carved by a high priest centuries ago. Look at the wood. Its patina. It has been held by many more than me. Although I've loved it long," Lily said. "I think it foretold our meeting. My ancestor must have had a vision of you."

"A vision of me wearing Lucifer's wings," Michael said. He raised his arm to dash the doll to the ground, but Lily was there before he could complete the move. She stilled his arm with her hands. Her body inadvertently pressed all along his side. Michael closed his eyes and swallowed. His Brimstone was completely damped. But their affinities still came together like pieces of a song. A verse and a chorus meant to be sung together.

"It's a lie. Whatever it is. Wherever it came from. It's

a lie," Michael swore. But he released the doll when she reached for it. He allowed her to take the ageless treasure in her steady hands.

"When you first stepped into my life, I thought the shadows that clung to you were wings. I'd always seen you like this," Lily said. She stepped back from Michael with the kachina cupped in her hands.

"You didn't say anything. Why were you carrying it in your pocket? And your flute in the other?" Michael asked. She followed his glance to the bed where the discarded flute lay. He had found it as well.

"My two prized possessions, Michael. That's all. I took them with me when I spoke to Ezekiel," Lily said. "For comfort. To boost my nerve. I don't know how any of this works. I follow instincts and urgings from the affinity or my ancestors. From the spirits I call. This isn't an exact science. It's more ephemeral than that. I wasn't using the doll against you. Not in any conscious way."

"But you admit you don't know how it works. So besides the affinity and Ezekiel's meddling I have to assume there might be other things at play between us," Michael said. He zipped pants he'd only pulled on without fastening when he'd left the bed. His accusatory tone was more acidic than his disbelief.

"There's more between us than I can explain. I agree," Lily said. His suspicions about the doll came dangerously close to the truth. She wasn't using the doll to manipulate him and she refused to use her affinity, but Ezekiel used her. Of that she was certain. She was hollow again. In the shower she'd been certain that the memory of their joining would be enough to keep her warm forever. She'd been wrong. Separation she might have been able to handle. But his reaction to her supposed betrayal was insurmountable. The secret of the kachina doll was nothing compared to the secret that Ezekiel wanted her to be Michael's queen. If he reacted like this to the doll, there was no hope of an amicable parting between them when their quest was over and he learned the truth.

He wouldn't refuse to be king. The doll foretold his capitulation to his duty. But she would have to walk away. She could never be his queen. She had lived without love for too long. He might desire her, but he would always resent her. The affinity they shared wasn't love.

"Wrap the doll and place it back in your pack. If I see it again, I'll burn it," Michael said.

He walked toward the bathroom without waiting to see if she complied. She let him go even though his impersonal brush by her hollowed her out even worse than before. She didn't go after him. She would hide the doll away rather than risk him destroying it. Besides, even she wondered about the tiny kachina. She had used it in the circle when she called the fire that burned the attacking Rogues. She had felt it grow chilled beneath her fingers when she'd confronted Ezekiel in the throne room. She'd been honest about not understanding exactly how her affinity worked with her kachina dolls and her flute. She was a conduit for greater powers than anyone could define.

The warrior angel went back into its wrappings with the ease of an object in the place it belonged. She would respect Michael's wishes until she was compelled to take it out once more. But she would use it again if she had to. Even if it meant risking his wrath. Lily placed it back in its spot in the bottom of her backpack. Michael hadn't told her to put the flute away, but she polished it while he showered and then returned it to its velvet pouch.

All the while, hot moisture burned the back of her eyes and her tight chest fought every breath. Her body was still tender from their lovemaking. That was the hardest thing to take. She tried to ignore the constant reminder of their passion every time she moved. It didn't match the hollow left inside her. Without passion, her tenderness was only pain.

As hot water sluiced over his body, its heat was a faint echo of what he'd experienced when he'd made love to Lily. He'd sworn he wouldn't let the Brimstone drive him. Finding the Kachina in Lily's pocket had shaken his certainty that he was in control. He'd had to completely shut down his burn to reassure himself that he wasn't a slave to it.

He wasn't.

But he was also incapable of being as cold as he'd been in the past. Lily was awakening the daemon in him. It wasn't only his blood. His heart throbbed painfully with every steady beat, filled with emotions much stronger than a human man could endure. He'd seen what being driven by those passions had done to his grandfather. He'd heard what they'd done to his father. And what those passions had left in their wake to the mortals they'd touched.

He wondered at Lily's place in the daemon king's plans. She was only a human woman in spite of her affinity. She was in great danger if the daemon king had involved himself in her fate. And if Lily was trying to influence Michael with her Kachina doll at the urgings of Ezekiel, she was playing with more fire than she could possibly imagine.

As water ran in rivulets over the scars that his daemon blood had caused on his human skin, Michael clenched his fists. He leaned his forehead against the tile on the wall. It was warm against the icy skin he'd managed to achieve.

He would protect Lily from all harm. Including the potential for harm he harbored in the daemon part of himself.

# *Chapter 13*

Peter was healing. He sat on the bed of a filthy motel and examined his leg. Though bone still showed beneath torn skin, he could see knitting was taking place. Evidence that the taint in his blood from selling his soul to Rogues was a blessing. The motel by the side of a secondary road had once been located on a route to the less-visited West Rim of the Grand Canyon. Fewer tourists chose the West Rim as a destination, but its proximity to Las Vegas and the efforts of the Hualapai tribe to increase tourism by installing a glass skywalk over the canyon had increased visitors. A new highway had finally been completed to reach the skywalk and it had left the tiny motor inn built in the 1940s all but abandoned.

Peter's room was small. The wallpaper was stained and yellowed by generations of nicotine and who knew what else. It wasn't a glamorous place to plan a trap for Samuel's daughter, but the Order had been a cruel and austere master. He'd endured worse as an acolyte. Much worse. He still bore the lash marks on his back and legs with pride. Only a psychologist would have attributed his constant anger and need for violence to the lashings he'd suffered as a child. He saw the Brimstone as an enhancement to his anger. His fury had joined with the Brimstone's burn to set his breast alight.

Once he had rebound his leg with fresh bandages, he rose from the hard, musty mattress and left his room. The door required a forceful wrench of its loose knob to open, but he kept his curses to himself. Discipline was required in this place. He was surrounded by daemons.

The group of Rogues he'd joined had succeeded. Its leader, Abaddon, had increased his importance a hundred-fold in the hierarchy of lesser daemons. Rogues were young compared to Loyalists. They had never walked in heaven.

But Abaddon had bargained with heaven for Lucifer's wings and they were now in his possession. If the wings helped him reclaim hell, he would probably lead the new Rogue Council or he might even claim the throne for himself. Peter had been a disciple of Reynard, the Brother who had killed Samuel himself. He knew how to speak to a dangerous leader who could kill him for one wrongly placed word. He had a long lifetime of practice.

Nonetheless, his heart pounded hotly in his chest when he sought out an audience with Abaddon. Reynard had been powerful. Abaddon was nearly a god.

Lying in his room wasn't an option even though his leg was still a gruesome version of its former self. Brimstone or not, the hellhound had left him with a permanent reminder that he wasn't immortal. That more than anything sent him to ingratiate himself with a powerful Rogue. There was residual power in Lucifer's wings. The closer he came to them the better.

Abaddon had taken over the lobby of the hotel. Its former occupant was nothing but a pile of ash left behind an abandoned Formica counter. The old manager had refused to kneel. Foolish. His punishment had been a slow and horrible immolation. Only Rogues, Peter and coyotes had heard his screams.

Peter stopped in awe when he saw the wings hung on the wall of the lobby. What should have looked ridiculous struck him with a shudder of wonder tinged with fear. Lucifer had boldly led a group of loyal Ancient Ones that had leaped from heaven to rule autonomously in hell. Any devoted member of the Order had been taught to abhor that level of independence. At best, a Brother could aspire to be the leading cog in a machine oiled by sweat and blood. It was his devotion to the Order that had brought him this far when they had been all but destroyed.

Abaddon sat beneath the wings on a worn armchair that managed to look throne-like because of his carriage and the aura of triumph that lit his features with daemonic light from his glowing eyes. Yet he hadn't claimed the wings for himself. He hadn't placed them on his own shoulders. There were still other powerful Rogues who stood in his way.

If he saw Peter enter the lobby or if he heard the incongruous twinkle of the copper bell above the door, he didn't glance in Peter's direction to confirm. In Rogue hierarchy, Peter was a human servant, worth only what he could offer. Before, he'd offered the possibility of catching Samuel's daughter. He'd failed. This time he'd dragged himself before these Rogues with the knowledge that the daemon king's prized ward was now accompanied by his prized heir. She could be expected to come for the wings with the prince…and the hellhound.

Peter's leg throbbed at the thought, but he'd given Abaddon a valuable advantage with the information he'd offered. He'd also offered advice, very careful to phrase it as humbly as possible. Peter had seen Lily Santiago rain down fire in defense of the daemon king's heir. His presence could be a liability to her rather than an asset if they took the half daemon and his hellhound by surprise. If they disarmed Samuel's daughter before she could play her flute against them.

Dozens of Rogues came and went, receiving Abaddon's attention while Peter waited. Sweat ran down his face as he stood with most of his weight on his good leg. Just as he felt as if he might collapse, Abaddon glanced toward him with a slight nod of his head. Peter nearly fell forward, but caught himself and forced a slow limp toward the Rogue. He was eager to help the future Rogue leader in order to establish his importance. Ingratiating himself with Rogues was one small step on his way toward leading the Order of *Peter* to ascendance.

# Chapter 14

Michael had always healed more quickly than an ordinary man. He was stiff and sore, but no worse for wear after the horrible battle he'd fought against the Rogues who'd come for Lily thanks to Grim and his real father. For once, he didn't regret his half-daemon heritage.

He also didn't regret the Rogues he'd cut down.

In times like those, when he was protecting someone, his affinity was so perfectly in tune with his Brimstone that he felt whole. Not like he was running from his destiny, but embracing it.

Then he'd woken up to find Lily gone and Grim had led him to the hell dimension to find her. His grandfather's ward. Michael had thought he was using Lily to help him find Lucifer's wings. Now he wasn't so sure if he wasn't the one being used.

Her doll had his face, but worst of all it had black wings.

It was the wings that shook him more than the likeness. He didn't like the idea that the doll had any sway over his future. Or that Lily was using her power to manipulate him just as the daemon king had tried to manipulate him his whole life.

He'd had to walk away. After their connection, the betrayal was too great.

He didn't realize he was looking for Ezekiel until he found him.

The daemon king was alone in a hazily lit courtyard that Michael remembered. It was a training field. Ezekiel was shirtless and sweating, going through sword-fighting forms with a broadsword that looked as worn and battle-scarred as the man who wielded it. He didn't stop when Michael walked onto the field. He did slow as if he was surprised. That, in itself, was a reward. It wasn't often he surprised his grandfather.

Michael continued toward a weapons rack without greeting. His Brimstone was banked, but it scorched beneath his skin. He needed to work off some of his anger. Ezekiel wasn't the best target. He was dangerous, at best. Deadly, at worst. But he was also more to blame for his current predicament than Lily.

If he had sent her into the desert to find and help Michael, then the daemon king was responsible for the danger she'd faced.

The very thought made Michael's scars begin to glow.

"To what do I owe this unexpected visit?" Ezekiel asked. He hadn't lowered his sword. He knew better. He didn't brandish it, but he held it at the ready, prepared for Michael's attack.

The clang of the weapons as Michael chose, spun and engaged his grandfather, metal blade against metal blade, rang out across the courtyard and jarred his recently healed injury. He grunted with pain, but he didn't cry out. Rather, he swung again and again, driving the seasoned warrior king across the gray grass in retreat.

"You. Sent. Your. Ward. Out. Into. The. Desert. Where. She. Could. Have. Died," Michael accused. Each word was punctuated by a swing of his sword and the clash of Ezekiel's parry. He wasn't fooled. He knew he was no match for a nearly immortal daemon warrior who had been sword fighting long before he was born. But each swing and parry released some of his heat so he wouldn't explode.

"You need help to retrieve Lucifer's wings," Ezekiel

said. Sweat ran down his brow and trailed over his hard, muscled chest in streaks. His scarred arms bulged as he held back Michael's advance. But his eyes glittered as if he was pleased, not angry.

"Is it help you offer me? Or is there some other game you're playing?" Michael asked.

His blade clashed with Ezekiel's again, but this time they'd reached the edge of a stone wall that encircled the yard. The daemon king's body didn't yield. His arm turned to steel. His feet planted into the ground like tree trunks and Michael knew the retreat was over.

"You need each other," Ezekiel said. He spoke softly as if he'd gone from warrior to diplomat following the last blow. Although their gazes locked over the swords between them, Michael knew the battle had been over before it began. He wasn't free to fight the daemon king. His family was beholden to the creature who had helped them against Rogues and the Order of Samuel. He had made a deal with Ezekiel and a daemon deal couldn't be broken.

"How do you know who or what we need? You're the daemon king. You come and go with the ease of smoke, often leaving us scorched in your wake. What gives you the right to interfere in our lives?" Michael asked. The glow of Brimstone had left his scars. They were back to pale reminders of the pain he'd endured because of his blood. The potential for pain that he could unleash on others if he wasn't strong enough. Control. Control. Control. He lowered his sword, allowing it to slide from Ezekiel's blade with a protesting shriek, long and low.

Then he turned away from Ezekiel's intense blue eyes.

He stabbed the tip of his borrowed sword into the ground and leaned against its hilt.

"The hell dimension is one of many worlds. You've traveled between worlds with Grim often enough to hear the whispers that also travel those dark pathways, but you're too young to have listened to what they have to say," Ezekiel said. He also lowered his sword, but he tossed it to the side as if it had been sullied by the conflict with his grandson. "I have had many, many years with nothing but those whispers for company. I listen. I heed. Time is fluid in the hell dimension, but even more so on the pathways between worlds. Wisdom from the past and foretelling from the future filter back to my ears."

Michael watched the daemon king stand beside the sword he'd thrown onto the ground. He looked more mortal than he'd ever seemed. It wasn't the sweat or the unusual furrows on his brow. It wasn't the battle scars. It was the pain. His words dripped with pain. His eyes burned with it. His hands clenched against it.

"I carry the weight of experience and knowledge that comes from eons and more worlds than a mortal could count. I followed Lucifer out of heaven, but I never imagined that the hell I'd find would be one as intricate and demanding as this one. I never imagined Lucifer would be murdered and I'd have to assume the throne. When I ask you to embrace your heritage, it isn't out of cruelty, Michael. It's because I won't always be able to do this alone," Ezekiel said.

"She's in terrible danger," Michael said. He had forced the sword deeper into the ground. He straightened without its support. Ezekiel nodded.

"Your birthday will be dangerous for us all. We need the power in Lucifer's wings to survive the transition and the threats that are rising. I never would have allowed her to leave the palace if it wasn't necessary," Ezekiel said.

"We will retrieve the wings. I can't promise more than that," Michael said. "Don't ask her for more than she can give, either. I won't let her burn herself out for you and I won't be manipulated into burning out of control."

"At one time or another we all burn, Michael. At best we can try to determine where and when," Ezekiel replied. "I'm glad you've both survived thus far, but there are worse challenges ahead."

"That's the only reason I'm not walking away. I won't leave her to face this alone," Michael said. He left the sword as a punctuation mark on the field. He didn't bid his grandfather goodbye. He just walked away.

"I never imagined you would abandon her. Your desire to protect is your greatest strength. Your father's devotion lives on in you," Ezekiel said to his back. Michael paused, but he didn't look back as the words seemed to settle heavily on his shoulders—like heavy black wings.

Grim was no longer reluctant to take her on the pathways he traversed between worlds. She didn't point out the hellhound's trust to his master. Michael was distant, untouchable. His Brimstone tamped down to a glow she could barely detect. He'd left her room after his shower, telling her to wait until he came back. It had been the longest wait in a life spent waiting. Grim had been the one who'd come to retrieve her. She'd found her father's sword where Michael had left it and she'd shrugged into her pack and followed the beast into the familiar corridors, wondering where his master had been for such a long time.

When they met Michael outside the entrance of the palace, she'd been too afraid to ask. All around the palace, the craggy mountains of the hell dimension were as familiar as the palace itself. It was a dark world, but its darkness was filled with natural beauty that belied some of its war-scarred history. She hadn't run from this majestic scenery or even the palace with its haunted walls. She had run away to fulfill her mother's request to help Eze-kiel, but also to leave the heart that was too scarred and full for her behind. How different would life in hell be if it had been possible for her to be Michael's queen without forcing him to marry her? If he had been free to join with her out of love and without obligation?

She would never know. The affinity was a part of her she could never escape. She couldn't prevent its power from influencing Michael.

"There's no need to speak. Grim will understand where you need him to lead us. Hold him here and think about what your spirits shared with you," Michael instructed. He demonstrated by grabbing a handful of the hellhound's ruff at his neck. The gesture was rough but affectionate. Grim's tongue lolled happily in response to his master's touch.

Lily stepped forward and reached for Grim's ruff. She moved too quickly. Michael didn't have time to move away. Perhaps his body betrayed him. His hand was still in the way when her hand burrowed into the hellhound's fur. Their fingers touched and when they did, Grim's hair turned to smoke trailing up and away from their hands. Michael jerked away. Lily grabbed for purchase and Grim's fur obliged by solidifying once more, but not before her heart leaped and pounded in her chest as if she'd been about to fall.

Michael ran his hand through his own hair, mussing it and looking pained. She could feel the fight. His Brim-stone had flared when their hands had touched. It took him a long moment to tamp it back down. Her affinity felt like adrenaline beneath her skin. And they were no longer sheltered behind palace walls. Even Loyalists could be af-fected by her lure. Though they tried to resist. It was time for Grim to lead them away.

"The Colorado River, Grim. On the West Rim of the

Grand Canyon," Lily said. Michael had told her she didn't need to talk, but she spoke to dispel her reaction to his touch. She also closed her eyes and envisioned the trail of the river that had been shown in the floor of Michael's earth-bermed home. She saw it and the map they had perused on the hood of Michael's Firebird. She saw the two come together as one, spirit guidance and cartography.

Grim's muscles gathered beneath her hand. She allowed him to slip from her fingers. He walked away on decisive legs that slowly disappeared into vaporous smoke as she watched until nothing was left but a wisp of gray from the tip of his tail.

"Come on. He's never very patient with those of us who only have two legs," Michael urged.

His voice was strained, but Lily followed him. It was the first step in a journey that would take her away from the only home she'd ever known and the only man she'd thought might love her in return if there weren't so many daemon manipulations getting in the way. But her legs responded when she forced them. One stride and then another. She'd enjoyed the respite. She could only hope the memories of her time in Michael's arms would live on in her dreams.

They materialized four thousand feet above the Colorado River suspended on a glass walk that enabled Lily to see the yawning chasm beneath them and the glorious canyon all around. She gasped and clutched for the metal railing that was also rimmed with glass, providing unobstructed views. Heavy winds buffeted her body and dark clouds converged in the distance. The weather explained why the horseshoe-shaped bridge was deserted.

"Damn it, Grim. A little warning," Michael said. He also held the rail, but in less of a death grip than she did.

No doubt he was used to the hellhound materializing in precarious situations. His monstrous companion only clicked along the walkway, disregarding the scratches his claws must be leaving in the glass. He led them to the outer curve of the skywalk. Lily followed with superhuman effort. The wind was hard to walk against. But worse than the wind was the feeling that nothing substantial was between her and the fall.

"I fail to see how a tourist trap is going to lead us to heaven," Michael said.

But Lily had forced herself to look at the curves of the river below and she recognized them from her vision and the map.

"This is where we begin. I'll need to summon again to see how we need to go on," Lily explained.

Michael and Grim had traveled faster across the glass walk than she could manage. She worried about hurting its surface. She'd seen magazine articles about the cantilever structure a feat of engineering embraced by the Hualapai tribe as a means of improving their economy. Visitors were supposed to wear covers over their shoes to protect the glass. They were intruding on tribal land. The least they could do was leave it undamaged.

Unfortunately, her caution allowed waiting Rogues to spring their trap.

Lily was grabbed from behind by her backpack, which was torn from her back. She cried out and only then did Michael whirl from the view to find her in the clutches of Rogues.

Grim responded without pause, loyal to the last, but his response had been carefully planned for and expected. When he winked out of existence at the curve of the bridge to reappear at Lily's side, a fireproof net was waiting. But more had gone into its construction than fireproof material. Each twisted joint ended in a spiked barb that pointed inward toward the beast it would contain. Each barb was black and tainted, poisoned by Rogue blood which was a reflection of their darkness. Daemons weren't damned, but they could deal in damnation. The barbs were long and cruel. They penetrated Grim's smoky fur instantly and he howled out in pain. Instinctively, he tried to gnaw at the barbs near his face, which only caused the poison to penetrate his mouth and tongue.

"Grim!" Michael shouted. He ran across the bridge, but the Rogues were ready for him, too. Lily struggled against the daemons that held her to no avail. Her sword, flute and kachinas were in the pack they'd taken. Michael still had the sword she'd given him. He reached for it in a fluid motion, faster and smoother than her eyes could track. But daemons were faster than half daemons. Michael's father had been an Ancient One. So he'd been bequeathed more power than the Rogues might have known, but they seemed eerily prepared for his strength and speed.

This time they had a net designed for him. Lily screamed when the barbs bit into Michael's flesh. She watched him fall. His Brimstone blood dripped down to sizzle and pockmark the glass.

Though fury shook her whole body, Lily stood helpless as a Rogue approached from the opposite side of the bridge. He wanted a grand entrance. He'd chosen the long way around. Behind him, a limping man followed. His entire manner was one of obedience to a master, but the deference his posture and movements showed didn't match the fury in his eyes. Lily recognized the robes he wore. The limping man was one of the corrupt monks who had stolen her father's name—the Order of Samuel. The Rogue daemon walked slowly, turning his face toward the approaching storm. As Michael and Grim bled, he sauntered.

His companion was pained by his limp. Lily could see the leg he favored bled profusely through the rough bandages that covered a terrible injury.

"Devil take you," Lily said.

Her words were carried to the Rogue and his toady on the whipping wind and he laughed in response. The monk wasn't as amused. His face flamed and he fisted his hands. The Rogue stopped his sightseeing then to approach at a more regular pace, but he paused over the prone bodies of the hellhound and the half-daemon prince. He looked down at Grim. He nudged a groaning Michael with one toe. Then he lifted his attention to meet Lily's horrified gaze. Unlike his master, the monk avoided Grim's prone form, skirting him even though it meant more steps on his injured leg.

"Samuel's daughter, I presume. I'm Abaddon. We haven't met, but you should know…" The daemon moved closer to her, stepping over his bleeding victims. Grim didn't move. He didn't shift a hair. "I *am* the Devil."

# *Chapter 15*

Lily was held on either side by two powerful daemons. Their heat raised blisters on her skin. She hissed at the pain, but, after, she bit her lower lip against showing them her reaction to their touch. Her affinity was wild in her chest. Like a murder of crows flapping for freedom against the cage of her ribs. She held it back. She tamped it down. She wanted these fiends to get no pleasure from manhandling her. They laughed and it was an even wilder sound than the wind whistling over and around the glass skywalk. The storm was coming closer. Part of her responded to the vibration of the glass. Her affinity was drawn out to the surface of her skin by the reverberation of sound. She tried to resist. Without her flute, without her kachinas to channel her abilities, rising affinity would only send the Rogues around her into a frenzy.

She particularly feared the ones who held her. Their heat, their excitement, was rising. They might tear her apart if either decided he wanted to keep her to himself.

"You came for these, I presume," Abaddon said, jeeringly.

A handful of Rogues carried a large object draped in a wind-tossed sheet between them. Glimpses of blackened bronze showed again and again as the wind blew. They stood near Lily and turned their burden until it was as it would have been on Lucifer's back. She remembered the wings worn on Ezekiel's back years ago when she'd first been delivered into his charge. He'd been very different from her beloved warrior angel, all craggy and battle-hardened. But she'd still been fascinated by the blackened wings.

Michael stirred and moaned. Lily jerked toward him, but her captors only laughed and held tighter. Then they laughed harder as she cried out with the sizzling of her skin. Her resistance was leaving her vulnerable. Without the rise of affinity to protect her, she would burn horribly from their heated hands.

Abaddon lifted one leg and placed his foot on Michael's back. He shifted his weight and the half-daemon prince cried out against the pain of the barbs being driven into his skin. More Brimstone blood flowed and hot tracks of fury trailed down her face in solidarity. She was glad of the wind. It whipped her hair to hide the depth of her emotion and it dried her skin.

Grim still hadn't stirred.

The angry monk had shrunk to the side behind the Rogues holding Lucifer's wings. He watched and waited. Lily suddenly knew he was more of a threat than he appeared. It wasn't only the anger in his eyes. It was his predatory air. Her affinity could sense the hunger in him. His blood was tainted by Brimstone and even though that taint wasn't as strong as daemon blood she could feel his burn and the darkness in it. He would wait patiently for his chance to claim Samuel's daughter. She felt more hunted than she'd ever felt before.

"You will help us as you've been helping Ezekiel and his bastard heir. We need your ability to track our enemies. Plus we just like it. A lot," Abaddon said. The hold on her arms tightened, but neither of the Rogues protested. They would yield her to Abaddon when asked. He was their superior.

They would, but would the angry monk? She thought

not. He acted as if Abaddon was his master, but he answered to nothing except his own fury. Its burn almost dwarfed the taint of Brimstone in his blood.

"I'm not a tool, especially not for you," Lily said. She ached for her flute, for her kachinas. She was the one who needed a tool to channel the affinity. She needed to control it in order to call the spirits and ask them for aid.

One of the Rogues that held Lucifer's wings cried out. The sheet had shifted and allowed his skin to touch the bronze.

The monk straightened and stiffened as if he prepared to lunge. She'd been right. He was only waiting to act on his own behalf. And Abaddon was too consumed by his power and importance to realize he had a traitor in his midst.

"Be careful. The council will decide who will wear the wings. Until then no one is to touch them," Abaddon said. He lifted his foot from Michael's back and stepped toward the wings. "Not even me," he continued. Lily could see the lust for power suffusing his face. His eyes glowed with Brimstone's fire.

The Rogue apologized for his slip, begging profusely for forgiveness. Abaddon was distracted by his efforts to dominate his subordinates.

Lily couldn't see where her backpack had been taken. It had disappeared in the threatening group of Rogues at her back. The wind of the approaching storm had grown impossibly fierce and damp. It buffeted them now with stinging whips of thick atmosphere. The clouds had come so close that the views had been obscured. Wind. Rain. And so much fire. Every Rogue around her burned with the heat of a thousand suns. Before the clouds enveloped them she'd seen the layers upon layers of earth that ringed the canyon.

All of the elements she could call waited for her to tap

into the power of her affinity to bring them to life. She just needed some way to channel it without her kachinas.

Lily sagged in the daemons' hold. Her burned skin sloughed off in their hands. The pain was excruciating. Her knees crumpled and she slumped to the ground. She landed, hard, because she'd taken her captors by surprise. The monk wasn't as surprised. He'd read her better than the daemons had, just as she'd read him. He leaped, but he hadn't judged her well enough. He thought she would go for her friends or for her pack. He landed several yards away from her actual destination. Before the monk could adjust or the Rogues could grab her again, she crawled the several inches necessary to bring her to one blackened tip of Lucifer's wings. The sheet had blown back to reveal its bronzed point. Lily fought against the pain to lift her hand and wrap her fingers around the longest feather.

And then she let her affinity go.

There were no dolls. No flute. No Michael. No Grim. There was only her and a bold decision to risk using Lucifer's wings as a channel for her power. And there was also the humming of the glass in the wind.

Daemons screamed. She'd heard those screams before. Fire had come to her. Blood burst into flames all around her. But Wind came, too. Humming the bridge and protecting Michael and Grim with the rain that followed when the natural storm clouds were swept over their motionless bodies. Lily saw steam begin to rise. It filled the air with fog.

She was ripped from her contact with the wings by Abaddon himself. He kicked her cruelly aside. But it was too late. Rogues burned. The two that had blistered her arms were already blackened corpses beside her on the ground. The angry monk had disappeared. He must have seen her heading for the wings and he'd wisely run away while she'd focused on his evil companions.

Michael was weakened from the tainted barbs. His Brimstone had been completely denied and tamped down even before he'd lost consciousness. He was protected when she called Fire. The rain cooled what remained of his Brimstone heat and soothed his skin.

Poor Grim hadn't moved since he'd first been snared.

Abaddon hadn't been controlling his Brimstone and he was fully a daemon, inflamed and burning bright. He howled at the churning sky as her fire engulfed him. But he didn't fall. He didn't join his fellows on the ground. Lily got shakily to her feet. The Rogue's leader stumbled away from her across the slippery glass skywalk he'd originally sauntered over to torment her. He fled. Beside her, Lucifer's wings were held upright by statues made of hardened ash that had once been daemons. Even in death, they hadn't been bold enough to allow the wings to fall to the ground.

Lily stepped to them even as she watched Abaddon make it to the curve of the horseshoe bridge. He looked back at her. She reached to touch the surface of Lucifer's wings again where the sheet fluttered open as if to grant her access. Clouds immediately rolled away. The storm dissipated as if it had never begun. Sunbeams stretched down from the sky as Abaddon climbed up and dived over the rail he'd melted in a mass of glass and steel from his heat. His clothes burst into flames echoing the sun. Then he fell out of sight.

He would never survive the fall. He might even dissolve into a cloud of ash before he made it to the ground. Lily pulled her hand from the wings. She backed away. Others would come. Others would always come. She fell to her knees beside Michael and Grim. Even drained, she found the energy to work on the nets. She found the openings and pulled them free. First Grim because he had been snared the longest. Then Michael.

"It's over. You're okay. You have to be okay," Lily said. It would never be over. It would never be okay. Outside of the palace she was a Rogue magnet. Inside the palace, she was a snare. An obligation that could never be escaped.

Neither Grim nor Michael responded to her pleas.

Lily got to her feet to search for her bag. She was too weak to risk using the wings again. She stumbled, light-headed and dizzy, through piles of ash where Rogues had fallen until she found the scorched remnants of her bag. Rain had soaked it. Fire had held back. Wind had swept rain in to put out the flames. The kachinas had saved themselves. First she pulled on a damp shirt that was black around the edges. She bit her lip when the material met her burned skin, but anything was better than the wind that stung at this height even after the storm. She gathered up the bundles of burlap and the velvet pouch of her flute. It had been singed, but was otherwise the same.

This was all she could do. It would have to be enough.

She staggered back to Michael's prone body and collapsed on her knees beside him. She barely had the energy to summon music from her flute, but she did her best. She allowed her affinity to rise with the music and hoped there was enough life left in Michael to respond. She played until her lungs protested before a slight aura began to glow. Warmth flooded through her. It stilled the shivers in her body and hands. It came from the man she wasn't allowed to love on the ground. The flute fell from her fingers and she leaned to press her lips to his.

The kiss was soft and over too soon. Michael's eyes fluttered open and she sat back.

"Grim is hurt and I don't know how to save him," Lily said.

Michael's pale hazel eyes changed into twin flames of leaping Brimstone, but it was still a struggle for him to rise. He didn't hesitate. He'd been near death, but he didn't pause with the news that Grim was in danger. She had come to realize that Michael protected those he loved with everything he had. The hellhound had been his life-long companion. There was no way that Michael would let him suffer and die without trying everything to save him. Lily reached to pull Grim's head into her lap while Michael walked unsteadily toward the place where the dead Rogues held Lucifer's wings.

"You win, Grandfather," Michael said. Lily's heart broke when he reached for the wings and ripped them from the ashy grip of the Rogue corpses. The hands holding them disintegrated. The macabre statue-like corpses crumbled and tumbled to the ground.

And her daemon prince donned his warrior angel wings for the first time.

He had worried that embracing his daemon half would mean he'd lost control. Instead he found ultimate control when his body accepted the weight of Lucifer's wings. When the Rogue Council had bronzed the wings, they'd allowed the molten metal to pool into a broad-shouldered mantel where the wings had once blossomed from Lucifer's mighty shoulders. The mantel rested on Michael's shoulders now and his Brimstone heat allied with the residual power in the wings to fuse them to his body.

But it wasn't only his heat. The protective instincts that always drove him and burned deep in his belly seemed to rise up and spread outward through the wings and beyond until an aura of energy glowed around him.

He was whole. Human and daemon. Brimstone and blood. Affinity and a fierce burn to protect. The throne was a dark threat on his future horizon, but, for now, the wings were a tool at his disposal to save his most loyal friend and companion. More than a tool. They were a part of him and they channeled everything he was and everything he could be with no part of himself rejected.

Lily's affinity blossomed in a powerful wave of admiration and fear. He was more beautiful than her kachina doll had ever been. More perfect. More noble as he sacrificed for Grim. He strode back the way he'd come on steady legs. He was no longer weakened. The residual power in the wings had burned away the Rogue taint from the barbs that had pierced his skin.

He stood over them. She couldn't read the expression in his eyes because they were consumed fully by the Brimstone glow. She wasn't afraid. His scars were old. His accident with his Brimstone blood had happened long, long ago. The burn didn't control him. He controlled the burn. But she did cry out when he drew her father's sword from its sheath and sliced it across his wrist with one graceful gesture. He knelt and allowed the blood to trickle over Grim's worst injuries on his face and mouth. Smoke rose. The hellhound yelped. Lily ignored the burns on her arms and the new burns on her hands where Michael's blood sizzled. But she did allow the affinity to rise. She allowed its aura to burgeon outward and upward until all three of them glowed with more than Brimstone light and smoke.

She looked up as tendrils of smoke curled up into the sky. Michael's eyes had dimmed. The hazel was back. He met her gaze.

"You saved us," he said.

Lily leaned into the uninjured hand he placed against her face. She tried to keep her eyes open. She wanted this moment to last. Then Grim stirred in her arms and struggled to rise. She let him go. Her affinity faded away. Nothing was left to hold her body in place. Her eyes closed. She fell away from Michael's hand. He allowed it to trail along her cheek. He didn't stop her fall. She slumped down to sprawl against the skyway's floor. Flying. Falling. It didn't matter which; with Michael her feet were never firmly on the ground.

Beneath her, the Colorado River continued its winding course that supposedly led to heaven. Her heaven would be in hell with Michael by her side, but her path to that place was as obscure as the pathway they'd tried to use to find heaven.

Peter had told them what to do and still they had failed. Abaddon had been too carried away with his newfound position. He'd had to display the wings. Now they were back in the possession of the daemon king. Thankfully, Peter had acted quickly to remove himself from danger. Samuel's daughter was more powerful than he had imagined. Even without the half daemon and the hellhound, she hadn't been defeated.

The roadblock the Rogues had created to stop tourist buses from entering reservation lands was dismantled easily enough. The handful of lesser daemons and human slaves Abaddon had left with the SUVs and cars simply drove away. Peter was sure that some visitor center staff had been killed. Rogues wouldn't let a few murders stand in their way.

None of them had offered him their blood to heal his injury faster. Even after he'd told them about Michael and the hellhound. He'd given them every advantage and they had left him to suffer for the months it would take his body to heal.

He'd miscalculated again. And he was no closer to his goal than he'd been before he'd sold his soul to the Rogues. He almost kept driving. It might be better to disappear and recuperate. His life would be long. He could hide while generations rose and fell and fought battles without him until he could make another bid for power.

He'd seen Abaddon fall from his hiding place behind the building.

His followers were still loyal to the arrogant Rogue.

Instead of driving away, Peter drove back to the motel. Abaddon was no mere mortal, but even a daemon wouldn't have survived that fall. Peter would tell the Rogues what he had seen. He would prove he was still loyal to their cause. If he helped them to retrieve Abaddon's body, then perhaps he could maneuver himself into a more powerful position long enough to use the lesser daemons before a new leader arrived. He might not have to wait generations to punish Samuel's daughter and the bastard prince.

# Chapter 16

Grim had risen to his feet, but he'd fallen after only a few strides. Michael had lifted him and carried him to the parking lot where half a dozen cars had been abandoned by daemons or workers who staffed the skywalk. He'd gone back inside then to check for survivors, but he'd come back out grimly shaking his head. It wasn't his fault that humans had died, but she could see him accept the burden of their deaths all the same.

Lily had climbed into the back seat with the hellhound. He'd rested his great head on her lap, seeming to relish her soft pats and reassurances. Michael hadn't mentioned the seating when he got behind the wheel. She'd watched him remove the wings and place them in the trunk of the huge sedan. She was afraid when he removed the wings that he would degenerate back to a weakened state, but he hadn't. They had driven for miles. Occasionally, their gazes met in the rearview mirror, but they both looked away.

The wings were silent, but both occupants of the car were completely aware of what they signified.

Even the static-filled radio station that Michael eventually chose after hours of surfing didn't drown out the sound of her heartbeat in her ears. Grim couldn't take them to the hell dimension. He was too weak. Lily would have to get them there. A sipapu portal would be their only means. And she would need to rest before she could summon the spirits to help her find one that hadn't been sealed.

It was fitting that she'd have to take full responsibility

for delivering Michael and the wings for his twenty-first birthday celebration where she would meet Ezekiel's beloved D'Arcy family for the first time.

Lily's head had slumped time and time again, but she'd managed to right it before Michael noticed in the rearview mirror. They needed to get as far away from the skywalk as possible. Their power had been epically released. Every daemon and all the damned in the area would sense her like a beacon. In order to rest, they had to run away. She tried to stay conscious. She fought the swoon that hollowed her insides out. Her body had been completely depleted. She'd nibbled the burned bars left in her backpack, but it wasn't enough. She wasn't sure she could consume enough this time. Touching Lucifer's wings had been a bad idea. She had no daemon blood. She was a human woman with a gift. Or a curse. Her affinity hadn't protected her from the scorch. It was as if she had been burned, inside and out.

Michael hadn't noticed. Not her weakness. Not her burned arms. She was beneath Grim's bulk and his shifting fur hid her injuries. But even though she was hidden, Michael balanced concern for her well-being with what needed to be done. They needed to get away, but he would know that she needed to refuel as soon as possible. He'd seen her summon before. He knew the physical toll summoning exacted. As the sun began to set, he pulled into a used-car lot that was almost ready to close for the day. Michael used a card from his wallet to call on the Turov resources. His stepfather's Brimstone-enhanced lifespan had resulted in extreme success. His vineyard had been uniquely overseen by a single man for a century and his wisdom and experience had paid off. As Michael exchanged vehicles, she stood apart from Grim long enough for Michael to see her arms through the thin material of the shirt.

"What did they do to you while I was unconscious?" he said. He came to her side, but he didn't touch her. He only examined her burns from a distance.

"It's not as bad as it looks. I'll be fine," Lily said.

"The first time I saw the friezes on the walls of the palace I was horrified. But the Rogues that did this to you deserve to be punished for eternity," Michael said, softly. He fisted his hands as he spoke and Lily suspected he'd like the immediate satisfaction of punishing them himself.

"Justice takes time. And penance even longer," Lily said. "Redemption is as elusive as Grim's smoke."

"You grew up in the palace. How did you ever become used to the carvings on the wall? The sentient stone. The tormented faces. The writhing figures," Michael asked. The money he'd offered the salesman for a quick, no-questions-asked sale had been enough to ensure discretion and speed. Before Lily swayed on her feet, the keys were in Michael's hand. He'd already placed Grim in the back seat of the car he'd bought. It wasn't a vintage Firebird, but it was the kind of old boxy sedan they would need. Nothing to spark interest as they traveled farther away from the skywalk.

"You've seen my rooms. They're kept separate from the main body of the palace. I've always seen them as a blessed retreat. No damnation allowed," Lily said. "But of course I saw the walls and ceilings whenever I walked along the corridors or visited other parts of the palace. My mother told me it was better than Oblivion." Lily hesitated before she continued, softly, "Ezekiel could do no wrong in her eyes."

"The souls trapped in the walls bother you as much as they bother me," Michael guessed.

"I'm bothered because Ezekiel can't let go of the past or the anger that corrodes his present possibilities," Lily answered. "The weight of all those condemned souls condemns him to sadness. When the walls of your home are tainted with Rogue hate, how can you find any happiness?"

"It was wrong when the Rogue Council used l'Opéra Severne's walls as a prison for Loyalists. It's wrong for Loyalists to do the same to Rogues within the palace walls," Michael said. "That's revenge. Not justice."

Lily met his gaze over the car's roof. When he became king, he would be the warden of a prison he hated. Yet another reason for guilt to gnaw at her heart. He had a deal with Ezekiel to deliver the wings. But how much would her affinity influence his decisions once he was in the hell dimension?

She got in the front seat this time. Grim was resting peacefully and she didn't want to shift his body again to make room in the back seat. Michael got in and drove the car to the nearest gas station to fill up the tank. Lily didn't have to ask him for food. He bought several bottles of juice and packages of nuts and sunflower seeds when he went inside to pay for the gas. He even opened the lid of the first two bottles for her and waited for her to gulp them down before he discarded the empties in the trash. She nursed the third, sipping small swallows as she thoughtfully chewed and Michael finally pulled away.

He headed south. In a different direction than they'd been traveling before, but still always traveling away from the structure they had inadvertently helped destroy. The sooner they were able to retreat to the hell dimension, the better. No witnesses had been left at the skywalk, but someone might have seen them driving away. They couldn't be certain that the money they'd given the used-car salesman would be enough to keep him from remembering a scorched girl, a giant hideous dog and a man with banked fire in his eyes.

Silently, Lily vowed to make Ezekiel donate the resources necessary to rebuild the bridge.

"I'm going to drive through the night," Michael said. "You need to rest. We'll stop in the morning. By then, maybe you'll be strong enough to perform another ceremony."

"I'm feeling better. Find a discreet place to stop and I'll find a sipapu with the spirits' help. And I'll lead us back to hell," Lily said. "Ezekiel won't be happy if we're late for your birthday celebration."

"You'd endanger your health for him," Michael said. He kept driving. There was no use to pretend she was stronger than she was with Michael. He would be able to sense her weakened affinity. She closed her eyes instead. She hoped he didn't put two and two together and figure out that she'd risk all for both of the people she loved, Michael and Ezekiel, even with no hope of love in return.

Lily was completely depleted. And injured. She hadn't let him look at the burns, but he could tell they were worse than she let on. He didn't give a damn about getting the wings to Ezekiel or showing up for his birthday, but he did know that Sybil could help Lily with the burns. His former nanny had helped to save him when he'd nearly burned up from the inside out as a baby. His brain burned with plans to keep Lily from Rogues, help her refuel, and flee to the hell dimension.

He didn't think about donning the wings again.

Not. Once.

They had released him after he'd done what he needed to do to save Grim. They'd practically leapt off his shoulders. He'd been compelled to take them off and stow them away.

He wouldn't easily forget the incredible feeling of being

wholly himself for the first time, but in a strange way he thought the feeling came more from using his Brimstone to save Grim than wearing the wings. The wings had helped him focus. They'd given his injured body strength.

But they still didn't call to him.

The idea that he might wear them for the rest of his life after tomorrow night didn't seem right.

But the idea that he needed to protect Lily from the daemon king and from her own desire to please the only father she'd ever known? That idea drove him through the night.

The needs of her depleted body had taken over around midnight. She'd fallen asleep with visions of an endless highway illuminated by headlights behind her lids. When she woke at dawn, she was ravenous again. The sight of a glowing car-sized waffle smothered in butter reflected in the windshield startled her, but then she blinked and saw it was a sign for a restaurant. Michael had pulled the car to a stop beneath the sign. He'd already let Grim out to explore. The sudden cessation of movement plus the sound of the car doors had woken her. Lily's stomach gurgled and she breathed deeply. Sweet dough and bacon scents filled the interior of the car. Okay. Her hunger had woken her. Definitely.

Unfortunately, she was in no shape to go inside and order. Her shirt had dried crustily to her wounds and the rest of her wasn't much better off. Michael was at the passenger-side door now. He opened it and handed her a plastic bag from a familiar discount store.

"First, we'll get you cleaned up. Then you eat. Real food. Not protein bars or snack food," Michael said. "There are some medical supplies in there, too, and the key to the restrooms on the side of the restaurant. It seems fairly clean for a sixty-year-old fast-food joint."

"And it has bacon." Lily practically drooled.

"Yeah. That was the deciding factor," Michael said.

He didn't reach to help her from the car. He couldn't. If they had managed to shake the Rogues, one touch between them would instantly make her a beacon once more. He held the door, but kept his distance while she got shakily to her feet. She had to grab the door to steady herself and they were suddenly separated by nothing but steel and glass. It wasn't enough barrier between them. Lily looked up into Michael's eyes. He simmered. The thrill of affinity rose in her breast, but she tamped it down. His jaw worked, clenching and unclenching, while he seemed to do the same.

"Go. Please. I'm starving, but even bacon isn't enough to distract me from you," Michael said.

Lily went. She was faint with hunger, but nothing would fill her as well as indulging their connection filled her. She would never be full again. She could be more comfortable and clean, though.

The restroom was surprisingly well-tended. It had a fresh stock of paper towels, antibacterial soap and plenty of hot water. The worst part of the whole process was peeling away the shirt from her skin. Once she persevered through that, she was able to wash and slather on an antibiotic cream Michael had purchased. The bag he'd given her also had a change of clothes and bandages. He'd been considerate enough to choose a soft loose shirt that didn't press on the gauze once she'd wrapped her burns. Its long sleeves hid her bandages. By the time she washed her face, smoothed her hair back, and donned jeans and sneakers, she felt almost human.

She was also pretty sure she was going to shock the waitress by how much she was prepared to consume.

* * *

The entire meal was a delicious, buttery blur with high-lights of warmed blueberry syrup and mountains of crisp, salty bacon fried up on a cast-iron griddle the size of their sedan. Michael ate only a little less than she did. Once they were both satiated, he tipped the waitress big to justify her numerous trips between the griddle and their table.

Lily sipped a mug of plain black coffee to offset the sweetness of the syrup. Only then did she think about the locals eating and drinking their usual orders at the Formica-and-chrome counter while Lucifer's wings sat in the trunk of a car behind their backs. The parking lot was full of old cars and trucks that were the contemporaries of the boxy used car they'd purchased. It had been a good call. No one would think there was anything beyond jumper cables and ancient flares in its trunk.

Grim had returned from wherever he'd gone to hunt his breakfast. He lay by the rear of their car looking like an oversize German shepherd. He guarded the wings. Not to mention her dolls and her father's sword.

"We passed a rock formation several miles back. I think that will be the best place for you to perform the ceremony," Michael said, quietly. She wanted to kiss the maple syrup off his lips. Of course, that wasn't possible. Instead, she wiped her mouth with the faded linen napkin and stood.

"Happy birthday in advance," she said. She wanted to tell him now, before they were at an opulent party in the depths of hell tomorrow night. And before she had to leave him there with Ezekiel and the D'Arcys.

"Do what you have to do," Michael said. "We need to get you to safety."

Had she ever been safe? The warrior angel kachina doll seemed to indicate that her future had been foretold before she'd even been born. And any future that forced her to choose between Michael Turov's destiny and refuge wasn't one that was meant to be safe for her. She wouldn't lure him to the throne, then keep him there. He had to know his decision to rule was entirely up to his own head and heart.

# Chapter 17

The rocks were high on a rise above the road, but accessible by a worn slope others had used before. Michael was able to park on a level area behind the formation so that the sedan was hidden from passing vehicles. With midday approaching, it was doubtful anyone would stop for photographs, as heat already shimmered in waves above the golden-brown earth warmed by a cloudless sky and glaring sun.

The largest boulder was roughly triangular in shape and Lily decided to utilize the shade it provided for her circle of kachinas. Michael stood with his back to her also sheltered by one of the rocks, but facing the road. He would see if anyone paused or turned their car onto the slope they had taken up the hill. Grim, revealing his true hellhound nature, had winked out of existence only to materialize on the rock nearest Michael. He was undeterred by the fact that its surface must have been as hot as the griddle they'd left back at the waffle house. He lay in the shadows created by taller boulders against the one he was using as a perch, looking like a shadow himself. He watched the road as well.

Lily left the Fire kachina wrapped and in her bag. She was hesitant to use it again so soon. It had become her most powerful element, one she wasn't sure she could control. She also left the warrior angel wrapped, but she did allow her fingers to touch it lightly as she gathered the other dolls. Its coolness soothed in the heat. The sudden tingle in her chilled hand felt like a hello. But she didn't want to antagonize Michael so she left it in the bag. Controlling his Brimstone was so important to him. He wore his scars like a constant reminder of what might be if he embraced his heritage. She didn't want him to think she consciously threatened that control. He had worn the wings to save Grim, but he hadn't worn them since. Just like her, he was led by instinct and experience. For some reason, he still rejected the wings even though he had worn them so well in that moment to save his loyal hellhound friend.

She didn't want to remind him of wings and daemon expectations. She didn't want to remind him that she might ultimately be a part of his capitulation to the daemon king's plans.

This was a simple ceremony she'd performed many times. She was asking her ancestors and her elemental spirits to help her find an open sipapu. One she promised to sanctify and seal when she was finished. To protect the old places. And to limit Rogues' abilities to travel to and from Ezekiel's kingdom.

Often the sipapu she found were amid nothing more than rubble and rocks in a long-ago-looted site. But a couple of times over the summer she'd managed to rediscover pueblos that had been forgotten. She'd been happy to point Native archaeologists to historic places for study and preservation.

The spirits were less likely to be mischievous if they knew her motives were pure.

Then again, she was participating in a scheme to place Michael on the throne of hell. Ezekiel had reasons—good reasons—for wanting his grandson to be the next daemon king, but she wasn't sure if *pure* could be applied to daemon manipulations. At best they could be ambiguous by

human standards because mortals weren't required to survive and thrive for centuries.

Only when she had readied Wind, Water and Earth
kachinas did Lily reach for her flute. Michael seemed to
know when to brace himself, as if he sensed her breathing
in behind him. She watched his back stiffen as she brought
the flute up to her lips. Just before she released air to blow,
he reached to hold on to the rock beside him. It wasn't a
lean. It was a grasp. He held the edge of the rock with tense
fingers and white knuckles. His whole body tightened.

And then her music began to fill the space around them.

She couldn't hold back during a summoning ceremony.
She couldn't control her affinity. She allowed the full swell
of her power to rise within her and then rode the release
of it as an almost visible aura of warmth exuded from her
every pore. Her affinity joined the music—warmth and
vibration, feeling and sound. Lily tried to focus on the
kachinas, but Michael was too close and the stiffness of
his posture was too much of a challenge.

It was too natural for him to be the one she called.

The aura that wouldn't have been visible to the naked
eye was visible to her heart. Like the heat she'd seen shimmering over the desert, the affinity vibrated the atmosphere between her and Michael. She watched it reach
him and envelop him. She watched his tension increase
a hundredfold.

Then he turned, and with his movement a rush of
heat rode the invisible waves of affinity back to her. Lily
tensed in response. Her eyes closed as Michael's Brimstone warmed her from her pursed lips to her stomach to
then curl enticingly lower. She continued to play, a pied
piper who was damned to call, call, call a man who didn't
want to follow her off a cliff.

But when she opened her eyes it wasn't only tension

she saw in Michael's broad shoulders and braced legs. His intense gaze was riveted on her playing—the breath that came softly from her lips, the pads of her fingers dancing on silver, the rise and fall of her breasts as she inhaled and exhaled—and in his eyes was anticipation.

The kachinas were forgotten. The spirits would have to wait. Her ancestors would have to continue to sleep. Because this song was for Michael, for all the affinity and Brimstone fire between them while they could still indulge it.

She played and he stepped toward her. Slowly but not reluctantly. He wanted to jump off the cliff she created for him with every breath, every sigh, and every slide of her hand. She didn't pause, although her breath grew lighter and shakier the closer he came. Not until he was standing directly in front of her did she allow one note to trail down to a long soft whisper of sound. Only then did he drop to his knees. With that sudden movement, her last note ended as his hands came up to rest against hers on the flute.

"One last kiss before we go to hell," Michael said. "I'll risk everything for one last kiss."

Lily didn't protest. She had no air left in her lungs to fuel any sound. Michael held only her hands as she held her flute, but she didn't pull away. She waited as he leaned down to bring his lips near hers. Close. So close. Dangerously close. But not close enough. The heat parched her lips, but he didn't soothe them. Not yet.

"One kiss, Lily. Worth dying for?" Michael asked. "We've got to be a beacon right now. Just from our hands touching."

He was right. The affinity throbbed between them with every beat of her heart. The unseen aura neverthe-less burned her eyes with a warm glow that caused them to fill with tears.

"I could face Oblivion with the taste of you on my lips," Lily whispered.

Flames leaped to consume the hazel in Michael's irises as he moved the hairsbreadth necessary to bring their mouths together. She opened for him, eagerly meeting the hungry thrust of his tongue. It wasn't tender or gentle. They had no time for slow seduction. He devoured and she hungrily explored all of the silken and rough textures of his mouth while their tongues tasted and twined and danced together.

Exhilaration claimed her with pounding heart and shaking limbs. Michael held her hands in a grip that was relentless, but that was all. He didn't embrace her. So she trembled for want of more—his arms around her, his body pressing her to the ground, the thrust of him inside her. But his lips became all of that to her because this kiss was all they had.

It was too long. Too indulgent. He discovered all the sensitive hidden crevices of her mouth that seemed to be wired directly to her most intimate nerve endings elsewhere when he teased them with his tongue. Her nipples hardened. And she tensed against the ache between her thighs. The vibrations when he groaned at the response of her questing tongue only increased her pleasure. Perspiration rose from their skin as steam. They were surrounded in a humid embrace in the middle of an arid day.

Lily imagined pulling her hands free from his controlling grip to fumble for the waistband of his jeans. She imagined taking this further than they could. Truly risking the chance of being captured and killed just so she could join with him one last time.

She whimpered into his mouth. She actually tugged against his hold. But a chill suddenly crept up her spine. Michael didn't release her hands, but he must have felt the sudden cold, too. He broke the kiss. He leaned his forehead against hers.

"I would risk death, but I don't want you at risk," Michael said. "I'm going to put some distance between us while you complete your ritual."

He stood and she rose along with him. Mostly because he still held her hands. Her knees were shaky. It was only with his help that she managed to get to her feet. He backed away, but didn't release her hands until he was at arm's length.

"Grim," Michael said. The hellhound was beside him instantly. "We're going to go for a walk while Lily does her thing. Not too far. Don't attempt too much."

Michael didn't say goodbye. He broke eye contact and followed the beast, who disappeared more slowly than usual as he walked away. Lily watched Michael dissolve from her plane of existence little by little from his ankles up, up, up the long length of his legs and spine. His broad shoulders and the shine of his hair went last.

He didn't look back.

Her body still trembled from his taste and touch even after he was long gone. She had no time to savor or regret. The Rogues would have felt the amplification of her affinity. They would be on their way.

Lily reset the kachinas that had fallen over. She quickly placed her focus entirely where it belonged. Or as much as she could muster when her body was still tender with needs that might never be met. This time the elemental spirits responded with messages from her ancestors in the form of visions in her mind rather than a map drawn on the ground. They left her with a magnetized feel for the direction she and Michael needed to travel.

There was an open sipapu nearby.

She gathered the kachinas and wrapped them and

placed them back in her bag. Somehow the warrior angel had come loose. A flash of black caught her eye. When she reached to wrap it back up, the sting of cold burned her fingers and she drew them back with a gasp to suck them back to life. How could the doll likeness be so cold when Michael was filled with Brimstone's fire? She thought about how a chill had come between them and how it had caused Michael to back away from their kiss.

If the chill had come from the kachina, it had probably saved their lives. The warrior angel seemed to become colder and colder every time she touched it, after years of dormancy. She wasn't sure what its chill meant, but it seemed more and more foreboding. She was used to being hunted by now, but the doll seemed to warn of unseen dangers.

By the time she was ready to get into the car, Michael and Grim had materialized nearby. This time Grim didn't climb into the back seat when she opened the door. Michael gripped his ruff and tugged before the beast loped away.

"He's going to keep an eye out for Rogues," Michael said.

"I'm sure they're coming," Lily warned.

"It was worth it," Michael said as they both climbed into the car.

"That's what scares me," Lily said. Too softly for him to hear over the roar of the engine. If he was willing to risk death for her kiss, he might accept the throne. For her. She couldn't allow herself to be the reason for that sacrifice. No matter how it might help her to win Ezekiel's heart. His fondness was reserved for D'Arcys. If she married Michael, she would be the closest thing to a D'Arcy that she could ever be, but did she truly want his love and approval that way?

If only he could love her on her own—as Lily Santiago—

and if only he would allow Michael to make his choice without daemon deals and manipulations. Then maybe Michael could be free to love her, too.

The Rogues had found where Abaddon's body impacted the canyon floor. It had been partially burned but mostly intact when he'd jumped from the skywalk. Much trouble had been taken to gather his remains together and bring them back for a ceremony that involved singing unlike any Peter had ever heard. He participated by bowing his head and biding his time. Abaddon's charred heart had been stabbed through with a daemon blade at the end of the ceremony. To "release" him to a state they called Oblivion. Peter imagined it much more likely he would wind up in hell. He kept the observation to himself.

"Friends," he began when the ceremony was over. "I have an idea of how best we can seek retribution for Abaddon's death."

He was rewarded for his service and patience by the gleam of a dozen pairs of daemonic eyes turning his way. Before he had completed his pitch for the continued hunt of Samuel's daughter, they all felt it—the call of Lily Santiago's affinity.

# Chapter 18

The sipapu was perfectly preserved, because the kiva where it was located had been created out of a natural cave rather than a hand-dug cellar. Whether there had been no pueblo above it or those structures had crumbled to dust long ago, Lily couldn't be certain. She thanked her ancestors and the elemental spirits when she climbed down into the shadowy hole in the earth to find what they'd been looking for. Michael climbed down after her, mimicking the use of naturally occurring rocks and ledges as stairs because the lashed wooden ladder was long gone, stolen or disintegrated by time.

Grim had already materialized below them. He was getting stronger and faster. More like his healthy self. Lily laid her hand on the top of his head when she passed him on the way to the dark circle of the sipapu portal in the ground. He allowed the pat. He didn't shy or fade away. They'd come a long way from his initial distrust.

But he did whine as if to tell her and Michael something.

"I know," Lily said. "I can feel them."

The Rogues were coming.

"Grim can help to take us through here where the opening makes his job easier," Michael said. He didn't wear Lucifer's wings. He carried them on his back, but they were wrapped tightly in a scorched white sheet and held like a backpack by ropes across his chest. He had used them to save Grim, but he wasn't ready to accept them as his own.

"I'll need to set up my kachinas here, in this world, and

call them to close the portal once we're safely on the other side," Lily said.

"But if the Rogues get here before you finish…" Michael began.

"They might destroy the dolls before I can close the portal," Lily said.

She was already crouched down to unwrap and place the dolls around the circle. She wouldn't have to use the element of Earth to widen the sipapu. Grim would help them pass. The doorway was open. He would only need to expend the slightest effort to dematerialize their physical bodies so that they could slip through.

Lily instinctively unwrapped the warrior angel and placed him to watch over the other kachina dolls.

Michael stood over her and the dolls on the floor. Tall, warm, real. The kachina that seemed to have been carved in his likeness was cool to her touch and it chilled her fingers to the bone. Michael's expression did the same.

"Don't protest. I know what needs to be done," she said. "He's been as much of a guardian to me as the daemon king has been. More so at times. He'll help in this. I know it."

"How can 'he' help when I'm going through the portal to the hell dimension?" Michael asked. He knelt to look closer at the doll he'd told her to keep wrapped and hidden away. She tried to stop him, but he reached to touch the kachina before she could react. His body jerked and the color drained from his face. He pulled his hand back quickly to cradle his frigid hand against his chest. Lily reached to touch his pale cheek, and when she did a reassuring flush of color returned to his skin. For a second, he leaned into her palm, but then he straightened and slowly stood.

"Why would a doll that looks like me be so cold?" Michael asked. His color had returned, but she could still hear the memory of ice in his voice.

She stood to join him, but didn't try to touch him again. Her fingers still tingled from the brief contact with his skin.

"I'm not sure. It hasn't always been cold. It was completely dormant most of my life. The temperature difference began to occur shortly after we met," Lily said.

"If it's representative of me, it should burn when you touch it," Michael said. It wasn't meant suggestively. He only stated fact. Yet Lily's cheeks warmed beneath his direct gaze.

"It's a kachina that was carved by one of my ancient ancestors. I don't know why it looks like you. I only know I've loved it since I was a young child," Lily offered.

It wasn't a declaration of affection for the daemon prince. Not quite. But it was more than she ever meant to share with him. This time he lifted his hand, but he didn't continue the motion to touch her face. He paused with his hand in the air between them. She waited for a touch that never came.

"You don't know me," Michael said softly. His melodic drawl seduced with no help from Brimstone at all. "You don't know the horrible fire that's within me or the depths of my struggle to deny it."

"Don't I?" Lily replied. "I've had my own struggles sheltered in a dark palace by a man who would be a father to me if only his heart would soften enough to allow it. You and I both fight fires in our hearts. You try not to burn. I try not to love. It's the same. You're more successful, that's all," Lily said. She turned from his uplifted hand. The one that could have touched her, but didn't. She knelt again to straighten the warrior angel, accepting its chill and wishing it would reach all the way to her heart.

"If I fail to control my burn, people might die," Michael said. To himself? To her? She couldn't be sure.

"It feels like death. To always walk alone," Lily said. "Better to brave the burn. Besides I've never met anyone who could control the Brimstone as you do. I don't believe you're capable of hurting anyone who doesn't deserve it. You would burn yourself up first containing the fire."

She reached for her flute, and it slid from its pouch into her hand like an old friend eager to play. Michael backed quickly away from her as musical notes rose from the breath she blew into the silver mouthpiece.

Lily ignored the rejection.

When the earth began to tremble beneath their feet, Michael called to Grim. She continued to play as she rose to follow. They stepped over the sipapu and even though it should have been too small to accommodate their bodies, Lily's stomach dropped as her body dematerialized and fell at the same time. Only moments passed before Lily found herself in the familiar great hall of Ezekiel's palace. There was a roaring fire in a hearth as large as a Volkswagen to welcome them, but she had no time to feel its warm glow.

Lily continued to play and from far away she heard the sounds of daemon shouts. The Rogues had found the sipapu. Would they destroy the kachinas before they could close the portal? Had she just sacrificed her beloved warrior angel for nothing?

Peter had been afraid they would have to face fire to follow Samuel Santiago's daughter to the hell dimension. He hadn't expected ice. Rogue screams ripped through the air around him as a monstrous shadow blocked their paths. Its wingspan was mighty and its reach was everywhere along the walls of the cave. Everyone it touched turned to a fleshly statue that fell stiffly to the ground with every ember of Brimstone fire sucked from their souls. The glow from daemon eyes only compounded the leaping shadows of the flashlights some of them carried so that they cried and shrank away from innocent shadows as well as the deadly one that hunted them.

"Lucifer! Lucifer is on the walls!" one daemon shrieked before he fell stricken to the ground, lifeless and silent.

"Lucifer is dead," Peter protested. He made his way toward the dolls Lily Santiago used to call her elemental spirits. The black one caught his attention, but before he could grab for it rocks began to fall from the shaking ceiling of the cave above his head.

Some of the Rogues had run away, but most lay on the floor as rubble fell all around them. He had sold his soul to reclaim power for the Order of Samuel. It was the Order of Peter in his mind now, although no one had gathered to officially change the name. He was the one who would rebuild and rekindle their purpose to defeat all the daemons and claim dominion over the earth. He only needed Samuel's daughter, and with her he would control Rogues and Loyalists alike.

The shadow had devoured all the heat in the cave. Peter shivered and dropped to his knees as a great wing stretched toward him. He reached for the doll and cried out in pain as his hand closed around it. His vision blurred, but he thought he saw his fingers turn black as if the blood that flowed in his veins was instantly frozen to ice and no longer able to feed his extremities.

When he fell, he fell far and long with the tiny kachina doll clutched against his chest.

The last murmurs of protesting earth faded away and Lily lowered her flute from her lips. She blinked and focused on Grim, lying by the enormous palace fireplace that made him a hulking black dog-shaped silhouette. Suddenly, her head grew light and her legs softened, but then there was a hand on her back. She didn't even try to step away from Michael's help. Unfortunately, accepting his chivalrous hand on her back too easily became stepping into his heated embrace.

They were safe. For a time. And until Ezekiel responded to their arrival, they were also alone.

Lily placed her flute in her hip pocket, and then twined her arms around Michael's neck while he seemed to wait and watch to see what she would do. Once he determined that she wasn't going to pull away, he strengthened his hold, pressing against her back with the palms of his hands to bring her fully against his chest. There was no reason they couldn't allow their affinity to rise and Michael's Brimstone to burn except for a million rational arguments she could think of if she allowed herself to debate the logic.

She looked up and met Michael's gaze instead. The leaping flames of the giant fireplace were no competition for the Brimstone glow in his eyes. All too soon he closed them, but it seemed to take forever for him to bridge the gap between her mouth and his. This time was slow. A steady claiming of this safe spot they'd found to fully explore her tender lips with his tongue. She gasped at the coil of heat that rose from her own depths to join with his Brimstone burn. But when he deepened his tasting past gasps and sighs to tease his tongue into her mouth, she wondered at his control over the fire in his veins.

He was hotter than hot, but he didn't burn her.

Together, their affinity amplified, but it was his concentration that buffered his burn.

While their mouths tasted and slid and sucked, Michael's hands roamed down her back to cup her bottom and lift her against him where a rampant erection distended his low-slung jeans. Lily moaned into his mouth and wrapped her legs around his waist to settle her ache against him.

His head fell back and he looked up at her from under hooded lids.

"I'm beginning to find that the palace is a much more pleasant place than I remembered," he said.

Tension claimed Lily's body and ice replaced heat in her veins. She pushed against his shoulders and he released her so she could drop to the ground. She backed away a few hurried steps to stand shivering by a fire that couldn't warm her. Ezekiel had known exactly what he was doing to use her and her affinity to lure Michael into wanting the throne.

"I'm dead on my feet. I need to rest and refuel," Lily said. "And you're the one who needs to deliver the wings to your grandfather." She tried not to notice how the dancing light from the fireplace illuminated the perfect angles of his cheeks and jaw and his lips swollen from her kiss. He nodded, but his intense stare saw through her excuse. Her body and her affinity cried out to step back into his arms. He had to hear them. And she'd even hinted that her heart would like to be there cradled against him.

She should tell him about Ezekiel's schemes. She should confess that she was torn between resisting them or succumbing for all that they would bring to her.

Instead, Lily turned and walked away.

She hadn't gone far from the light of the fire and the glow in Michael's eyes when her foot tapped against something in the dark corridor that led to her rooms. She stopped and bent down to retrieve the object that had rolled from her foot to the base of the carvings on the wall. Her hand recognized the warrior angel kachina before her fingers closed around it. She gasped in surprise and lifted the doll to the soft glow of light fading behind her.

The tightness in her chest eased as she saw the tiny doll hadn't been damaged. None of the other dolls had come through the sipapu portal, but somehow she wasn't surprised that this kachina had managed to follow her here. The light from the fire in the great hall didn't illuminate the hallway very well. As she straightened with the doll in her hand, her eyes skimmed the riot of carved stone all around her. The walls and ceiling were covered in the faces and limbs and figures of condemned Rogues—some would say damned—and her pause to pick up the kachina had nearly given her time to bring individuals into focus. Fortunately, the odd shadows created by the shifting flames of the distant fire kept the faces indistinct.

Lily shivered as one particular shadow passed near her on the wall. It was only the cold kachina in her hand that caused her chill, not the shadow. But she backed away from the wall, blinking, as the shadow seemed to grow larger and larger. It was only her imagination that gave the shadow a set of enormous wings beginning to unfurl. She blinked again and it became more of an indistinct blob once more.

Clutching the precious kachina that had somehow found its way back to her, Lily hurried on her way. Her rooms would be warm and welcoming and shadow-free. She never felt comfortable near the carvings for long. The smooth walls of her bedroom called. She needed to recover before tonight. If she knew Ezekiel, there would be a dinner fit for a king to welcome Michael "home." There might even be D'Arcys already at the palace in preparation for the Brimstone prince's birthday celebration.

She would meet the "daughters" Ezekiel loved for the first time, and one of them happened to also be the mother of the man she couldn't allow herself to love. She had to bolster her nerve and brace herself. The tiny warrior angel doll wasn't much to carry with her into a challenging evening, but it was better than nothing at all.

# Chapter 19

Michael was able to find his usual suite without much trouble. He'd visited the palace every summer since his sixteenth birthday. Odd now to think that Lily Santiago had been here all along. Ezekiel had never introduced them. Of course, Michael had been younger and less able to control his Brimstone, and Lily had the strongest of connections to her father's affinity as his only child. The affinity his mother and aunt had inherited because of Samuel's Kiss and the affinity that flowed through him was nothing in comparison to Lily's. It might have been a disaster if they had so much as touched each other's hands when they were young and inexperienced. The idea that he might have harmed her with the fire that had horribly scarred him as a child caused his chest to tighten and constrict his lungs.

He shrugged out of the burden he carried and discarded the wings on the bed. The room had that neglected air of a place reserved for someone who had no affection for it. The furnishings were fine but sparse and Spartan in design. The rugs on the marble floor were still plush and new because no one but the occasional maid ever walked on them. And yet the whole palace felt different to him now that he knew it was Lily's home. Seeing it as her shelter made him warm to it in ways he'd never imagined he could.

Her rooms had been filled with color from Southwestern elements her mother had brought from their former home—wall hangings, rugs, woven blankets, paintings and pottery—in reds, golds and soft umber browns. Not to mention kachinas of every shape and size on hand-hewn shelves of petrified pine. He'd made love to Lily there— and meant it—surrounded by color and light.

This empty room seemed petulant now. A teenage rebellion against heavy expectations and dark designs. He'd done everything he could do to show Ezekiel that he wasn't interested in being a king. And now that he was so close to delivering the wings and walking away there was a compelling reason for him to stay: Lily.

She would never be safe outside of the hell dimension. She was the beautiful Firebird from his stepfather's Russian fairy tales kept in a gilded cage. He'd always felt empathy for the bird in the tales. He'd been trapped in his own way by Ezekiel's expectations. But he'd always known he had a choice in his future. To accept the throne or walk away. Lily's blood gave her no choice. Unless to live or to die was a choice.

He would do anything to keep her safe. The drive to protect her roared in his ears and caused his heart to pound as if there was an unseen foe in the room that had to be vanquished. Did doing anything include accepting a throne that seemed to repel him?

Michael found the bathroom and wardrobe well-stocked as usual. The clothes had seemed to magically grow with him because he rarely saw a glimpse of the servants who changed them out with bigger and more mature choices as he grew. Everything he needed to prepare and dress for dinner had been left where he would find it. He donned the dark suit in the front of the closet in spite of the luster of the fabric. Ezekiel's taste was more evident in the wardrobe than his own, but he couldn't complain because he was certain he could have chosen whatever he'd wished if he'd participated in its tailoring at all.

He did omit the tie and he left the white shirt open at

the neck. He wondered at the perfect fit, but not for long. Sybil's needle was evident in every perfect stitch when he eyed it closely, and Sybil was never wrong.

When he came to the cuff links, he paused. They were bronze and stamped with a stylized *L* he'd seen often before. His uncle, John Severne, had a whole collection of brooches with the same emblem. He'd taken them from Lucifer's Army, one by one, before he'd come to realize he fought on the wrong side. Thoughtfully, Michael added the fasteners to his cuffs. First one. Then the other. They glistened when he moved, each *L* highlighted against the white linen of his shirt. John Severne's grandfather had sold his soul and the souls of his children and grandchildren for longevity and success. Severne had rebelled against the Rogues who owned him, risking his soul to save Michael's aunt Katherine D'Arcy. He'd also helped to save Michael and his mother when Michael was only a newborn by ordering his hellhound Grim to Michael's side forevermore.

To this day, his uncle Severne was intimidating. Maybe because Michael always felt like he'd stolen his uncle's dog. As a baby he'd had no say in the sacrifice, but he sure as hell wasn't giving Grim back now.

With Italian leather boots and belt, he was ready to face his grandfather. As if on cue, a tap sounded at the door and Michael opened it to reveal a young daemon boy in old-fashioned livery holding a silver tray. He thanked the child, who was probably older than he was, as he reached for the fine linen stationery note in the middle of the tray.

The "boy" hurried away without waiting for a reply. Of course it was from Ezekiel. He was waiting in the throne room. The only response he expected was Michael's attendance.

The wings gleamed darkly in the low light of the room's lamps when he unwrapped them from their burned covering. They would fit him perfectly if he placed them on his back, but he wasn't ready for that just yet. Instead, he tucked them under his arm and carried them without ceremony to the man who would wear them first.

The daemon king wore his suit with much more aplomb than his grandson. His was not loose about the neck or anywhere else for that matter. Every inch of the fine silk, linen and brocade hugged him like a second skin, and the sheen of obsidian fabric matched his hair and the shadowed glitter of his eyes. His skin might be craggy and scarred from centuries of battle, but he wasn't only a warrior. He was an angelic being who had chosen to fall and that self-dominion was evident in every graceful move his body made. He was hardened by battle and imperfect in every way and yet still so beautiful that every eye followed him when he moved through a room, including the damned eyes on the walls.

"Michael, you return in triumph, I see," Ezekiel said. He rose from the throne and moved toward his grandson with his arms outstretched. Physically demonstrative, daemons were often overwhelming in their intense affections. But his grandfather was also wise. He paused and waited for Michael to step into his arms before he hugged him ferociously. It was a conquering hero's hug. Yet Michael felt niggling doubts about who was the conquered and who was the conqueror.

"We almost died for these. Even Grim. I hope you appreciate what we went through to get them," Michael said.

"I was devastated by the necessity of the risk. I hoped it wouldn't turn into a sacrifice," Ezekiel said. Michael stepped back from his grandfather and dropped down to one knee. He'd been taught to be very careful with daemons and especially with the daemon king. But he'd also been taught to give him the respect he was due. He had reclaimed the hell dimension from Rogues. He had helped to save Michael's mother and his stepfather from the Order of Samuel. Ezekiel wasn't their enemy, even if a daemon king could never be trusted.

"Lucifer's wings," Michael said. He presented the wings to his grandfather by lifting them up horizontally with both of his palms spread beneath them. Ezekiel paused for a moment, looking down at him with inscrutable eyes before he nodded his head in approval and reached to take the wings.

"You bring me the wings, but…you don't refuse the throne?" Ezekiel asked. "We had a bargain between us."

"I'm…not ready to refuse…yet," Michael said. It was a mistake. He should close the deal between them now as he delivered the wings. To wait was to diminish the power of their agreement. But he couldn't make the decision to abdicate the throne without talking to Lily first.

"I accept the wings," Ezekiel proclaimed. The universe paused around them. Michael's chest squeezed as air moved sluggishly through his lungs. Now. Right now, he could say that he refused the throne and the deal would be done between them. It would have been a struggle to speak, but that wasn't what stopped him. The taste of Lily's lips. The glaze of passion in her eyes. The gleam of tears. Her hips welcoming him and meeting the thrusts as they joined together. The odd feeling of taking flight and finding home whenever he touched her hand. Those memories stopped him. But most urgently the feeling that she was in danger and she needed his help. The urge to protect Lily drove him mercilessly beyond the point where he'd originally intended to walk away.

The moment passed. Oxygen filled his lungs. His body shifted to the side as the molecules of atmosphere loosened around him. And Ezekiel turned away, casually, as if deals were meant to be broken.

"Your parents have already arrived. They'll be at dinner. As will your aunt and uncle. And Sybil, of course," Ezekiel said. Several servants had rushed from the shadows to help him with the wings. He had turned to allow them to place the wings on his shoulders, where they settled as if they belonged. There was no noise or flash of light, but Michael's affinity felt the rush of ancient Brimstone power quicken the room. Suddenly, his grandfather was even more daunting than before. "And Lily."

Michael didn't flinch when Ezekiel lifted the direction of his gaze from the cuffs he'd straightened to meet Michael's eyes.

"She almost died," Michael repeated. It was an accusation. Probably one only a Brimstone prince—and a D'Arcy—would dare to throw at the daemon king. "She was badly burned."

There was an imperceptible flinch then. From Ezekiel himself. One that might have been missed if Michael had blinked.

"She is my ward. I have protected her for fifteen years," Ezekiel said. It wasn't an apology. It was only a statement of fact.

"You weren't protecting her out there," Michael said.

"She saved you. She helped you retrieve the wings. And now you are back where you belong," Ezekiel said.

"She's back where she belongs. Safe behind the palace walls," Michael said. "Nothing is more important than her safety." The desire to protect Lily burned hotter in his heart than his Brimstone blood. It was almost as if the need to guard her against harm fueled that muscle's every beat.

"Yes. All is well," Ezekiel said. But his body was tense

and his eyes seemed to search Michael's for a mutual understanding he couldn't find.

"I'll make my decision tomorrow night," Michael said. He'd seen the flash of bronze on Ezekiel's wrists, where cufflinks identical to his own starkly gleamed against pristine white. He still didn't know himself what his decision would be. Lucifer's wings. Lucifer's throne. An entire realm to rule. Judge, jury and executioner as well as king.

And Lily.

She would soften the weight of the throne, but in a way, wasn't she as trapped as the faces and figures that horrified him on the walls? Was accepting the throne actually the best way to insure her safety or would he only be turning the key in the lock of her beautiful prison?

# *Chapter 20*

Sybil was the closest person to a loved one that Lily had in the palace. The daemon seamstress had been like a mother to her since her own mother had died. Where Sophia had been openly warm and demonstrative, Sybil was outwardly cool, calm and collected. Lilly saw the banked fires in her dark eyes, though. Her affinity couldn't be fooled. Sybil was old and wise; her emotions were tempered and hard in ways that only intense burning in the past could have achieved. She'd been hurt. Badly. So she buried herself in her work. She cared with needle and thread, with lush fabrics and incredible designs. The passions she'd once allowed to rule her heart as other daemons did, were now completely expressed in the clothing she created.

She was waiting to fit Lily into a gown for the evening.

When Lily arrived exhausted and injured, Sybil jumped into action. She wasn't demonstrative with her affections, but she cared with every practicality she could proffer. With her long life and wealth of experience, her knowledge often approached the supernatural even when Brimstone and affinity weren't involved.

"Ezekiel risked much in allowing you to run away," she said as she tended to Lily's arms. The herbal ointment she smoothed gently over the burns on Lily's arms had a medicinal scent, but it wasn't unpleasant.

"He has a plan," Lily said. She sighed as her pain disappeared. Then she gasped when the redness on her arms began to fade.

"Doesn't he always?" Sybil replied. She placed the lid back on the ceramic pot that held the ointment. "He tries to manipulate the universe, never imagining that the universe might get the better of him." Sybil set the ointment on Lily's dressing table. "Several more applications and you won't even know you were burned. I used the same remedy on Michael when he was a baby. But his burns were much worse. Even I couldn't prevent the scarring or stop his pain. I helped. I eased. It was all I could do."

"It must have been very bad. He fights his Brimstone to this day," Lily said. The burns on her arms no longer pained her and they had nearly faded away. Her skin was still tender, but it was smooth.

"He's the strongest man I've ever known, and I've known many strong men," Sybil said. She followed the revelation with more practical concerns. "Now, I need to add soft sleeves to your gown for the evening."

Lily bathed and dressed for dinner as if she was preparing for the gallows. Her every move was reluctant and slow, but also deliberate and careful. How could her makeup possibly matter? And yet she took extra time and effort to apply it flawlessly. She shadowed and shaded and contoured until she wore a perfect mask of the woman she'd like to be.

Good enough to meet the D'Arcys.

Her baroque wardrobe was filled with beautiful clothes supplied by Sybil, a nearly immortal seamstress with a gift that would rival that of any designer in the couture world. When she opened the elaborately carved mahogany doors, she saw a new addition hanging in a snowy white garment bag on a hook on the back of the door. She could tell by the way the garment bag was rounded out by the full skirt of the dress it contained that this must be a new dress for the birthday celebration tomorrow night. Looped over the hanger by their straps was a pair of high-heeled sandals that possibly gave some hint to what the bag contained. They were deep, dark blue but dusted by sparkling diamanté dust so that they shimmered with the slightest movement.

Lily couldn't resist. She dreaded the birthday celebration even more than she dreaded the dinner tonight, but Sybil was an amazing artist. She had to see what the daemon seamstress had created for an event that was supposed to be the most important this palace in hell had ever seen.

She reached trembling fingers to unzip the bag and reveal the fabric beneath.

The room was softly lit by several lamps, but when the navy chiffon was released from its confinement, it glittered as if it held the light of a thousand stars. Lily gasped and touched several of the tiny gems that illuminated the endless layers of sheer dark fabric.

Sybil had made the dress out of the Arizona night sky, or so it seemed.

Lily's heart palpitated and her breath came quick as she remembered the escape she'd made with Michael when he'd said, "Run with me." The feeling of weightlessness in the pit of her stomach and the exhilaration when they flew.

It was difficult to zip the bag, but she forced herself to carefully press the dress back into its protective covering once more. Now anticipation warred with fear of what tomorrow night would bring. Paired with her nervousness for tonight it was almost too much to bear. She wanted to wear the dress for Michael and dreaded the appreciation that might turn to betrayal in his eyes once she confessed her part in Ezekiel's scheme. Michael thought he was immune to her influence, but no one with Brimstone blood could be that strong.

She hadn't intended to be bait. She hadn't intended to be a lure. She hadn't intended to want to become his bride.

But all of those had come to be just the same.

Once the ball gown was zipped back into the garment bag where its presence would torment her now that she'd seen it and touched it, Lily reached for the more simple dress Sybil had intended her to wear to dinner.

Of course, in Ezekiel's palace no one dressed simply.

Sybil had created all of her dresses. Even the less elaborate ones. But one had new soft sleeves that Sybil had added while Lily bathed. The pale blush sheath ended high above her knees, but it featured a trailing overskirt that fluttered when she walked because it was composed of hundreds of jagged silk pieces. Under each piece a patch of darker organza added texture. The overskirt tickled her legs softly and highlighted their sleek, fit lines with every step as her skin showed against the pastel material. The bodice was satin. It was form-fitted and smooth. It hugged her breasts with a neckline that seemed to suggest she had a curvier figure than she actually possessed. The new blush sleeves were the softest organza. They were lighter than air and full so they didn't press against the tender skin of her healing arms.

Simple for hell. High style for anywhere else. And not nearly suitable armor for her first encounter with the D'Arcys who had haunted her since she was a child.

Lily chose shoes that matched the bodice of the dress— smooth satin—in a slightly darker hue. Then she paused to look at herself in a floor-length mirror her mother had brought from Santa Fe. Against her dark hair and eyes, the light colors of her clothes and makeup shone. In fact, against the whole room her outfit nearly seemed to glow, as it would wherever she went in the palace tonight.

She probably should have worn something black and

nondescript. She should have opted to blend into the background and give the D'Arcys center stage. But for some reason the very thought of that made her square her shoulders and lift her chin. The lamplight caught her eyes, and they glittered in the mirror with a dark determination she suddenly embraced.

This was her home—for now.

She would never be queen of the castle, but tonight she was the hostess. She wouldn't be a wallflower even if she was only the daemon king's ward.

Sybil knew her. The dress had pockets hidden beneath its silk patches. Perfect for her flute and her warrior angel. Lily put her oldest treasures within easy reach before she headed out the door.

Michael accompanied Ezekiel to the dining room. A glance from his grandfather to his bare neck seemed to suggest he had been expected to wear a tie, but nothing was said. His suit rivaled any of the designer clothes in his closet at the vineyard so he was fairly certain, tie or not, he would do his mother proud.

Of course, it wasn't his mother he thought of first when he entered the large room made cozy by the candelabras that lit only the table and left all else in shadows—except Lily Santiago. She was in soft pale silk. The rest of her was anything but muted. Her dark chestnut hair gleamed. Her chocolate eyes glittered. Her skin so perfectly contrasted the fluttering dress she wore that when she moved, her long legs drew his attention time and time again. Her outfit glowed in the shadowed room, but it was Lily herself who shone.

She was talking to his mother.

He flinched with guilt when he realized he hadn't noticed anyone else in the room for several minutes. He'd been totally transfixed by Lily. She laughed at something his mother had said. And then Victoria D'Arcy Turov saw her son.

Only a man related to her wouldn't have seen her first in a crowded room. She was still a stunning diva even though she no longer graced the opera stage. She proudly wore the sparkling dust of silvery streaks in her scarlet hair. And as usual, she wore matching red for her dress and shoes.

"Michael," she said with the husky voice she now used to sing contemporary popular music. She'd injured her throat when she'd saved him as a baby from an opera house fire. It hadn't been the last time she'd saved him. They were both scarred from his first burn when he'd almost combusted before the affinity they shared had helped him to control it.

"Victoria, I'm so glad you've all come," Ezekiel said.

Did everyone notice that his mother faltered ever so slightly when the daemon king spoke her name? Did anyone else see his stepfather, Adam Turov, move to place his hand supportively against his wife's back? Or that seconds later his aunt, Katherine D'Arcy Severne and her husband, also came to stand beside Victoria as if they were presenting a united front to a threat that had just entered the room? Is that how they would all treat him once he was king? Would accepting the crown burn the last of his humanity away?

"Now that Ezekiel and Michael are here, we can all take our seats and dinner will be served," Lily said. The whole room looked to Samuel Santiago's daughter and seemed to release a long, pent-up sigh. Because Lily smiled as if this were a normal dinner party and not a dinner party in hell. She glowed with humanity in her inhuman home.

She led the way to the table, which just happened to bring her near him. Even as his mother hugged him and kissed his cheek in hello and his aunt did the same, even as his uncle and stepfather shook his hand, Michael was entirely focused on Lily. She brushed by him. He felt the soft tickling silk of her tattered skirt against the leg of his pants. He breathed in and tasted the slightest ozone hint of rain that always seemed to hover around her like a delicate perfume.

Without thinking, he reached to take her hand. He needed to stop her from walking away. But it was a mistake because when he touched her bare skin, everyone in the room held their breath again. He spoke into the stillness rather than let her go.

"You've met my family… Victoria and Adam. Kat and John," he said. It wasn't a question. It was a statement he'd already confirmed with his own eyes. But for some reason introductions he hadn't seen weren't enough. He needed to introduce Lily to his family. "This is Lily. Lily Santiago. She helped me retrieve Lucifer's wings."

As always when their skin came into contact with each other's, the heat had flared in his blood and the seductive song of Lily's affinity surrounded their slight connection with an almost perceptible aura. Lily looked from his hand on hers up to his face. He spoke to his family, but he didn't look at them. He looked deep into Lily's eyes instead.

"Samuel's daughter is my ward," Ezekiel interjected. He was oh so casual. He didn't have a casual bone in his body and everyone in the room knew it.

"So…you used her to help you retrieve the wings," Adam Turov said. He wasn't looking at Michael when he spoke. He also didn't question. He looked right at the daemon king as if his statement was an accusation.

Michael's hand tightened slightly on Lily's and her eyes widened. It was true. Of course it was true. His stepfather wasn't a daemon but he'd lived a very long time. He perceived things that younger people never would. His long life had given him an almost psychic-like ability to notice and absorb everything about his surroundings, including everything about the people in them.

Lily licked her lips and, damn him, he wanted to kiss her even in that moment when her nervousness gave her away. She had helped him in order to help Ezekiel. He should have known it all along. Everyone in the room was aware that the daemon king moved them like chess pieces in an elaborate game only he understood. And of course his grandfather would try to use Lily's affinity to seduce him to the throne.

"Something smells delicious," Victoria said. Her voice was brittle. He could hear her displeasure in every sharp shard. But she knew better than anyone that hell wasn't the place to displease the daemon king by attacking his ward. Besides, like Lily, she'd been manipulated by the daemon king more than once in her life.

"Ezekiel always lays a sumptuous feast," John Severne said. His cultured French accent was more melodic than a modern one would have been, influenced more closely by Old World tones. Like Adam Turov, he'd once sold his soul, and the Brimstone in his blood had given him a longer-than-mortal life. He'd lived in his family's opera house in Baton Rouge as the city grew up around it, and though a new one had been rebuilt in place of the old one that had burned to the ground, l'Opéra Severne and its master were still haunted by days and nights gone by. "The devil's charms are seductive and sweet."

Michael knew it was meant as a warning for him. Even if everyone in the room sympathized with Lily, they would still want him to be careful. He loosened his fingers and allowed Lily to pull away. She lowered her eyes until her lashes created shadows on her cheeks, which seemed suddenly pale. Her hands went to her skirt and she swept it aside to sit in a chair beside the head of the table. Her place. Near Ezekiel. Of course.

What had it been like to lose her real father and find herself in hell? She hadn't had a choice. And once her mother had died she'd been left with no one but Ezekiel.

The seat meant for him was on Ezekiel's opposite side, across from Lily, but Adam Turov moved forward to take it, earning a look of reproof from the daemon king himself. Victoria sat beside her husband. That left three more seats. He should have taken any but the one beside Lily. They were all warning him with their eyes and actions to keep his distance from his grandfather's ward. He should have listened, but didn't. He pulled the chair out and sat next to her, so close that he could smell her rain-kissed skin. Adam frowned, but Michael ignored it. He'd seen her hands linger on her skirt where two small bulges on either side were mostly hidden beneath fluttering silk. She had her doll and her flute and she touched them for courage. She wasn't as comfortable in hell with his family as she seemed. The telling gesture made him want to sit by her in spite of Ezekiel's schemes. Or maybe because of them. Lily was being used. Ezekiel's plans would consume her and she might just allow it. She loved the daemon king. Michael's chest burned with anger that Ezekiel would use her vulnerability against her. Everyone seemed shocked when he took his seat. They all paused, even Ezekiel. But then the daemon king's face relaxed into a lazy, crooked smile.

"Please. Be seated, Katherine and Severne. Let us begin," Ezekiel said.

"Yes. Let's," Michael said. Suddenly, he knew his control was enough. The daemon king's scheme would fail because he wasn't ruled by the Brimstone in his blood. He had spent his life controlling it so that no one around him would be hurt. He'd protected his friends, his family and his lovers. Even Lily who tempted his fire unlike anyone ever had. He'd had his scars to remind him what his daemon blood was capable of. He'd never let it hurt anyone again. When and if he accepted the throne, it wouldn't be because of Lily's affinity. He would never use her the way others wanted to use her. She deserved better and he would damn well give her what she deserved.

He was cold as ice by the time the first course was served.

Lily escaped the parlor off the dining room shortly after the party had retired there to drink after-dinner cocktails. She had wanted to be bold and brave and claim her place at her guardian's table among the people he actually loved. Instead, she'd ended up feeling that she'd been placed squarely on the side of the devil against them all.

They didn't love Ezekiel.

He was a hard being to love. She and her mother had always known it. But it was harsh irony that the D'Arcys didn't care for the creature who placed them before everyone else in his life. It made her useless quest to gain his affection even more tragic.

And Michael.

He had looked at her through the eyes of his family and found her wanting. They hadn't openly challenged her or Ezekiel, but she'd seen the caution in their eyes. She had yet to make her full confession, but she could see the truth dawning in him. She had grown up in hell seeking the approval of the daemon king himself. He was the only father she'd ever known. What did it matter that her real father had been a veritable saint? Hell was her sanctuary. She deserved any taint it had left on her heart.

"You're a quick little thing," a throaty voice said from out of the darkness of the corridor she traversed.

Victoria D'Arcy stepped from the shadows. The silver streaks in her hair glinted in the torchlight of the sconces placed sporadically to illuminate the palace hallways. Lily could see anger in the tight lines of her face. She was still beautiful, maybe even more beautiful than she'd been when she was younger now that she had a lifetime of emotion swirling in her eyes.

"You left before we could talk," Victoria continued.

Lily had stopped. She stood and waited for Michael's mother to draw closer. In this light, her dress looked nearly black.

"I wouldn't have known what to say," Lily said. She had agreed to help Ezekiel lure Victoria's son to the throne of hell. She hadn't agreed to bind him to the throne. That's where she would draw the line. She wouldn't bargain herself to make him a king. In fact, she would risk her life to keep him from making a forced decision.

But Victoria couldn't know that yet. Lily would tell no one that she planned to run away. She couldn't risk Michael trying to stop her. It would be too easy to succumb to his persuasion.

"You came here as a child? You've lived here since you were small surrounded by these chaotic walls?" Victoria asked. She nodded toward the walls that surrounded them and the figures Lily had learned to avoid looking at directly.

"My father knew Ezekiel was the only one who could keep me safe from Rogues," Lily replied. She reached into her pocket and held the warrior angel in her hand. The doll was cold. Colder than she remembered.

She was startled then by the sudden warmth of Victoria's embrace. The woman came forward and wrapped her in a fierce hug and squeezed her tight against her petite frame. The scent of sweet Firebird wine enveloped her.

"I also had a dark childhood. Don't run away from me so quickly. I don't blame you for what Michael must face," Victoria said into her hair. "My anger is for Ezekiel. And for Samuel, too. This gift that's both a blessing and a curse. It ties us to beings that would consume us with their love."

Tears burned the back of Lily's eyes but she blinked them away. "Don't run away" was different from "Run with me," but they were both invitations she was going to have to refuse.

"Ezekiel isn't human. He asks too much. His gaze is always on an eternity of what-ifs that don't take into account our finite time on earth. His love is a harsh taskmaster, Lily. Don't let it crush you," Victoria said.

"I have nothing to fear from Ezekiel's love. It's reserved for…others, but I promise I won't hurt Michael," Lily said. The words came from somewhere in the bottomless pit her chest had become.

"Don't be so certain where Ezekiel's affections lie. He's an enigma. But rest assured, I'm not afraid you'll hurt Michael. I'm afraid you'll continue to hurt yourself," Victoria said. She leaned back and looked down to the cold place around Lily's pocket she must have felt during the hug. Lily pulled her hand and the warrior angel out of her pocket.

When Victoria saw the perfect likeness of her son, she gasped. She reached to take the tiny doll from Lily's hand, but she jerked back her fingers when she felt the icy cold.

"It was never cold when I was a child. My ancestor carved this. Before Michael was even born. It's getting colder and colder and I don't know why," Lily explained.

"He was nothing but a cold shadow the last time I saw him. A frigid shadow that protected us after he died," Victoria whispered. Her pupils had gone large and haunted and her skin was deathly pale. Against it, her hair was vivid even in the shadows. In spite of the cold, she touched one finger to the warrior angel's face. "It's a perfect likeness."

"When I first saw Michael, it was as if the doll I'd always treasured had come to life," Lily said.

Victoria looked from the warrior angel up to Lily's face. Her eyes widened.

"You thought this doll looked like…my son?" she asked.

Lily nodded, confused.

"Lily, this is Michael's real father," Victoria said. Her voice shook. "He was an Ancient One. He fought with Lucifer himself. He sacrificed himself to save us all when Reynard tried to hurt us. Michael is very like him, but… the wings."

So the little kachina she had always treasured wasn't Michael Turov after all. He didn't have wings. And he might choose to never wear Lucifer's wings. She'd thought the doll was a prophecy about Michael taking the throne. She'd even thought it might mean that he was destined to be a part of her life.

It had all been a mistake. The kind of wishful thinking a woman might fall prey to when she'd grown up in the depths of hell, longing for more.

"He was very cold. So cold he was dangerous to touch or be near. Deadly in shadow form," Victoria said softly. Suddenly, her attention went to the carvings on the wall. She narrowed her eyes to look into the shadows from face to face. "I lingered and loved him still even though the chill might have killed me."

"It's worse if you focus on them. They become…restless," Lily warned. She reached to place her free hand on Victoria's arm, but the other woman continued to look at the carvings as if she was searching for something…or someone.

"He dragged Reynard into Oblivion. Or so Kat thought. She watched them disappear in flames when the opera house burned, but I wonder…" Victoria said.

Lily tried to stop Michael's mother from stepping toward the carvings on the wall, but the other woman pulled away from her restraining hand. The warrior angel had taken all the warmth from her other fingers. They were numb. Suddenly, Lily wasn't able to grasp the doll and it fell to the floor.

She and Victoria watched the doll begin to roll inexplicably toward the wall. Faster and faster as if it was pulled by an invisible string.

"No," Lily said. The doll had always been her treasure, but it was no longer a comforting object. If it didn't represent Michael, it represented a daemon she'd never known. One that had died, but somehow managed to live on as a vengeful shadow. What if he lived on still?

"He won't hurt us," Victoria said. "He would never hurt me."

"I'm a threat to Michael. I've lured him back to hell with Lucifer's wings and hell is the last place he wants to be," Lily said. Fear blossomed in her heart, making it as cold as her hand.

The warrior angel came to a stop against the base of the wall and then it plinked with the sound of wood on marble as the force propelling it brought it upright again on its wooden feet.

While their attention had been fixated on the doll, an amorphous shape had begun to converge from all the leaping shadows caused by torchlight on the wall. Many shadows became one large shadow looming above them on the wall.

"No, Michael. She's not our enemy. She's just a young girl, a pawn, like I was when we first met," Victoria said.

Wings had begun to unfurl from the shadow and the corridor had noticeably chilled. Lily shivered and her teeth clicked together. She wrapped her arms around her body and backed away. The hallway was shadowed from end to end. There was nowhere to run.

"I won't h-hurt him," Lily promised. Yet still the shadow continued to grow. One of the wings had actually started to stretch out and away from the wall toward her face.

"Michael will never forgive you if you hurt her. And neither will I," Victoria said. She had placed herself in between the shadow's wing tip and Lily's face.

Without thought, Lily reached to place her hand on Victoria's shoulder. Through the fear, she allowed her affinity to rise. Victoria stiffened, but then she began to sing. Softly, at first, but then louder and louder Michael's mother sang a French lullaby. Lily dug for her flute with her free hand. She brought it out and lifted it to her lips and began to play. She joined Victoria's song.

The hallway grew warmer. The shadow diminished. Before long, the only shadows that were left were ordinary ones cast by leaping firelight.

Victoria's song faded away. Lily allowed her flute to fall from her lips.

"I loved him, once. And he loved me. As a daemon loves, you understand. Terrifying, forever, both dark and burning bright. Michael fights his Brimstone blood. And it's right that you should try not to help Ezekiel hurt him. But please, understand, my son is a daemon prince, Lily. If you think loving Ezekiel as a daughter loves a father has been difficult you must try to understand that loving a daemon as a woman loves a man is likely to bring *you* pain," Victoria said.

She had followed Lily to warn her. But it wasn't the warning that Lily had expected.

Lily dropped her hand from Victoria's shoulder and the other woman slowly moved away. She bit her lip to keep from confessing that it was too late. She was already hurt. She would carry this pain with her forever once they were parted. Or at least as long as she survived.

## Chapter 21

Lily couldn't face her empty rooms. There was only one place that seemed to offer enough warmth to offset the discovery that her warrior angel was a threat. She hurried up deserted stairways that led farther and farther away from guests and servants. It had been months since she'd visited this part of the palace and the hallway sconces were long cold, but she found her way easily in the dark

The conservatory was perched on the roof of one tower far removed from anyone who would disturb her. Ezekiel had given her the key shortly after her tenth birthday when she was old enough to come and go as she pleased. The great glass-walled arboretum was a Gothic wonder of spiderweb wrought iron and thousands of glass panels that rose into a dome high above the trees and plants below. It was tended by gardeners who always disappeared discreetly when she entered and tonight was no different. She barely caught a glimpse of a man with a bucket of tools when she turned the key and slipped inside. He vanished down a spiral staircase that led to storage rooms below.

Warm, dry air embraced her with an artificial atmosphere completely separated from the palace. She closed the door behind her and leaned her back against it. The scent of desert flora filled her nose as she breathed deeply. But best of all, sunlight caressed her chilled cheeks.

Ezekiel had brought a little of the Southwestern desert into the hell dimension with daemonic manipulations she didn't understand. She supposed if Grim could travel pathways between worlds, then sunlight could as well. Within the great glass conservatory, one didn't look out at the purple glow of the hell dimension. A soft, hazy desert sunshine bathed the glass with light.

Now that she'd seen the actual desert, the light in the conservatory soothed her even more. It had always been a sanctuary for her, a secret garden surrounded by hell's shadows. She tried not to think what it would be like to leave it behind for good, to know that she could never return.

Instead, she wandered over the pathways to visit all of her favorites—the desert lilies, the climbing trumpet vines, the prickly pear cacti, the towering saguaro.

She paused to trail her fingers along the petals of one desert lily. She was saying goodbye.

Her heart pumped with slow, painful beats in her chest, the only noise to break the silence in the wake of her decision.

"You left the key in the lock," Michael said. He came around the corner of the path, startling with his sudden presence, but also with the glint of sun on the gold strands that shone in his brown hair.

"I'm never disturbed here," Lily said. The brass key with its stylized *L* and burgundy tassel had been a bauble to wrap and give to her on her birthday. After all, the gardeners came and went without the need of keys.

Michael continued to approach and the petals of the flower Lily touched began to tremble. She tried to draw back her hand, but Michael was there before she could move. His hand covered hers on the lily's petal.

"You're shaking," he said.

"I'm cold," Lily said. And it was a lie. The conservatory was very warm even though the sunlight was an entire world away.

"I'm sorry I've disturbed your retreat," Michael said, guessing the real reason for her trembling fingers.

"It was always temporary. The shadows are waiting just outside," Lily said. She looked from his hand on hers up to his face.

"I never knew there was a garden up here," Michael said.

The tension in his face and the intensity of his gaze weren't softened by the lightness of his hand or his lowered lids. His fingers were steady, but he wasn't unaffected by their contact. She was warmer than she'd been before. A flush suffused her skin, caused by Michael's heat and her own rising affinity within.

"It was a birthday present from Ezekiel," Lily explained.

Michael's eyes widened in surprise and his attention left her for a moment to look up and around at the elaborate garden and engineering marvel of the greenhouse itself. He tilted his chin and sun seemed to worship his angular cheeks and the chiseled perfection of his masculine jaw.

"He gave you the sun," he said softly. He closed his eyes briefly and then opened them as he looked back down at her again.

"I… I never thought of it like that," Lily said. "Ezekiel is the king of daemons and daemons are…grand creatures. He tilts worlds based on mere whims." She shrugged and pulled her hand out from under Michael's. She was uncomfortable talking about her relationship with the daemon king.

"If you say so," Michael said. But he looked at Lily with narrowed eyes as if his mind was focusing on speculations he hadn't pondered before.

"I'm his ward. He made a deal with my father to protect me. That's all," Lily said. "Giving me this garden was easier than spending time with me and my mother."

"I've never seen so many lilies in one place," Michael said, gesturing to the profusion of petals around them. "It's breathtaking."

"That's the affinity making you short of breath," Lily said. Her own lungs were having trouble processing the oxygen necessary to keep her breathing normally in his presence.

Michael allowed his fingers to trail down the lily and she watched, transfixed by his rough fingers on the delicate silk of the petals. Then she gasped when he lifted his hand to touch her face. Each ridged pad sent a thrill of response from her sensitive skin to other neglected places that longed for his caress.

"You call to me, Lily. But I don't think we can blame it all on the affinity," Michael said softly. He seemed to savor the feel of her skin beneath his fingers, tracing the soft hollow of her cheek down to the edge of her lips. She breathed out, carefully trying not to move, but the exhale caused her mouth to open slightly and his attention was drawn down. He lightly touched his thumb to the swell of her lower lip and Lily inhaled sharply. She tensed as fire coursed from his touch to her entire body, igniting erogenous zones she hadn't known she possessed.

"It's your Brimstone blood," Lily said. "You can't resist the way we're drawn together."

"Can't? I've controlled my burn for years. Something else draws me to you. The need to warm. To protect," Michael said. He teased his thumb across her lip, a rhythmic, whisper-soft caress again and again. "You're missing the fact that I don't want to resist, Lily. Especially here where there's no danger in indulgence."

He leaned down then to replace his thumb with a sudden press of his lips to hers, but he slowed immediately to carefully capture the lower lip he'd been teasing between his teeth and bathe it with his tongue. All the while he kept his eyes open and watched her reaction.

Her knees went weak. Molten heat flowed between her legs. And the rest of her fell from a great height where she'd been trying to keep herself distant from the seductive daemon prince who challenged her every resolve.

Michael caught her. He wrapped his arms around her and kept her on her feet, pressing her against his solid, hot body. She reached for his suit jacket and crumpled his lapels in her fists. No longer focused on staying on her feet, she only wanted him closer. He complied by deepening the kiss. She opened for him, mouth and soul. Perhaps she was saying goodbye to everything she held dear, but Michael didn't have to know. He couldn't know. If this was farewell, she wouldn't hold back now.

"I don't want to invade your refuge, Lily. I want to be asked. This is your garden. Your palace. Your home. Invite me inside or I'll walk away. I'll show you just how much control I have over this damned Brimstone in my blood," Michael said.

He said it all against her lips and he punctuated each word with long, slow tastes of his delving tongue. She was burning from the inside out so much that she wondered how she hadn't turned to ash and blown away. The aura of affinity was full force around their bodies and he scorched against her skin. Could he walk away? If so, he was stronger than she was. Her legs had stopped responding from the second his mouth claimed hers. But he was right. It wasn't only affinity and Brimstone. She was hungry for Michael, the man, the daemon prince who was caught in otherworldly manipulations as she was caught.

The man she would lose before she trapped him on the throne he'd always hated.

"Please. Stay. This garden has always been the place I

came to forget the world outside. We can forget together," Lily said.

"Already done. Every time I taste you everything else fades away," Michael said.

A rush of adrenaline shot to her heart, causing it to pound as he punctuated his words by lifting her off her feet. She grasped his shoulders, but didn't protest when he sat her on the edge of a raised stone wall that enclosed the beds of desert lilies. Not even when he joined her and pressed her back to crush the flowers beneath their combined weight. She didn't mind the springy earth beneath her or the prickles of the greenery. The mashed petals released a sweet, fresh scent that enveloped them. The scent combined with the hint of smoke that always lingered on Michael's skin when his Brimstone heat had risen in response to her touch.

Michael shrugged out of his jacket and spread it beneath her head and shoulders when she lifted to accommodate the gesture. She noticed he took extra care around her arms even though they no longer pained her. Then he looked down as if he found her laid back on the tuxedo and crushed flowers a compelling vision framed by the pale blush of her rumpled silk gown.

He had a halo of sunshine around his hair and his face was in shadow. But she could still see the familiar sharp angles of his cheek and jaw. She reached up to touch the side of his face. He stilled beneath her fingers, drawing in a breath and holding it. The kachina might have been a likeness of his real father, but he was still her warrior angel. He would be forever, even when they were apart.

"Not a very soft bed," he said.

"It's perfect," Lily argued.

"Your burns?" he asked.

"Sybil helped me. They're almost healed," Lily said.

She could see shadows shift over his eyes as her words reminded him of his burns and how Sybil had tried to help him long ago, but he won the war against bad memories for once.

His eyes cleared and he reached for the fastening ties of her overskirt. He slowly began to manipulate the knots that held them together. His attention stayed on her face as she breathed in with every tug of the strings he pulled and softly released each gasp as the ties loosened. Until her hand caressed from his face to the opening of his shirt and pressed against the heated skin of his neck; then his eyes closed and he hissed in a sharp inhalation of reaction.

Her overskirt slid open and spread beneath her. It provided another layer of padding on top of the flowers, an impromptu, bohemian quilt of patchwork silk. There could have been shards of glass beneath her and she wouldn't have noticed. Not when Michael moved his attention from the released fastenings to the skin of her legs that had been fully revealed.

Her fingers trembled on the buttons as she worked to open his shirt while his calloused hand lightly smoothed from the edge of her sheath's skirt down to her knee and back up again, to find soft warmth between her thighs.

"You're softer than your namesake's petals," he whispered. Then he moaned and closed his eyes again because she'd finally worked all of his buttons open to find the muscled expanse of his chest and the flat plane of his lean stomach. He sucked in air as she caressed softly over the white ridges of his scars, banishing the memory of pain with the current rush of desire.

"Could you walk away now?" Lily asked. He slid his hand under her skirt to cup her hip, and her breath came faster. Her skirt rode up high on his lower arm. She was light-headed with need. Her heartbeat wasn't isolated to her chest. It had claimed other parts of her as well, thrumming a call for his touch between her legs.

"Would you want me to?" Michael countered. He'd opened his eyes again to watch her as he teased his hand closer and closer to the apex of her thighs.

"No. Don't go," Lily gasped.

"I'm not going anywhere," he said. It was a low groan, a sensual promise. One Lily opened her legs to encourage. He took advantage of her movement, sliding his hand over the silk underwear she wore beneath her sheath. Silk was no real barrier, but it was too much. She moaned in protest at the thin scrap of material preventing his touch from finding her throbbing clit. "No, Lily. I couldn't walk away. But it isn't the Brimstone that rules me. It's you."

He pulled her underwear down in a soft, swift move that left her completely bare to his fingers. He tossed the silk to the side and his fingers returned to seek and find the focused point where her pulse throbbed. Lily cried out, swiftly claiming a sharp orgasm against the tender expertise of his calloused fingers under his intense, watchful eyes.

And then he swooped down to devour her cries with his hot, hungry mouth while he continued to pet and play her. There was no rush. They didn't have forever, but they had tonight with no Rogue threat hunting them down. He took advantage of the decadent hours stretching ahead of them. Gently filling her with thrusting fingers and questing tongue.

Lily luxuriated in the tastes and textures of his mouth—wine-sweetened, rough and smooth—but she also sought further access for her own explorations of his beautiful body—scars and all. She fumbled blindly for his belt and was rewarded by deep groans of approval. She arched her hips against his fingers as they mimicked the connection she craved, but she wasn't distracted from the need to release his erection. He bulged beneath the trousers she struggled to loosen. His heat called to her. She impatiently unfastened his button and brought his zipper down.

He pulled back from the kiss and they both looked down to where her hand reached to slide his underwear out of the way. His freed cock sprang forward to bump against her mound. But he continued to use his fingers to rhythmically fill her even as his penis teased against her.

She tensed and her intimate folds squeezed his fingers as intense pleasure arched through her again, buoyed on by his attention and the thick, throbbing evidence of his need.

Lily reached for her own top. She shifted and ripped the smooth silk down to expose her breasts. The dress was ruined. She didn't care. He rewarded her boldness by leaning down to suck one distended nipple and then the other. He bathed the pink tips of both globes with his hot tongue while she reached to grasp his erection in a trembling hand. He arched his back into her grip and Lily held on the best that she could against his enthusiastic thrusts.

The aura of affinity competed with sunlight around them. And Michael's eyes glowed with twin flames.

"Who we are brings us together—including the legacy in our veins," Lily whispered. "Don't deny your Brimstone. You don't have to resist it or control it. Not with me."

She urged him closer and his hand slipped away to grasp her hip. She opened for the wider girth of his erection and he settled between her thighs. He was engorged and it was a tight fit, but she was slick and ready, eager for the jerk of his impatient hips as he filled her.

"I can't resist, Lily. I lied. There's no controlling this. Not now," Michael said. Beads of sweat evaporated off his brow as quickly as they rose up on his skin. A slight haze of humidity surrounded his half-naked body as she held on to the frenzied movements of his hips and met them again and again with her own.

"No control. Not now," Lily repeated against his neck as she nipped his salty skin. Later she would worry about regaining control. Later she would worry about sacrifice. For now she rode the pleasure as it claimed her one more time. She cried out as he buried himself all the way to her womb with a final thrust that brought his own release. His heat filled her and they were closer than they'd ever been for long moments until they fell back down to the reality of crushed flowers and the scent of earth.

He didn't care if the wings tried to reject him for the rest of his life. He would wear them for Lily. To protect her. He'd felt the same wholeness when he'd worn them to help her against the stone Rogues. The same satisfaction in finally having a tool to channel the protective instincts that burned in him as surely as his Brimstone burned. That they'd immediately rejected him afterward didn't matter. He didn't care if he had to endure the pain of ill-fitting wings. He would wear them and he would convince her that he wanted to. That he accepted the throne. He embraced it even as he embraced her.

She was so warm in his arms. And it was a replete, soft warmth unlike any he'd felt before. He hadn't been seduced or manipulated. He loved. And if it was as passionate as a daemon loved so be it. He was half-daemon after all.

Michael's grip eased only after hours of sleep. Lily watched him as the distant sunlight from another place and time tracked across another world's sky. He was as miraculous in her garden as the sunshine. It didn't matter if the kachina had foretold the presence of his father in her life. She would always remember what it had been like to love the warrior angel she'd always loved—in the flesh.

Finally, when twilight settled over the garden, she disengaged herself from his heavy arms and rose. She did the best she could to dress in the crumpled remains of her dress. The torn bodice necessitated her borrowing the tuxedo jacket. He didn't wake. He slept the deep sleep of the satiated on the lily garden's ground.

This time she left the key in the lock when she slipped away. She would never visit her sanctuary again. Michael had blessed her with a memory that would have to heat her in its place.

Somehow she wasn't surprised when she found Grim at the top of the first stairway as if he was keeping watch over their tryst. She was taken aback when he turned and led the way instead of staying with his sleeping master. But she was glad of the company. The staircases and hallways were cold and dark. Far more chilly than she remembered. She didn't think the sconces provided heat as well as light, so the cool shadows spooked her. Grim padded with sure-footedness toward her rooms. He knew the way. He always knew the way. As long as the destination wasn't heaven, he could find it.

She avoided looking too closely at the riot of carvings on the walls. When they finally reached hallways where torchlight gleamed, she tried not to jump at shadows on the wall. The chill was probably only a reaction to leaving Michael's Brimstone heat. She would have to get used to the cold.

Once Grim escorted her to her bedroom door, he sat and waited for her to go inside. He didn't follow her. He also didn't walk or fade away.

"Are you protecting me? Or keeping an eye on me to protect your master?" Lily asked. Grim was more intelligent than an ordinary dog. He could sense and see things that even some humans wouldn't see. He might understand that her bargain with Ezekiel was still in play. He might not understand that her decision had already been made to thwart the daemon king's schemes.

"Whatever your reason, I'll accept a watchdog for tonight," Lily said. "But beware of cold shadows."

Grim's eyes swirled with fire and his tongue lolled from his mouth. Sitting at attention, his head almost came to her shoulders. No wonder he acted like he had little to fear.

Lily slowly entered her rooms and shut the door behind her. She placed Michael's jacket on her pillow and went into the bathroom to wash away the soil from the garden. Afterward, she pillowed her cheek against the jacket that held Michael's smoky scent and slept fitfully, less afraid of shadows than she was of the man who might come to find her in her sleep.

At first Peter was trapped in an endless scream he fought against for hours that seemed to stretch on for an eternity. His entire focus was on closing his wide-open mouth, which had unaccountably turned stiff and unresponsive. His force of will was still strong. Several times a living presence passed him in the darkness and he was enlivened, better able to feel and move.

Finally, he brought his lips together.

Only then, when his focus slowly shifted elsewhere, did he understand where he was.

Peter spent hours ending his first scream as a carving on the walls of the daemon king's palace in hell. Then he spent several more hours opening his mouth to scream again.

# *Chapter 22*

Michael's birthday dawned with the hazy glow of purplish sky that lit every day in the hell dimension. But on the day of a special celebration the usual demands of discretion were lifted from the servants in the palace. The hallways and rooms bustled with a constant flow of lesser Loyalist daemons that were rarely seen as they saw to the needs of arriving guests and the decor and amenities necessary to care for them.

Lily avoided conversations.

She might regret not saying goodbye to the daemons that had cared for her for years, but other than a stack of notes she carefully placed in her writing desk to be discovered later, she didn't intend to acknowledge her plans in any way. She couldn't risk Ezekiel's finding out that she was making unusual rounds among the servants. He would never let her go. Of that she was certain.

She did risk discovery when she left her rooms to visit her mother's grave. Fortunately, the importance of the party preparations kept most too busy to notice her passing. She planned her course along less-traveled halls and used a side entrance that few others utilized.

Before she visited the cemetery, she stopped at the stables. The great stone stalls weren't made for ordinary mortal horses. Mounts larger than draft horses carried daemons into battle, but most of the stalls were empty now that the Rogues had been driven out of the hell dimension. Lily spoke to all the creatures that nickered at her as she passed. She wasn't intimidated by their giant bony bodies, sharp teeth or glowing eyes.

Reaper was waiting.

He was the most ferocious of them all, but even though he'd once carried the daemon king on war-torn fields, he took the apple from her hand with careful movements. If anyone had seen her leave the palace, they wouldn't realize she was visiting the beast to say goodbye.

Once she was clear of curious eyes, she hiked up a craggy hill behind the palace and the stables to the cemetery beneath an ancient willow-like tree. Unusual plants and animals thrived under the lavender light of hell's skies. Grim followed behind her this time, trailing after her instead of leading the way. Out of respect or uncertainty, she couldn't be sure. He had stayed smoky and vague inside, but he had fully materialized by the time she reached the black marble tombstone on the crest of the rise.

There were cut desert lilies left to dry on her mother's headstone. Lily fingered their brittle petals. She hadn't placed them there, but many of the servants had loved Sophia. Someone could have asked a gardener for the flowers. Sophia had brought a human woman's passion to the halls of the palace—warmer and softer than its master's.

Not to mention the laughter of a human child.

Lily had been happy in the hell dimension. Often. She'd been freer in captivity than she'd ever been in the outside world.

"I know you would understand," she said. "I have to set him free."

Of course there was no answer. Grim sat in the distance too far away to hear her words, but her heart still pounded in her ears for saying them and her palms grew moist. She took a handful of petals and crushed them in her fingers before sprinkling them over the grave in a flurry of pale gray. She watched them float to the ground.

Her mother had asked to be buried here. Near her daughter, she'd said, but Lily had known she had also wanted to remain close to the daemon king. Did her unrequited love linger here even in death? Or had she found peace?

The hot knot in Lily's chest said the ache of unfulfilled love was never eased.

She reached into her pockets for the familiar velvet pouch and her warrior angel kachina. Her hands met flute, but not doll, of course. She'd abandoned the doll in the hallway. A lifelong habit was hard to break. She focused on loosening the pouch inside her pocket and pulling the silver flute out into the purple light. Once it was in her hand, she sank down to her knees beside the scattered lilies on her mother's grave.

Lily had no desire to disturb her mother's rest if poor Sophia had managed to find it, but she needed to play here and reclaim the memory of the loving lesson times they'd shared. Her breath was weak and soft at first, but the song grew in strength. It was a Hopi lullaby. The first song she remembered and the first one she'd played. She didn't intend a summoning. She hadn't brought any of her kachinas. Nevertheless, a cool breeze wafted over the grave, stirring the crumbled flowers into petal dust in the air. Lily watched them flutter and float, hover and fall. The willow-like tree had long draping limbs filled with crinkled leaves. It seemed caught in perpetual winter. The breeze stirred its dry branches into a cacophony of sound. The sibilant hiss of leaves brushing together created whispers whose meaning she couldn't quite ascertain. The insistent noises skittered along Lily's senses. The hair on the back of her neck and arms rose to attention.

But she continued to play.

She refused to be too afraid to use the gifts she'd been given. She sought answers and guidance. She might have lost her precious doll, but she still had her flute and the ability to use it to dwell in the aura of her affinity. Eventually, the breeze stilled and a warm energy filled her, called from her own heart. She was Lily Santiago, Samuel and Sophia's daughter, and she would not be a pawn in Ezekiel's game to bind his grandson to the throne.

Lily came to the end of the lullaby and allowed the last note to fade. She lowered the flute from her lips. Looking down, she noted that there were no dried petals left on the grave. They had all been swept away.

Grim was a dark shadow behind her. Waiting. Watching. She rose and slid her flute back into the pouch in her pocket.

"One day I'll see you again, but not here," she said softly. The headstone that held her mother's name and the years of her birth and death had a sleek, dark surface. Lily started when her movements mirrored in its surface. Her heart leaped with a quickened beat. She could see a distorted reflection of herself in the obsidian marble. That was all. But she was pale and her hair was wild. Reflected in the grave marker, she was unfamiliar. As if a different woman rose to head back to the palace.

And maybe she was.

She was no longer conflicted.

Desperate. Afraid. Filled with dread.

But determined.

She turned to follow the path down the hill without noticing the figure of her guardian silhouetted against the purple sky. He looked down on her and the palace from a taller rise as she walked away. Grim paused. He raised his horrible muzzle in the air and nodded at the daemon king before turning to follow Lily Santiago inside.

\* \* \*

Michael woke alone, stiff and dirty and naked. He was confused for several seconds as his mind processed his surroundings. It was definitely daytime, but the sky above was dark. He finally processed the myriad panes of glass and the whistle of a gardener in the distance, thankfully before the gardener came his way.

It was his twenty-first birthday, a day he'd dreaded his whole life, but he didn't have to ask himself why he hurried to shrug into his clothes.

Lily.

She was bound to hell by the powerful affinity her father had bequeathed her. She wasn't safe in the outside world and it would never be safe for them to be together anywhere but the hell dimension. This palace was her refuge. Somehow that made it more appealing to him than it had ever been before.

Did it matter that his grandfather might be using Lily to bind Michael to the throne? No one liked to be manipulated, but he had grown up dealing with daemons. Nothing was straightforward. Nothing was simple. Lily was an innocent caught in a web that Ezekiel had been weaving for centuries. Even when she succumbed to the irresistible attraction between them, he could sense her reservations. He was disappointed to wake alone, but he had to admit there was also a rush.

He was the stepson of a hunter. Adam Turov had hunted Rogue daemons for years and helped their victims. Lily might want to run away from Ezekiel's schemes, but Michael wasn't prepared to just let her go. The rush he felt was the thrill of the chase. His whole life had been building toward this birthday and this celebration. The palace was abuzz with preparations as he stalked down the stairways that led to his rooms. Servants curtsied or bowed as he passed as if he had already assumed the throne, but Michael had only one thought on this mind: the hunt was on. Tonight wasn't only about his birthday and the throne. Tonight was about showing Lily that they were meant to be together in spite of all Ezekiel's manipulations. Not because of them.

Lily went back to her room, no doubt creating gossip because of her new hellhound companion. Grim shadowed her without making a sound, but his materialized presence was enough to cause a stir.

"I guess it would be too much to ask for you to stay invisible?" she asked under her breath. "I'm fine. Not even a chill bump to be seen." If he had been able to speak, Grim might have pointed out that she avoided the walls and even the most innocuous shadows all the way back to her bedroom.

When she arrived at her door, Grim took up his post again with a vigilant pose—ears up and forward, shoulders stiff. She had to admit his presence was reassuring for now. Later, he might interfere with her plans, but she would worry about that when the time came.

Her room met her with peace and darkness. There was no bustle here. No party preparations. But she'd had a visitor while she was gone. The ball gown had been taken from the garment bag in the closet and spread across her bed. The bed was king-size and yet it still didn't accommodate the voluptuous layers of organza that spilled over its edges. The diamanté gems featured heavily on the bodice and then were scattered with more subtlety on the skirts, but the sparkle was compelling. Lily stepped forward and lifted the dress gently. She watched the soft lamplight glimmer on the gems in the fabric as they reflected the light. The shimmer also revealed the deep midnight blue of the dress and the intricate weaving of hand-sewn silver threads holding the garment together.

Sybil had outdone herself this time.

She couldn't have known about Lily's fascination with the night sky over the Arizona desert. Yet the dress perfectly called forth the memory of flying through that sky with Michael beside her. She was both eager to try the dress on and loath to begin an evening that could only end in resolute sadness. But she would dance and dine with the Brimstone prince. She might spend hours in his arms tonight. No ordinary designer could have provided a dress worthy of her last night in hell.

# Chapter 23

It took time to master the art of movement in his nearly paralyzed form, but Peter was nothing if not persistent. The increased activity outside his prison of the frieze helped. The more daemons that passed, the more he and the others trapped in the walls found themselves enlivened.

The response was chaos, mostly. There was no method to the madness of movement around his frozen form, only shifting, swirling and screaming as he had when he'd first found himself trapped.

Peter had been trained well by the Order. He spent hours reaching one hand out from the wall. Inch by inch he fought against whatever force had placed him in the purgatory of the palace walls. Once his hand reached forward into the shadows of the corridor, he worked to follow it with his arm. One goal drove him, as it had for many years. He would have Samuel's daughter and her affinity for his own.

She found whisper-soft ivory undergarments folded on her pillow. The absence of a corset didn't worry her. She was certain the dress would fit her perfectly. Sybil's creations never needed help or adjustment. The strapless bra was light as air when she lifted it to place it against her skin and made of a material that was translucent, yet it conformed to her curves with the right amount of support. She couldn't help glancing in the mirror as she pulled the equally translucent and airy thigh-high hose over her legs.

After her night with Michael in the garden, the ensemble suggested numerous enticing possibilities. The idea of his calloused hands sliding against the silky hose…

Lily turned from the dress before she allowed herself to be carried away with a sultry scenario that could never be. She didn't need help with the ball gown. Sybil's designs were always easy to manage no matter how luxurious they seemed. In spite of the numerous layers of organza, the dress was light and went over her head with ease.

As she'd imagined, it settled on her slight curves like a second skin. Made for her by a seamstress more aware of her measurements than she was herself. Her arms were completely healed after several applications of the ointment Sybil had given her. They were no longer tender or pink. She stepped into the starry sandals and then allowed the skirts to fall to the floor. Their sweep was perfect. Not awkward or confining. They moved with her easily as she crossed the floor.

It was time. The celebration would go until midnight and by that time Michael would have to make his decision. It was a poignant countdown with a foregone conclusion. He would agree to be king. It wasn't in a D'Arcy to back down from a challenge, even if it warred with their very nature.

Lily had to ensure that she wasn't part of his decision—for or against—even though his choice would sever their connection forever.

His tuxedo was midnight blue with a sheen that reflected and refracted the candlelight as he moved. Lily watched him for long moments from the shadows. The snowy white of his silk shirt was the perfect contrast to the tie that matched the tuxedo save for the diamond chips that sparkled there like stars.

Sybil had designed their clothes to be complementary. All of the guests including the D'Arcys would know that they were meant to be seen as a couple. Ezekiel's orders? Or had the daemon seamstress taken it upon herself to play matchmaker with two people she had watched over since they were young?

Lily couldn't hide for long. Even in the crush and whirl of a ballroom filled with Loyalist daemons in their best finery, her starlit ball gown had been designed to shine. She'd only managed to go unnoticed this long because Grim had disappeared rather than escorting her with full hellhound ferocity into the ballroom. She had no idea where her vigilant watchdog had disappeared to, which added one more concern to her evening. She needed to know where he was in order to avoid him when she had to slip away.

Michael saw her before she had braced herself sufficiently to step from the shadows. Had he been watching and waiting for her to appear? He turned fully toward her and walked several paces her way, but then he stopped. When their eyes met, she'd been pulled forward as if by a string attached somewhere deep in her chest. He stopped when she came into the glow of the candlelight and he wasn't the only one. All around the room, guests paused in what they were doing to turn toward her with audible sighs of admiration. Lily froze and looked down at herself, drawn by a soft glow she hadn't expected. In her dark bedroom, the dress had sparkled. In the candlelit grand ballroom of Ezekiel's palace, it shone.

There was more sparkle than she'd seen sewn into the fabric of her skirts. Layers upon layers of soft midnight illusion held millions of tiny multifaceted gems and they all seemed positioned perfectly to catch the light. The crowd began to clap softly. Sybil deserved the applause and the quiet murmur of surprised admiration that flowed around the room.

Lily, however, was torn. The look in Michael's eyes was unfamiliar to her. He didn't join the applause. He only stared as if he'd been struck. The candlelight was equally brilliant if more subtle on his tuxedo. He gleamed darkly. He was the shadow—the shining night sky—to her galaxy.

"Take him a glass of champagne, love. I warrant his mouth has gone dry," the daemon king said. He'd come up beside her and he lifted one of her hands with his and pressed a long-stemmed crystal glass full of golden liquid against her fingers. She grasped when he let it go so it wouldn't fall. He backed away and was swallowed again by the crowd, a crowd that seemed to swirl around her and Michael at a slight distance as if the rising affinity created a force field between them that kept the blur of others away.

Her feet weren't rooted to the ground. She discovered she could take a step toward him and then another. He only stood and watched her approach. He didn't help her narrow the gap. He didn't smile. His face was unreadable. His hazel eyes leaped with candlelight, movement and then the glitter of her dress.

She held the glass out to him when she came as near as she dared.

"Happy birthday," she said to break the silence—and the tension. She hadn't realized her breath had been held until he blinked. The slow lowering and raising of his lids freed her to expand her lungs. He reached for the glass and brought it back to his lips in a sudden move that startled her as if he'd unfrozen when she spoke. He tilted his head back and drained the sparkling champagne in several long swallows. Lily watched the workings of his throat as the liquid went down. He placed the empty glass on a passing tray and scooped another in a smooth move that surprised because his attention was still fully on her. He offered the fresh glass of champagne to her.

"You're stunning tonight. I fear Sybil might have to retire. She'll never equal this. For you or anyone," Michael said.

Lily took the glass from his fingers, carefully, so as not to draw the room's attention again if they touched. She hoped he didn't notice that the golden fluid shimmered with movement as she raised the glass to her lips. She sipped its chilled sweetness, but it didn't cool her. Michael's Brimstone caused perspiration to form on her upper lip. The room was full of Loyalist daemons, but they were distant warmth compared to the man beside her. Ezekiel? Possibly. He often buffered her affinity. He might be as responsible for the bubble around them as they were themselves.

"It reminds me of the desert sky," Lily said. She'd torn her gaze away from his. It was too easy to grow dizzy from the kaleidoscope of reflections in their depths. Or the emotions she couldn't read. "Do you remember asking me to run away with you? The sky that night?"

"I remember every moment with you," Michael said. "Especially the stars…and the sunlit lilies crushed beneath us."

Lily's attention flew back up to his face. She licked her lips and tasted perspiration and champagne.

"You avoided my touch when you took the glass. But Lily, this is my birthday and I have to touch you. Say you'll dance with me and damn the consequences," Michael said.

"I'm here to dance," Lily said. "All night long."

This time, she drained the champagne. The effervescent bubbles in her nose matched the ones in her stomach. He took the glass as she lowered it and placed it on another tray. Then he took her hand. Ezekiel's buffering or not, when they touched the whole room seemed to pause again. Lily could feel the perusal of hundreds of gazes. She glanced around as she followed the tall figure of the half-daemon prince to the dance floor. Most of the faces were a blur—except for a lady in red who was, of course, Victoria D'Arcy. Her arched brow and wild crown of scarlet curls were vivid against the rest. By her side stood the daemon king. He, too, stood out against all others—tall, dark, lean and ever watchful.

Lily looked away from them both.

They were the first on the dance floor. The black marble shone stark as obsidian except for the slight tracings of white that might have been mistaken for wavering seams of natural discoloration in the stone if it weren't for their intricate spiderweb patterns.

Michael didn't wait for her to come into the circle of his arms. He pulled her onto the dance floor and then turned to meet the momentum he'd caused. She was pressed flush against his broad chest with her skirts crushed and his hands splayed on the curve of her back. It wasn't a waltz position. It was an embrace. One she didn't fight. Instead, she wrapped her arms up to cup his neck. She gloried in the heat of his skin and the silky texture of his hair against the back of her fingers. The glow of three immense chandeliers in the high cathedral ceiling of the room created a halo around his head. His face was cast into shadow. He was angelic and mysterious in that moment even without wings, but he was also solid beneath her hands and sturdy against her body. The kiss happened without thought or pause. He leaned to accept an invitation she had instinctively made with a tilted chin and open lips. In spite of the shadows and the halo of light, the press of his lips was salty and real. As was the hot, moist thrust of his tongue. Desire arced from his teasing probe to her nipples and the flesh between her legs that was still tender from the night before. Remembered pleasure heightened the current thrill of his touch. His hands kneaded low on her waist. Champagne and wood smoke blended in the sweet soft and rough textures she explored with the quest of her own tongue.

And then the music started.

Other couples joined them on the dance floor at a slight distance, but close enough to disturb their intimacy. Michael lifted his lips from hers and after a slight protest of tightened fingers on the back of his nape, Lily let him. Tonight was for dancing before it was for goodbye.

"Later," Michael murmured above her ear. She didn't contradict him. There would be no later for them if he accepted the throne before midnight. His deal with Ezekiel would be done and her only recourse to not be a part of it would be to run away. Her heartbeat quickened as if she was already in flight. She didn't need the adrenaline to tell her by freeing Michael she would be risking death.

She would be the walking dead without him anyway. If Rogues hunted her down outside the hell dimension, she would fight and then accept the consequences. It would be the least she could do for the man she...

Her eyes were closed and her cheek was pressed to Michael's chest. His loosening hold and a pause in his steps disturbed her thoughts. She raised her head and opened her eyes to see the daemon king behind Michael's shoulder. Her dance partner released her and stepped away with one final squeeze of her hand. Michael passed her to Ezekiel and only then did she know that her guardian had cut in.

"Shall we dance, Lily?" Ezekiel asked. As usual his words had myriad meanings. They'd been dancing around her affinity and his plans for his grandson all along.

"For a little while longer," Lily answered. She accepted his hand in place of Michael's. As far as she remembered, she'd never touched his hand before. It was calloused and scarred, nicked from a thousand battles. It was also perfectly formed, with long, elegant fingers and symmetrical lines. He held her hand gently, as a gentleman, not a warrior. And his smile was dark, but fatherly in the candlelight.

"I'm sorry there haven't been more celebrations such as this in your life. You obviously enjoy it," Ezekiel said.

It was true. Even with the tension of the night building to an inevitable heartache, she had enjoyed the music and the movement with Michael and she enjoyed Ezekiel's grace. The dark shadows of the palace had come alive with colorful guests, laughter, flowers and a tangible excitement she wasn't immune to even though its cause would prove tragic to her heart.

"We've been at war with Rogues. Not the best time for parties," Lily said. She'd had her flute for music, and the lessons with her mother had been happy times full of dance and song.

"If we don't dance, then what are we fighting for?" Ezekiel countered. He was slightly taller than Michael and leaner. He was full daemon and an Ancient One at that. His otherworldly features, so angular and perfect in spite of his scars, had been created in heaven itself. He had followed Lucifer when he'd fallen. He'd been one of the original seekers of autonomy in another world.

She looked up at him and examined his face. For the first time she noticed a pinched quality around his eyes as if his nearly immortal life of intrigue and fighting was beginning to take its toll. She couldn't help it. Her hands tightened on his shoulder and against his fingers.

"Michael will be a good king. You weren't wrong about that. You were only wrong in trying to use me to guarantee his acceptance of the throne," Lily said.

"He doesn't care. He would give up heaven and earth

for you," Ezekiel said. A full orchestra of daemonic musicians played the waltz that fed their movements. Lily only had to hold on to the daemon king and he did the rest—effortlessly graceful and fluid as he whirled her around the floor. Her head grew light and her breathing was rapid, but she didn't let go.

Not yet.

"I care. I would have him give up nothing. And especially not for me," Lily said.

"I have to admit, I wondered. If he would even be here tonight. If he would live up to his heritage. His real father was extraordinary and even now he is tireless in his watch," Ezekiel said.

Lily nearly stumbled over her own feet at Ezekiel's words. Had he known about her warrior angel? She had always carried it everywhere with no thought to hiding it from the daemon king. Had he known long before she did that the doll was a likeness of Michael's father and that her abilities might call whatever was left of his soul to life?

"Victoria says he still exists as a frigid shadow who watches over her and Michael," Lily said. Her words were breathless and soft from the exertion of the dance in an athletic partner's arms and from fear. What other beings did Ezekiel manipulate for his own ends?

"He was a Guardian. That unique calling didn't leave him when he fell to earth or when he became a lover and a father and a friend. Though I would say Victoria might be surprised whom he considers his charge," Ezekiel said. "Michael is the son of a Guardian. He has proven to me that his blood runs true by his care and concern for you."

"And you will reward him with a throne he doesn't want," Lily said. He was impossibly hard against her hands. Like immovable stone that lived and breathed and danced. "I won't help you force him to be king."

"I never imagined you would, Lily Santiago. Your blood also runs true. It has been the great joy of my life to see you learn and grow into your own heritage. Your affinity is the purest I've seen outside of heaven," Ezekiel said.

This time Lily did stumble, but the daemon king didn't let her fall. He saved her from the missteps her surprise had caused, and with effortless strength he placed her back on her feet.

"Perhaps you didn't know that Samuel's gift came from heaven itself. What is the affinity if not the ability to tune in to the music of the universe? Love is the language of the stars, my child. No doubt Sybil created your dress for this evening as a nod to your ability and where it came from," Ezekiel said. "Those of us who've walked those pathways don't speak of it often. Even as we make a place for ourselves apart from our creator, we miss that connection. That's why those tuned in to it call to us. We remember. We long. We ache. Even as we're determined to live independently in this dimension."

"I thought the desert sky..." Lily said softly.

"Entire galaxies in the palm of his hand...and people think I'm intimidating. But I see that my grandson is eager to reclaim his place in your arms." Ezekiel led her off the floor with deft turns and several smooth strides.

"I never knew. I thought my father's affinity was a random freak of nature, an arrangement of chromosomes or an accident of birth," Lily said.

Several servants had converged on them with trays when they'd seen their king leave the dance floor. Ezekiel plucked two glasses with a regal nod of approval and handed one to her. She sipped the cool dark liquid and an explosion of flavors from the Turov pinot noir caused her to close her eyes in pleasure.

"This wine is an accident of birth. It's also the careful

result of love and obsession. Random and planned. Such is life. Such is ruling a kingdom…or the universe," Ezekiel said. "You came into my life like a song. Love on two gangly legs. I had been planning for your arrival my whole existence without knowing when, who or how. Have a good night, Lily. Don't worry too much about daemon deals and sacrifice. Blood will out."

Ezekiel moved away and Lily watched him as the crowd parted like the Red Sea for Moses. Though she doubted Moses had ever worn a shimmering tuxedo that rode a man's muscles like designer armor.

Her resolve hadn't wavered. No matter the daemon king's talk of heaven and hell or her as a young girl. He'd sounded almost…affectionate…but she knew better than that. He had been a distant authority figure at best. A frightening unknown creature at worst. She had loved him and still did in spite of his manipulations. But he had never loved her. His treatment of her mother had been her greatest warning that he preferred D'Arcys. Kindness and care wasn't love. He had held them at a distance because there was no room for them in his scarred heart. Perhaps he grew sentimental because he thought she would marry Michael and become the closest thing to a D'Arcy she would ever be.

The thought made her ache. Worse to be so close and yet so far from her guardian's love.

Fortunately, she saw what Ezekiel had seen and the sight completely distracted her from old pain. New pain sliced through her, hollowing out her gut and causing her hands to clench.

Michael stood near the wall of the ballroom. He propped one foot behind him and balanced his guitar on his knee. She wasn't surprised to see his guitar. It was as much a part of him as his legs or his hands. A different sight froze her in place and chilled the blood in her veins. Behind him a larger frieze than in any other room besides the throne room roiled with unnatural movement. The carved figures came and went from the surface of the marble as if it was as malleable as mud. Their mouths opened and closed as they silently shrieked. And a giant shadow had unfurled its wings on either side of Michael's broad shoulders.

The ghostlike entity that Victoria claimed was Michael's father had just cast its vote for the new daemon king. What stabbed at her heart was that she didn't disagree. He would make a fine king. She would like nothing better than to share the only home she'd ever known with him. Only her affinity stood in her way. She couldn't be the chains—no matter how seductive—that bound him to the throne. He could never truly love her if he wasn't free to travel and sing and walk in the light. The highlights in his hair would dim. His voice would grow rusty. His heart would be shuttered to her forever.

He didn't know it now. Maybe he would even welcome a weighted choice rather than a free one. If he chose for her, his own conscience could be clean. But she couldn't let him choose the darkest of fates because of her. She'd grown up with the souls on the walls. She was used to the coming and going, the torment and the occasional loss when a soul winked out either to Oblivion or... She watched as Michael remembered that it wasn't a bare wall behind him. She watched him drop his foot down and move away.

She saw the walls as a necessary pause, more of a purgatory than damnation. She could tell that Michael didn't feel the same way. Could she blame him? His real father had been trapped in walls like these at l'Opéra Severne before it burned. Victoria and Michael had almost died.

He saw that her dance with Ezekiel had ended and he placed his guitar against the wall. His father's shadow had diminished to nothing, hidden in the shadows of the dancers that shifted across the wall. No one else had seen anything unusual in the shifting shadows, but, then again, most avoided looking directly at the walls. A new waltz had begun.

Lily drank her fill of Michael as he moved toward her. As with the daemon king, the crowd of guests parted almost in unison to let him pass. He didn't notice. He was far too focused on her face. She could feel the flush on her cheeks. As he came closer and closer, his Brimstone heat caused her temperature to rise. Maybe. Or maybe she could have reacted to his sensual grace if he had been wholly human without a drop of daemon blood at all.

Finally, he stood near her. Nearer than necessary, but not near enough. She wanted to be alone with him. She wanted their midnight-blue garments to be piled together on the floor, a sparkling heap intertwined. Suddenly, she was exhausted from merely planning to run away. She didn't want to go. She wanted to succumb to his kisses and experience the slide of their naked skin together again.

"You look as if you're done with dancing," Michael said. He touched her cheek and her whole world stilled. Dancers spun around them. Her heartbeat thumped slowly in her ears.

"I need to be in your arms," she confessed. His fingers slid down to tease along the line of her jaw and she tilted her chin to meet his gaze. His eyes had narrowed. He knew something was amiss.

"Ezekiel upset you," he guessed. He was wrong. The turning of time upset her. They were closer to midnight on Michael's twenty-first birthday, which meant they were closer to the decision he would make that would drive her away. And she was upset that she was too close to all she'd ever dreamed of before it would get ripped away.

"I'm used to your grandfather. He doesn't bother me," Lily said. But she stepped against Michael's muscular chest even though he hadn't opened his arms. If he was surprised, he recovered quickly. His hand dropped from her face to her waist and his other hand reached for hers on his chest.

"You're used to Ezekiel and to hell and to this palace," Michael said against her forehead. His lips were hot. Her skin seemed hotter. He said it like he didn't understand how she could be even with years and years of practice.

"It is my home. He's the only father I've ever known," Lily said.

Michael pulled her away from the dance floor. The waltz was a slower tempo than the one they'd danced before. The sound of the music filtered out through several sets of French doors that led onto a stone terrace. He pulled her through one doorway as if he followed the delicate vibrations of music on the night air that teased into the stuffy ballroom, beckoning partygoers outside.

The terrace was lit by colorful silk lanterns. They had been crafted with intricate designs cut into the fabric. Light spilled through myriad shades and shapes, creating kaleidoscopes on the stone as the breeze stirred them to gentle movement. The dark purple sky above them didn't provide much light. But the soft glow paired with the lantern light was enough to urge Michael into the more private shadows created by the skeletal trees that formed a ring around the terrace. They moved close together and yet she was still jealous of the hairsbreadth of air that came between them.

"You're home to me," Michael murmured into her hair.

She wanted to sink into the warmth offered by the sentiment. It was every bit as warm as his embrace. But she couldn't indulge in the fantasy his murmur seemed to offer.

"You never wanted to come here. You made a deal with

Ezekiel to deliver the wings. You intended to buy your freedom with them. I can't let you be influenced by my affinity. It isn't fair," Lily said. "I never meant to manipulate you the way the daemon king has manipulated his loved ones for centuries."

Michael stopped. He drew back to look down at her face. She was at a disadvantage. The lantern light fell on her face, but it was behind Michael's head. His face was in shadow. She could hide nothing from him while she stood in what might as well be a spotlight. She willed away the flush that heated her cheeks and the emotion that must swim in her eyes. There was a soft halo around the golden tips of his hair, but his features were hidden. At best, there were deeper shadows that outlined his angular cheeks and his strong jaw. She couldn't see his lips—whether they were hard or soft. She couldn't see his eyes—whether they were cool or full of flames.

"You're right. I never wanted to come here, but I also never gave this dimension a chance. I defined it by what my preconceived notions had been. I was repelled by the carvings on the walls and by Ezekiel's expectations. It isn't your affinity that has changed that. I'm not being manipulated or influenced," Michael said.

His hands had been holding her for the waltz, but he moved them now to cup her face. Lily shivered beneath his gentle touch and the pleasant roughness of his calluses against the sensitive skin of her cheeks and neck. He brushed his thumbs along the sides of her mouth and she moistened her lips with her tongue. Then he held her more firmly, as if she was capable of slipping away. He leaned toward her and she was rooted to the spot— waiting, longing, craving.

"You've opened my eyes, but it isn't because I'm unable to control my Brimstone. If you told me to let you go, right now, I would. I would stop if you didn't want my kiss as much as I wanted to taste you. Our connection is compelling, but I'm strong, Lily. I've had to be my whole life to handle my daemon blood," Michael said.

He paused as if he waited for her to protest or plea. She held her breath, but she slid her hands up his lapels to the hot skin of his neck, then she buried her fingers in his hair. It was the permission he'd needed to softly press his lips to hers.

She gasped in reaction to the sudden thrill of contact, and he took advantage of her open lips to deepen the kiss, slowing and thoroughly teasing and tasting the silken depths of her mouth with his tongue. She pressed closer against him and it was her movements that became hungrier. He tasted of wine and wood smoke, flavors that would forever cause instant arousal because they reminded her of him.

Her heartbeat quickened, but her blood seemed to warm and thicken. It flowed languidly through her veins to spread heat and tingling awareness throughout her body. Her legs grew weak, but his body was hard and fully capable of supporting her weight as she sagged against him.

He was strong. Sybil had said he was the strongest man she'd ever known and Sybil had known the daemon king for an eternity. She'd known Severne and Turov. She'd known Lucifer and Michael's father.

Lily gave herself to the kiss, completely succumbing to the pleasure of swooning in Michael's arms because she felt the glimmer of hope stir in her breast for the first time.

Maybe he sensed her capitulation. He gentled his mouth. He lowered his hands to her back. He pulled his lips from hers and buried his face in her neck, where he nuzzled the delicate skin beneath her ear while she tried to steady her breathing and her feet on the ground.

"You have to give me the chance to prove that I'm clear-headed in this decision even as I'm far from clearheaded over you," Michael said.

# *Chapter 24*

The atmosphere had changed. He wasn't the only one who noticed. More and more entities around him—daemon and damned—began to press out from the walls that held their souls in limbo. He was well ahead of their frenzied efforts. All but one of his legs were free. He ignored the state of his new body. It was more marble than man, with gruesome striations of stone rendering his form dark and mottled in the dimly lit hallway. In the distance he could hear music and laughter. But the Rogues who broke free from their prison filled the shadows with guttural moans as if they were the undead returning from their graves.

Peter grasped at his lifelong obsession because his mind was vague.

Samuel's daughter. Samuel's daughter. Samuel's daughter.

It was her amplified affinity that called them from the walls. Hers and the combined call of others with the same gift, albeit in lesser degrees. The affinity and the weakening hold of a daemon king preparing to step aside for his successor.

His mind might be sluggish and striated with stone like the rest of him, but he knew one thing…the throne must remain vacant for the Rogues and their human slaves to rise. His fellows must have known the same because they struggled to free themselves from the friezes. He sank down to the floor on his knees. He needed to summon the strength to make his way toward the throne room and he needed to wait for an army of Rogues to join him. It was a diminished army. A gruesome army disfigured and deformed. But he was one of them now. The Order was no longer his driving force. To tear down, to destroy, to corrupt—these desires consumed him.

As midnight approached, the party became a crush of revelry. Champagne and stronger spirits had flowed heavily throughout the night and there were no partygoers more passionate than a hall full of daemons preparing to welcome their new king. Lily was swept up in an atmosphere thick with a joy that edged on desperation.

*Love us. Lead us. Save us.*

Near-immortality made the fallen more desperate than most for strong, steady leadership. They had survived the loss of heaven, the persecution of human hunters and the battle for hell and now wanted more than anything to live in peace. Lucifer had promised his followers autonomy, but he hadn't promised them it would be easy.

Lily danced with Michael off and on throughout the night. But she also danced with his stepfather, Adam Turov, whom she found almost as hard and scarred as the daemon king. He was a genuine hero, a man who had sold his soul to escape from the Order of Samuel and then spent his long, long life saving others from the enclave that had kidnapped him and nearly killed him as a child. She found him to be fascinating, intimidating and a fit match for one of the women who had loomed larger than life over her own childhood.

And then there had been John Severne. He still burned in spite of reclaiming the soul his grandfather had sold to the Rogue Council when he was a mere boy. Ezekiel had gifted him with a hint of remaining Brimstone for helping Katherine D'Arcy save her sister from Rogues and the Order of Samuel. The slight burn suited his brooding Parisian good looks and Baton Rouge charm. He deserved the title of Master of l'Opéra Severne. But there was a mysterious edge to his artfulness that flustered her when they danced. Michael's aunt Kat was a brave woman to have explored those mysteries. Nevertheless, he was a Southern gentleman who spun her around the dance floor with a masculine grace just shy of Ezekiel's own.

So she faced the D'Arcys and she survived.

Even though their eyes followed her all night long. She feared that Victoria's and Kat's affinity would certainly lead them to understand that she wasn't celebrating with the rest of the crowd. She feared that Adam Turov's and John Severne's prolonged lives would lead them to read her secrets in every glance and sigh.

And with every turn in Michael's arms she held a little tighter and lingered a little longer after the music died. She didn't trust the flicker of hope Michael's strength caused in her heart. Her affinity was an impossible obstacle between them even as it irresistibly drew them together. How could she ever be certain that he was functioning under his own free will?

A late Viennese waltz had her gasping for air in a dizzy whirl around the room. She focused on Michael's eyes. They glowed with flames outlined in darker green, all hazel burned away. She held his shoulder and his hand with ferocious grips, but he didn't protest. He was more than strong enough to take it. He took the weight of her whole body, propelling her over the marble floor effortlessly, their gazes locked. The rest of the dancers were blurs at the corners of her eyes.

She was in flight. With Michael, she always flew even when her feet were on the ground.

But midnight loomed and the daemon king was well aware of the passage of time. He was suddenly there, tall and immovable in their path. They stutter-stepped to a halt. Michael caught her to his broad chest so she wouldn't trip and fall.

"The decision is yours, but it's time for it to be made. Our deal has weakened my hold on the throne. As midnight nears my hold grows weaker and weaker. The walls are restless," Ezekiel said.

The music had ended as abruptly as their dance. All the other couples on the floor and around the great ballroom faced Michael D'Arcy Turov. They watched and waited. Silence had claimed the whole company. And in that stillness a new sound rose, the rustling and moaning of the walls. Beneath the candle chandeliers, the walls that shivered with the shadows of thousands of tiny flames now also moved with hundreds of figures straining their arms and hands and faces out and away from the wall. The sight illustrated what must have happened in other parts of the palace. It explained the distant sound of tramping feet.

"There isn't much time. Lucifer's wings await a new... master," Ezekiel said.

Michael straightened. He nodded to his grandfather. Lily could feel him slipping away even as he still held her.

"No. There has to be another way," she protested.

"My whole life has led to this moment. My legacy is my own to face," Michael said. He held her hands against his chest. She could feel the steady beat of his Brimstone-fueled heart. The crowd was already breaking apart and heading toward the throne room. Michael moved with them. She had to let him go. Although they left the room together at first, the press of people interfered and too soon their hands loosened. Then she lost her hold on his fingers.

Ezekiel led the way. She and Michael followed. They were no longer touching, but still close. The rest of the crowd surrounded them in a press of finery and tipsy enthusiasm. But in spite of the soft noise the guests made, Lily could hear the strange moaning and shuffling coming closer behind the crowd of Loyalists. And, even worse, the walls were alive with the grasping hands of the damned as they tried to break free. The heat of all the Brimstone around her that had risen from fear and fury scorched her skin.

Then there was a scream. One of the guests had made the mistake of looking behind them in the long, dark corridor that led to the throne room. Bad enough that the walls were lined with grasping and grabbing arms and hands, but the Rogues and their human slaves who had managed to fully manifest from the walls were a gruesome sight as they lurched and crawled and clawed their way toward the Loyalist daemons. Lily cried out when she saw them. At her sound of distress, Michael stopped and pushed through the mass of panicking subjects to her side to grasp her hand again.

His assumption of the throne was no longer a leisurely process with the pomp and circumstance of a ritualized occasion. It was now a desperate bid to save their people from harm.

Lily could see the D'Arcys and their mates herding the Loyalists away from the Rogue threat. She saw Victoria reach to stop Adam Turov from using the double small swords he'd drawn from hidden scabbards beneath his tuxedo jacket on his back. The merciful gesture caused tears to prick her eyes. The half-stone, half-flesh creatures that had escaped the walls were more monsters than men, but this manifestation shouldn't be their last act before Oblivion no matter how much evil had fueled it.

Ezekiel reached the massive double doors to the throne room first and he flung them open as if they were made of air. His people poured in after him and dispersed along the edges of the room, keeping a safe distance from the walls. The carvings were alive with movement here, but they hadn't been able to break free. Perhaps the residual power in the great bronzed wings that waited on the throne had held them in the walls.

Instinctively, the crowd had left a wide path for its future king from the open doorway to the throne. The daemon king had hurried forward and he waited for Michael. He stood behind the wings, ready to place them on his grandson's shoulders.

There was no time for goodbye. There was no time to reveal the entirety of Ezekiel's scheme to Michael before he claimed the throne. The lurching Rogues had already closed the gap. They were feet away from grabbing the slower Loyalists who hadn't yet made it through the double doors.

"Go. I know what to do," Lily said.

Michael touched her face. It was a stolen moment they didn't have. But only that. No more. His hand slipped away and he turned to hurry toward the wings he'd never wanted to wear.

Lily reached into her pocket. Adam Turov was ready with his swords and Grim had suddenly materialized beside his former master, John Severne. They had fought against daemons, side by side, for a hundred years before Severne had given Grim to Michael because he was a tiny baby who needed protection from the Order of Samuel.

Every item of clothing she owned had been made with pockets to accommodate her flute and her warrior angel at her request. Her ball gown for tonight was no exception. She pulled out her flute and brought it to her lips. She turned away from the sight of Michael stepping up on the dais that held the throne.

He would be lost to her.

But their relationship had been doomed from the start.

Lily began to play. She courted death, but she forced fear from her thoughts. She played her mother's Hopi lullaby. She played and she released the hold on all the affinity she held in her heart. The Rogues shambled to a stop after the first few notes. Their hands went to their ears. They fell to their knees. Victoria and Kat prevented their husbands from attacking the pitiful creatures that began to crawl toward the pure love that Lily channeled.

There was risk that they would tear her apart when they reached her. They still moaned and groaned in protest and clawed at the marble beneath them. They gibbered and cried and howled with occasional tortured screams.

But Lily played.

And Michael accepted Lucifer's wings. The instant the wings were placed on his shoulders, Lily could feel their power. She continued to play the song that had brought the Rogues to their knees, but when Michael's heat outshone all other daemons present, she turned. He stood before the throne with Lucifer's wings on his shoulders. The empty suit of armor beside the throne was dwarfed by his presence. Every Loyalist including Ezekiel had dropped to one knee. Lily's legs went numb and she fell to her knees as well.

But she played.

Behind Michael a great shadow had grown on the wall. It was as large as a dragon, but shaped like a man. Its wings spread wide while she watched and suddenly it wasn't only her song influencing the Rogues. A chill had spread over the whole crowd, but from that chill the power of Michael's Brimstone rose up. It was magnified by Lucifer's wings. It joined with the aura of her affinity and called the Rogues toward the shadow on the wall.

They all climbed to their feet and moved forward as a

herd. She continued to play, but though they came closer to her, too close, so close that she could smell the corruption of tainted Brimstone, their herd parted around her body. Only one paused. She recognized him from the attack at the Grand Canyon. He was the most gruesomely malformed of them all. More stone than man. The black striations of marble pitted and striped his flesh in uneven jagged slashes.

"D-daughter of S-Samuel. M-mine," he croaked. With horror, she recognized the monk from the bridge. Like Reynard, he must have sold his soul to the Rogues. He'd lost his life sometime since she'd seen him last and he'd wound up in the walls of the palace just like his Rogue allies. His hands reached for her, but suddenly Grim was there. He stood between her and the creature. He growled a warning even a monster could understand. And the thing shuffled back from the fearsome hellhound. It moved around Lily as she forced herself to continue to play. Her affinity and Michael's worked together as the Loyalists watched on bended knee.

Only when the first Rogue walked straight into the shadow on the wall did Lily understand that her warrior angel was helping them return the creatures back to their prison in the frieze. They seemed almost relieved, with each one hurrying faster to join its brethren back in an all-marble state.

"Our affinity is a blessing and a curse. We disturbed them. We called them forth," Katherine D'Arcy said. She had come to stand beside Lily where she knelt. Lily allowed her flute to fall from her lips only after the last Rogue reentered the wall. She was completely drained.

Victoria joined her sister and together they helped Lily up from the floor. She welcomed the support. Her affinity had waxed so strong and then waned. The sight of Michael coming toward her crowned as the new daemon king was almost too much for her to bear alone.

She had been part of Ezekiel's plan all along. Michael had been lured to hell in spite of her better intentions. Her only recourse was to give him a choice now that his deal with Ezekiel was done. If she left the palace, he would be free to step aside. His assurances weren't enough. She had to be sure that he wouldn't be held here against his will by her affinity.

"This is wrong. I don't know how I could have prevented it, but I feel its wrongness to my bones," Victoria said. Her throaty voice shook and her grip on Lily's arm trembled.

"I feel it, too. It's as if the affinity is out of tune," Kat said quietly.

Was her despair magnified by this wrongness in the affinity they spoke of? Lily wasn't sure. The music that normally filled her was overcome by a breaking heart. She pulled away from the other two women and stood as tall as she could manage to meet the new daemon king. Michael was burning bright. His Brimstone blood fully embraced for the first time.

But she searched his eyes and found the uncertainty in the affinity that they all felt. He was his mother's son, too.

"Ezekiel used me to entice you to the throne. It was his plan all along. He knew that you wouldn't be able to deliver the wings and walk away. He counted on my affinity to bind you," Lily said. "I'm sorry. I tried to warn you."

"I knew what I was getting into as soon as I discovered you were my grandfather's ward. He plays us all as chess pieces in an elaborate but deadly serious game," Michael said. "All of us. How can I hold it against you?"

In spite of the crowd, he lifted his hand to touch her face. The power of the wings he wore zinged into her skin and penetrated all the way to her heart. But its warmth didn't heal. It only highlighted her pain.

"I'm here for you, Lily. Affinity or not. I'm here for you," Michael said. "You can't live at peace outside of the hell dimension, so I'll make my home here with you."

It was a confession that cut her to the core because it was a truth she'd suspected all along. He had accepted the throne because of her. It didn't matter if the affinity had influenced him or if he was capable of feeling pity for her without the affinity's call.

"I won't keep you here," Lily said.

Somehow she managed to turn away from his soft touch. In front of an audience of thousands of eyes including the eyes in the walls, Lily walked away.

# *Chapter 25*

The second the walls consumed the horde; Michael felt Lucifer's wings release him. They still sat on his shoulders, but they were no longer connected to him as they had been in the first few moments when he'd used them to help Lily. The rejection was physically jarring. It slammed against him and took his breath, but he ignored the pain. He would overcome it. He would learn to wear the wings. For Lily.

The jubilant crowd tried to close in around their new king, but Michael pressed through the hundreds of daemons to follow Lily. The power in Lucifer's wings helped to part the sea of figures all around him without any direction from him at all. She had looked devastated. Her skin had been cool to his touch for the first time. And she wasn't steady on her feet. She'd used too much of her affinity to direct the horde back into the walls. Even with his help, she had used so much power that she'd stood in a glorious halo of energy. Her shining black hair had swept around her face blown by a wind he couldn't see. And Lily had played to save them all.

She'd played to save him from the throne. She thought she'd failed. He had to convince her that he was happy to be the new daemon king as long as she was by his side.

The wings didn't sit well on his shoulders. And he felt like something was wrong. But one thing drove him down the dark hallway… Lily was oh so right.

The walls were strangely still and silent around her as she dizzily made her way back to her rooms. It was only her light head that made them waver in and out of focus. She wasn't prepared to faint in front of an audience. Fortunately, she made it away from the throne room and the crowd before she found herself on her knees once more. Her legs simply collapsed beneath her. She couldn't go on. It was physical weakness caused by her effort to control the Rogue horde, but it filled her with shame because it matched her emotional state too well.

She was defeated—in and out.

Normally, she would hide her pain and fear, but her body wouldn't cooperate. She wilted to the floor with only her tightly clenched fists against the black marble indicating her desire to rise. The rest of her refused to follow her iron will's command. Except her tear ducts. They listened. Her eyes burned, but she refused to allow one salty drop to fall. She swallowed, repeatedly, and the unshed moisture settled in a hot knot in the middle of her chest.

She couldn't even protest when strong arms lifted her up from the floor and crushed her tightly against a familiar chest.

"You controlled those Rogues with every ounce of affinity you possess. You didn't even falter. I've never been so terrified. They swarmed around you like a pack of ravenous zombies. And you didn't blink," Michael said. She was able to lift her hands and hold his broad shoulders, but her grip was weak. He kept her from falling with his steely arms. The skirt of her dress trailed down to create a starry train behind them. His voice was a deep masculine vibrato against her, reassuring even as it pained her to know there was no permanent reassurance to be found.

Lucifer's wings swept artfully down his back, familiar and strange. She'd seen them. She'd touched them. She'd allowed their power to flow through her. Now they should be a part of Michael, seamlessly joined to the power he possessed because of his Brimstone blood and the affinity he'd inherited from his mother.

Yet her affinity revealed that the wings didn't sit well on Michael's shoulders. It was as if someone had tried to place two magnets together on opposite poles. He wore them, but they hadn't become a part of him...yet.

In time, surely, they would. He was the daemon king. He had accepted the throne.

Even in her weakened state, Lily made the effort not the touch the wings. It was difficult. If Michael and the wings somehow repelled each other, Lily found her own affinity drawn to the blackened bronze with a force she could hardly withstand. She trembled against it and Michael held her closer.

The heat of his skin comforted and tormented at the same time.

"You need to get away from the walls and the crowd. Your affinity has been bombarded by Brimstone all night long. I'm sorry if I'm hurting you. I'll leave you alone as soon as I get you to a safe place," Michael said.

"It's the wings. They're tormenting me with a call I don't understand," Lily murmured. Her head whirled. She couldn't even note which direction they traveled or how long they walked. It wasn't until Michael placed her carefully on a soft bed she didn't recognize that she realized he must have used Grim to help them leave the palace.

"This is Nightingale Vineyards. Probably the safest place you could be besides the palace. My stepfather has an army of daemon hunters who guard this place out of gratitude and loyalty. You can rest and recover here," Michael said. "I'll arrange for some food and drink."

He left the room and Lily lay in the blissful silence. Only her curiosity caused her to fight sleep. The slightest hint of freshly struck matchsticks filled the air along with scents of polished wood and leather. She blinked against her exhaustion and pushed herself up on her elbows so she could see where Michael had brought her.

It was a luxurious bedroom with heavy masculine furnishings and richly colored textiles on pillows, curtains and bed linens. But it was also worn in the way that only a room that belonged to someone could be. There was a leather jacket thrown over an armchair by the fireplace. The bedside table was cluttered with magazines, books and *guitar picks*.

He'd brought her home to protect her.

This was his bedroom. The scent of matchsticks was his scent. One she'd grown used to in the time that she'd known him. It was appealing and sultry and uniquely Michael. It rose on his skin from his Brimstone blood. Because even when he'd denied his heritage and tamped it down, the burn was a part of him.

Michael came back in the room with a tray full of food. She glimpsed fruit, thin slices of beef and cheese, and a bottle of wine. He swept the bedside table's detritus to the side and placed the food within her reach.

"I managed to raid the kitchen without disturbing anyone. Which is a feat in this house, believe me. Especially when you're decked out with a pair of bronzed wings," Michael said.

"You should be in the palace. Not pilfering snacks for me," Lily said. She'd already reached for several bites. Michael didn't look any less regal for his consideration. She was certain she'd been right about this being his bedroom. Especially because she'd noticed an empty guitar stand in the corner. But he seemed too big for it now. A tall, magnificent winged creature that cast a beautiful angelic shadow on the wall.

He reached for the wine and released the cork with

practiced moves he must have perfected from years of observation and practice. He filled two glasses with the dark pinot noir.

"Champagne is nice, but this is more fitting. Aged twenty-one years. Will you share a glass with me before I go?" Michael said.

Lily nodded, but froze when Michael responded by shrugging out of Lucifer's wings. He set them aside and flexed his shoulders before he reached to hand a glass to her. Lily closed her eyes against the longing that swept over her senses. The pull of the wings was nearly as strong as the pull of Michael's Brimstone once the wings weren't in the way.

"Should I leave now?" Michael asked. She must have looked as if she was ready to swoon. But it was pleasure, not weakness, that threatened to claim her.

"No. Stay," Lily said with her eyes still closed. She felt him move closer. She breathed deeply of his matchstick scent. It was both sharp and warm in her nose. Slowly, she lifted her lids to find him standing over her with the glasses in his hands. She reached up and he gave her one of the glasses as he sipped from the other. Maybe his mouth had gone as dry as hers. She should urge him to go. This was nothing but prolonging the torture of goodbye. "Stay," she repeated.

"Until they drag me away," Michael promised. He drained his glass and waited for her to sip from hers. In his bedroom, the wine tasted different. The bouquet influenced by the scents of Michael himself. It was exquisite; deepening the swoon of desire she'd experienced moments before.

Finely attuned to her mood, he reached to take the glass that almost slipped from her fingers. He placed it on the table while she sank back to lie on her side, curled toward where he stood. Her dress was a riotous crumple of sparkling organza against the dark chocolate of his bedspread, but she was too weak to fight with the voluminous skirts to straighten or remove them. She needn't have worried. Michael reached for her dress and carefully smoothed the airy layers. Lily closed her eyes again to claim the tickling anticipation of his silky manipulations of fabric—brushing, brushing, brushing—until he found the fastenings he sought.

Her eyes flew open then to watch his face as he slowly began to undo the endless line of buttons down her spine.

"This is cruel engineering on Sybil's part," Michael said. He met Lily's gaze and held it as button after button released to his deft fingers. Her breath came no easier when her bodice loosened. The look in his eyes kept her lungs constricted with anticipation. This was stolen time. She didn't tell him the dress could be pulled over her head without loosening a single button. Instead, she appreciated the lingering necessary to undo each and every diamanté sphere.

"Your hands are shaking," Lily said. "And your fingers are like fire."

He paused. Flames flickered in his eyes as well.

"I burn," Michael said. "I've tried to deny it, but I've never been able to deny it with you."

She'd cleaned the plate he'd brought her before he'd poured the wine. Her energy was returning. Lily was able to reach up and touch his flushed face with fingers that felt cool against his skin.

"You don't have to deny your Brimstone blood for me. Never," Lily said.

He had come to the last button where the fitted bodice ended and the skirt began. Only at that point did the unfastening reveal skin in between where her bra ended and her panties began. His hot, calloused fingers found her bare lower back and he caressed lightly there and over the swell of her bottom, which must have peeked from the slipping organza dress as it opened.

The call of the wings was still there at the edges of her senses. But it only heightened her affinity. Now that she'd fueled her body, her hunger for other things rose. For Michael. For his burn. For their connection and the pleasure it magnified between them. She would have to deny herself that pleasure for the rest of her life. For now she begged for it with the arch of her back and his name on her lips.

"This dress is incredible, but nothing compared to the woman wearing it," Michael said.

He moved to gently take the bodice of the gown and pull it down her body. She rolled to her back to accommodate the dress's slide until she was left in nothing but her underclothes. The flames in Michael's eyes had leaped higher. Only the dark green rims of his irises showed. She flushed beneath his fiery gaze. But when he swooped down with hot lips to claim uncovered skin—the swell of her breasts above her bra, her lower stomach above her panties, the tops of her thighs above the garters that held her hose—she cried out.

He joined her on the bed, kneeling over her prone body, to better linger over his kisses.

Rivers of heat flowed from everywhere he pressed his mouth to form an expectant pool in her stomach. His kisses against exposed places became tastes. His moist tongue teased from the top of her hose up to her inner thigh and the pool became a hot flood between her legs.

She reached for his hair, curling her fingers into its silky waves. She held on because she was flying again. She hadn't eaten enough. Her head was still light. Michael's hot breath teased over her mound. The thin silk she wore was no barrier at all. She moaned and he rewarded her reaction with a long, teasing kiss, nipping and nudging until her hips bucked beneath his mouth.

He reached to free her breasts and they spilled over the tops of the bra he pulled down. He captured both globes in his hot hands, moaning when he felt the tight buds of her distended nipples against his palms.

Lily flew. Her entire body tensed and then found release against the heat of his mouth. In that intense moment, the aura of her affinity reached out to the wings. It was no longer under her control. They were across the room. She didn't touch them. But somehow she tapped into their residual power as if they had been placed on her back. The amplification of Brimstone and affinity swept over their bodies and Michael reared back to rip off his shirt and tuxedo jacket. Buttons flew. He had no patience left.

She helped with his belt, but he was too impatient for her fumbling to wait for buttons and zippers to come down. He ripped his trousers loose and down as well. She heard the fabric tear.

He was naked over her. His half-daemon body was as carved and exotic as she remembered. If she could have been with him for a lifetime, she would have been surprised each and every time she saw him. Angular, but muscled. Perfect, but scarred. Lily was suddenly strengthened by the connection her affinity had made with Lucifer's wings. She rose up. She pushed Michael down. He allowed it. Fisting his hands into her hair, which had been loosened as she came against his pillows.

But he didn't try to control her moves. He allowed her to go where she would. And she did as he had done. Pressing kisses against his exposed skin. Only she sought out his scars. When he realized what parts of him she intended to worship, he gasped her name in protest, but she ignored his tightened fingers and the tension in the skin beneath her lips.

"You are incredible because of the trials you've endured," Lily whispered against his scars.

From his arms to his chest and down to his thighs, she trailed lingering kisses punctuated with flicks of her hot tongue.

His Brimstone blood heated beneath her lips. The scars of his former burns began to glow with a soft red light. Lily followed the light. He wasn't pained. She could tell from his gasps and groans that he was pleasured by the burn. He was no longer afraid of his daemon blood. They controlled it together. It was theirs to enjoy. To bank and build. To stoke and release.

And then she held his perfect erection with both of her hands to reward the bravery he'd shown as he'd allowed her to kiss his scars. She bathed the sweet, salty head of him with her tongue before engulfing him with the sheath of her hot mouth. He was too well-endowed for her to take all of him comfortably, but she persisted. It was her turn to be brave. He rewarded her with shudders and jerks and her name said worshipfully time and time again.

She found she didn't mind the stretch or having to hold her breath, but she did ache to replace the suction of her rhythmic mouth with the hungry heart of her. She needed to fill herself with him. So when he reached insistent hands to pull her up she gloried in the strength of his arms. He pulled her panties off and tossed them away as she moved. She was too intent on where she wanted to be to worry about the ruined silk. She mounted him with his help to position her in place. His cupped her bottom and spread her and impaled her on his swollen shaft.

Lily flew again, but she moved to take him even as she did. The power of the wings flowed over them. The aura of affinity glimmered around their joined bodies, reflecting and enhancing the glow of flames in Michael's hooded eyes. He arched to claim every inch of her, fighting against the constriction of her muscle spasms until he tensed and shuddered with his own release.

She kissed him them. Gently devouring the gasps of her name that continued in repetition like prayers. She would remember his wine-flavored sighs and his perfectly sculpted lips. She memorized them then. Not the hard wooden ones she'd always known, but the real ones she loved.

When Grim arrived, Lily woke Michael with a hand against his cheek. He opened his lids and his hazel eyes focused, but he didn't smile. The time they'd stolen away from the palace was over. Somehow, Lily knew she had to brace herself, but she wasn't prepared for the vacuum she experienced when Lucifer's wings were back on Michael's shoulders. She was hollowed out inside and her affinity barely hummed somewhere so deep she didn't feel she could reach it. She dressed to fill the silence. The ball gown covered her nakedness, but it was no longer breathtaking. It was a crushed, lopsided version of its former self.

Michael placed the leather jacket she'd seen on an armchair over her shoulders and Lily accepted the gesture. Sometimes it was cold on the pathways Grim took between worlds. She hugged the leather around her as Michael dressed from his drawers. He pulled on jeans and a T-shirt with the faded logo of a classic band followed by a worn jean jacket. Only when he was dressed did he reach for the wings as if they were an afterthought he'd rather forget.

Nonetheless they were impressive on his shoulders. Again she noticed the angelic shadow he cast on the wall.

He was striking with the wings on his back even though he was more human than the cold shadow of her warrior angel.

But she could feel the repel between him and the blackened bronze all the way across the room.

He had closed his eyes and clenched his jaw as soon as the wings settled on his shoulders. Lily didn't go to him. The magnetism between her and the wings was still there. For some reason, they called to her and resisted Michael.

"Are you ready?" Michael asked.

Grim waited, but his fur was already shifting to hazy smoke.

"Yes. It's time," Lily said.

They followed the hellhound out into the hallway, but he disappeared after several steps and they did as well. There was only the prickle of changed atmosphere on exposed skin to signify their passing from one place to another. In moments, they were back in Lily's rooms in the hell dimension. The natural silence of Nightingale Vineyards was replaced by a pregnant one interrupted by occasional whispers and distant sibilant sighs.

"Grim will stay with you while I meet with Ezekiel," Michael said. "There's more to being than daemon king's heir than wings and a throne."

"You aren't the daemon king's heir anymore. You are the daemon king," Lily said.

Michael's jaw was still hard. She could see that the wings pained him. But when she stepped toward him in sympathy, he backed away as if his pain increased.

"Send Grim to me if you need anything," Michael said before he turned to respond to Ezekiel's summons. Grim walked out with him. No doubt the hellhound would take up his usual sentry duty in the hall.

A servant brought a tray to Lily's rooms shortly after

Michael was called away. He knew she needed to replenish. There were desert lilies in a vase on the corner of the tray. She touched their petals with hesitant fingers. The night in the garden came back to her senses full force—every touch, every taste and every thrust. She'd already packed her backpack. It waited beside the door. But it was practical to sit and eat the thin slices of cheese and the fresh buttery roll. She wasn't stalling. She would have to run far and fast, and she needed all the strength she could muster. She avoided the glass of wine that accompanied the food. The deep dark color and the earthy black cherry bouquet identified the liquid as Firebird pinot noir. It would forever remind her of Michael's kisses. There was no reason to court that torture. Not yet.

She changed out of her ball gown, sadly recalling her desire to wear it earlier in the evening. Worn jeans, a black T-shirt and black hiking boots replaced organza and sparkling heels. She pulled on Michael's leather jacket even though it would still be summer in the desert. There was a chill deep in her bones that no amount of layering would warm away. The more distance she put between her and Michael the colder she would become.

For as long as she survived.

She wasn't going to give up without a fight. She'd chosen more kachinas from her mother's collection and she'd packed them along with her flute. She felt the absence of her warrior angel keenly. But she wasn't alone. She had the memory of her mother and father. She had the song in her heart that told her freeing Michael was the right thing to do.

She had another reason to run. The call of Lucifer's wings was incessant and it was interfering with Michael's ability to tap into their power.

Finally, in the early hours of the morning when all was hushed and still, Lily shrugged into the straps of her backpack just as she had several months before. Only this time she didn't plan to return. She'd already checked the hallway. For whatever reason, Grim was not there. She was grateful and regretful at the same time. She'd like to ruffle the mutt's smoky fur one last time.

Instead, she dipped a finger in the neglected glass of wine and smoothed the pinot noir over her lips. In spite of her earlier thoughts, she would leave the palace with the taste of Michael's kiss on her mouth.

Ezekiel wasn't without power even though he was no longer the daemon king. After he met with Michael, he knew it was time to set the last stages of his plan in motion. Grim wasn't happy. He whined and paced from within the cage where Ezekiel had tricked him with an enormous bone from a creature a mortal man would have found impossible to name. The bars of the cage were sanctified with Latin prayers. Grim avoided them in his pacing, but the prayers diminished his power and kept him from dematerializing.

"Trust me," Ezekiel scolded. Grim only growled, whined and paced some more.

He wanted to do his master's bidding. He wanted to watch over Lily to keep her from running away. But the former daemon king had another plan. One he'd brought forth decades before.

Lily had to run.

She had to be lost in order to be found.

She needed to embrace her power and discover her aptitude.

Most people thought that Ezekiel had planned for decades for his grandson to assume the throne, but those people were blind, including the woman he'd always intended to be queen.

Grim didn't come when he called. Even if he hadn't been wearing Lucifer's wings, the dependable hellhound's lack of appearance would have alerted him to trouble. He'd wanted to check on Lily without disturbing her after his meeting with Ezekiel. He'd wanted to give her time to adjust to the idea that he'd chosen the throne. Of course he understood that Ezekiel had used Lily to get to him. It had worked. He had been drawn to her as anyone with Brimstone blood would be drawn. She had awakened the burn in him after years of tamping it down and ignoring that part of himself. It was also true that the wings didn't sit well on his shoulders. He wanted to shrug them off and replace them with his guitar. Even though he'd learned to accept his Brimstone and his daemon heritage, the wings felt wrong somehow.

As if they belonged to someone else…

That feeling had to pass because he had to wear them to keep Lily safe. He'd already used them to protect her from the Rogues and the damned. In those moments, they had fit him perfectly. When her aura had risen up and connected with his Brimstone power and the power of the wings, he'd found his true purpose.

Protect Lily at all costs.

Not because of her affinity, but because of who he was—a D'Arcy, a Turov and the son of an Ancient One. In that moment, passionate song, fury and flame had united in him as it never had before. He had banished the Rogues back into the wall through an icy shadow that seemed both horrible and familiar. It, too, had exuded a protective vibe.

Now he was left with a crown that seemed to fit him wrong.

It wasn't until Grim didn't respond to his call that he felt in his element again. His Brimstone flared. His affinity rose. Something was wrong. He'd wanted to allow Lily time to recover and he trusted Grim to alert him to trouble, but now he knew his struggle to accept Lucifer's wings had distracted him from danger.

He didn't know how much danger until Ezekiel and Grim met him at the door of Lily's rooms.

"She's gone. She won't last in the outside world. She had to have known that. They'll hunt her down and this time they'll find her alone," Ezekiel said.

Michael slammed through the door, barely pausing to hear his grandfather's words. He knew the room was empty before he looked around. The air was still. There was no song. Lily's starlit gown lay crumpled on the floor. He stooped to pick it up. He cradled the airy folds against his chest. He wanted to hold Lily. To protect her from all who would harm her. She'd lived a protected life that was actually anything but safe. And her guardian, the daemon king, was the greatest danger of them all.

"You drove her to this," Michael said.

"Yes. I did. But not for the reasons you suspect," Ezekiel said softly. "Find her first. Save her. Protect her as only the son of a Guardian can protect her. And then you'll both understand."

Michael allowed the dress to fall back to the floor. But when he turned to claim his hellhound from Ezekiel's grip, he was stopped by the tiny wooden sculpture his grandfather held out in his hand. It was Lily's special kachina doll. The one she'd called her warrior angel. The one that had his face.

"Your father's name was Michael, too," Ezekiel said.

"Take this to Lily. It's time she accepted it back into her possession. She has nothing to fear from your father. He's been protecting her all along...until her true Guardian could assume his role."

Michael remembered what Ezekiel had said to him when he'd first visited the hell dimension.

*I will protect the throne for you until that day.*

Michael's heart swelled and his chest tightened at the same time. He reached to take the kachina from Ezekiel's hand. He felt its chill when his hand closed around it, but it was more familiar now. He recognized it from the shadow that had helped them against the Rogues.

"There's a reason these wings don't sit well on my shoulders," Michael guessed.

"You already have wings bequeathed to you by your true father," Ezekiel said. "It's time for you to claim them. His sword has also been waiting for you. Beside the throne. You need to retrieve it before you go to her. It's yours. Your legacy."

Michael reached to take Lucifer's wings from his shoulders, but Ezekiel stayed his hand.

"No. Take them with you. She'll need them to save us all," his grandfather said. "I'll follow with our people, but an army won't be enough. Rogues and their human slaves are converging. They've been coming together for months. The ones you both fought were only the leading edge of a vast movement. Retrieve the sword. Take Lucifer's wings to her. And follow your heart. Your heritage will show you what to do," Ezekiel continued.

Michael hoped it was true. The night before, his heritage had united in his veins. He'd followed its guidance and nothing had felt more right. But the idea of Lily out in the world open to attack with no one by her side hollowed out his bones. Nothing was enough to fight that. Not Lucifer's wings or a tiny kachina doll. Or the dusty old broadsword he'd tried and failed to brandish as a teen.

Ezekiel finally released Grim, and his loyal hellhound came to press against his side as if he was apologizing for being tricked by the daemon king.

"I will die to protect her," Michael said. The words came up hotly from the churning depths of his gut. Grim knew he was ready to go almost before he did. The hellhound disappeared beneath his fingers and he felt his material form follow along. First to the throne room and then to Lily. To Lily's side. She never had to fight alone as long as there was breath left in his body.

"I never doubted it or you," Ezekiel said to the empty room. He'd manipulated everything, including time itself, to give Lily the Guardian she deserved as queen of the hell dimension. He only hoped all his efforts hadn't been for naught as he turned to gather the Loyalist daemons who would help Lily return to her throne.

The throne room was cold and dimly lit. He and Grim materialized midstride and Michael continued without a break in his step. Grim ran by his side. Michael took the steps to the dais with one leap and landed in a kneel before the dusty suit of armor he'd once thought so large.

Slowly, he rose and reached for the sword.

He'd known the display was meant as a memorial. He'd just never known it was a memorial to his father and a placeholder for his own destiny. But hadn't he been drawn to the sword over the throne all those years ago? He narrowed his eyes as his hands closed over the hilt of the sword as if it had been forged for his grip. He looked up and measured the breadth of the hammered shoulder plates with a glance and found, to his surprise, that they might not fit him now because they were smaller than his.

He had grown.

His Brimstone still burned uneasily in his veins, bubbling up like lava he didn't quite trust, but he was easily able to brandish the broadsword with the muscles fueled by hell's fire.

There was no reluctance in him when it came to using this sword to protect Lily.

Grim whined and paced, stirred by the coming battle and Michael's growing fury.

When his Brimstone seemed to ignite the blade in a shimmering crimson heat wave, Michael didn't resist. He raised the blade aloft and pointed its tip at the sky. For Lily. He would burn for Lily with no reservations.

He'd been cautious for too long. He carried the scars of his near-death experience with him always as a constant reminder of how his inability to control his first Burn had almost killed him as a child. He'd burned in his nightmares and fought the burn during every waking moment. It hadn't been death he'd feared. It had been the idea that he might harm the weaker beings in his life. Humans. Loved ones. His family. His friends. That had been the Guardian nature he'd inherited from his father driving him with a passionate instinct to protect.

But it was time to put caution aside.

His fire was required to help Lily. He'd had twenty-one years to learn to control it and now it was time to use the control he'd honed. He would loose his Brimstone fire through his sword as a Guardian to the throne. He would risk immolation to save her. He no longer feared his burn would hurt the woman he loved.

# Chapter 26

Lily had taken one of Ezekiel's pathways. It had been a strategic risk. If she had summoned her kachinas to use a sipapu portal, she might have alerted Michael. This way she only risked running into the former daemon king, and though it felt like Russian roulette she hoped he would be too busy feeling triumphant to be traveling at 3:00 a.m. the first morning of his retirement.

It wasn't until she dematerialized that she took out her flute. She'd known where to enter from observing the daemon king's comings and goings, but she would need her affinity to guide her. She'd never tried to direct her travel, but she knew it was possible because of Grim. Regardless of where he dematerialized, he followed the paths to where he or his master needed to go. Lily had left her kachinas unwrapped in her bag. She played to call them in the same way that she "walked" between worlds. The idea of her flute and the idea of her hands and lips responded to the idea of playing even though she had no physical form.

She walked when she was sure she was being led in the direction she needed to go. It seemed a long time of wandering before her materializing feet finally met firm ground. She stepped into the gloaming light of an Arizona sunset with her silver flute in her hand and the last notes of a Hopi lullaby fading into the coming night.

But something was wrong.

She had expected to begin as she'd begun months before. Slipping into the desert to run and hide and run some more. She'd planned to continue her work to close the old sipapu portals until no more could be found. Then she'd planned to wander the world to escape detection.

She hadn't expected to be met with a wall of Brimstone heat so fierce that it dried her eyes and stung her skin. It was as if she'd stepped into the glaring noonday sun instead of desert twilight. Lily griped her flute tightly. It was her only weapon. She didn't have Grim or Michael by her side. She was no longer buffered by Ezekiel or his immense Gothic palace.

On the horizon, she sensed a stirring. She squinted and strained to see into the distance in spite of the waning light. Suddenly, the silhouettes clarified. One after another after another. She'd materialized in a canyon. Near her feet was what appeared to be a natural drought-caused crack in an ancient riverbed. Ezekiel's portals often showed themselves in ways that mortal eyes wouldn't understand. Disguised in plain sight.

But using this one had placed her at strategic disadvantage.

She was surrounded by an army of Rogues. She could sense their Brimstone and their hunger from a great distance. Time in the hell dimension was liquid and its anomalies often bled over into this world. They had known she was coming. Just as Ezekiel had built the palace for her before she was born. Mortals called it fate. Some religions called it predestination. Ezekiel was adept at reading the whispers that foretold the future as they came back through the pathways between worlds, but some whispers became shouts that anyone could sense and hear. Her affinity had radiated from this portal before she'd even known she would use it.

Lily was here. She was always going to be here. To face an army alone.

She knelt and shrugged out of her backpack. Her dolls rattled together without their wrappings. She took them out, looking at each one as if she might never have another chance. Her mother had carved each doll—Fire, Wind, Earth, Water. They held her mother's love as well as her beliefs and her artistic heart.

Lily had never been alone.

She placed them carefully in a sacred circle. She missed her warrior angel. He should be here, too. To help her take a final stand against the darkness. A large full moon had begun to rise. The Rogues on the rim of the canyon were thrown into stark relief by its light. They knew she had come. She could feel their excitement as they were each alerted to her presence by her affinity.

Her song was back, full force. Whatever interference she'd experienced when she'd been resisting Lucifer's wings had disappeared. A cool wash of adrenaline chilled and stiffened her spine. She crossed her legs, straightened her back and lifted her flute to her lips. This time she didn't play a lullaby. She played a battle song. It wasn't one she had played before. Knowledge of it rose from the kachina dolls as she played each note. And with it rode an energy she'd never experienced before. It was the aura of affinity in a loop. From her to the dolls and back again. From her to her ancestors and back again. From her to the elements and back again.

She didn't understand the increased power until Michael and Grim materialized out of the shadows across from her glow. Grim's hackles were already up and his legs were splayed wide. His intimidating maw was open and she'd never seen his teeth so large and jagged. He lifted his nose to the sky and howled. The noise rent the still night air into a million jagged pieces that seemed to stab her ears. But she continued to play. She rose to her feet as she played.

Michael commanded the move by his presence. He didn't howl at the moon or bare his teeth, but he was as ferocious as his hellhound. His eyes were flame and his fists were clenched around a sword she recognized. The empty suit of armor in the throne room stood without a weapon now.

Lucifer's wings seemed to shriek in her senses.

"I'm sorry, Lily. I can't let you run away again. Not without following you wherever you feel you have to go," Michael said.

She wanted to step into his arms. She didn't. Instead she played even louder. Using her affinity and the power she absorbed from Lucifer's wings to amplify her sound. The Rogues on the horizon had begun charging down the ragged incline to attack. But her elemental spirits responded to her call.

Wind whipped her hair into her eyes.

Rain began to pour.

Before long the damp strands of hair were like stinging lashes against her skin.

And still she played.

Grim had rushed to meet the Rogues and their human slaves. Screams began to rip through the night as lightning flashed. Michael moved toward her instead of going to join Grim in his fight. Her song stuttered as her breath grew light. The wings were too close. Their power joined her aura. She couldn't resist. The magnet was too strong.

"Stop resisting your heritage, Lily. Haven't you learned anything from my mistakes?" Michael said. He came to her and looked down at her as she played her flute. He touched the side of her face. "Ezekiel sent me. We misunderstood all along. The throne was never meant for me."

He stepped around her, being careful not to disturb her playing. But his firm, warm hands on her shoulders made her tremble, as did his breath against her ear when he leaned down to speak from behind her.

"Brace yourself. This is going to burn," he warned.

She didn't know what he intended to do until the fire settled heavily on her shoulders. She expressed her scream through her flute. And the Rogues began to burn. Only then did Michael join Grim. At first she thought that her warrior angel had somehow materialized from the walls of the palace because there were great shadowy wings outspread on either side of Michael's tall, muscular form, but it was him, all him, as she'd known him to be all along.

He wielded a sword she'd only ever seen displayed on a suit of armor by the throne. But it was her song amplified by Lucifer's wings that had set the sword into flames. Every Rogue he met with the blade disintegrated into ash, but there were so many. As she continued to play, she realized that Michael and Grim protected her in a determined circle just as they had before. Her guardians. Her protectors. While she waged war.

They would lose.

There were too many pressing down from the canyon walls against them. As Rogues and human slaves poured into the canyon, more replaced them in wave after wave. Lily played. Her elemental Fire spirit consumed Rogue after Rogue. Michael fought. Grim savaged. But they would lose. The numbers were against them even with the power in Lucifer's wings magnifying her affinity.

Or was it? Her affinity was love. The wings had magnified her fire and her fury and, yes, those things were rooted in her heart, but she had yet to truly tap into the possibility that the power of her affinity could be increased.

She loved Michael. But long before she'd allowed herself to love him, she'd loved her mother, her warrior angel…and Ezekiel.

Lily continued to play, but she changed her intention. She infused her song with the ache of her emptiness—for the ones she'd lost, for the one she'd never had. She called. With all the affinity that Samuel Santiago had bequeathed his daughter. She called. Lucifer's wings burned through the leather jacket she wore. They turned it to ash and it fell away in a sudden cloud of gray particles carried on the wind. Her T-shirt remained, but she could feel it scorch and she could smell burned cotton and flesh. She didn't scream. Not even when the base of each wing fused with her naked skin.

She fell to her knees with the pain. She didn't notice that the wings that had become a part of her were no longer bronze. They were bare and black as raven's wings, but they were malleable. They folded behind her and draped on the ground. She didn't scream because she continued to play. To an observer, she might have seemed a pied piper calling the Rogues to their doom as they poured over and down the cliff's edge to the death of Michael's sword or Grim's teeth. But in reality, she called others. She called them with all her heart.

And they came.

The crack in the earth in front of her widened. It yawned wide and belched smoke like a wakening volcano, but from its depths, instead of lava came the Loyalist Army materializing out of the shadows in full battle regalia. Ezekiel led them. He wore his old armor like a second skin as scarred and hardened and strangely beautiful as his first. He rode forth on a pale horse that was second only to a hellhound in hideousness. Reaper. He was a mighty destrier more bone than flesh with flaming eyes and a mouth full of razor teeth. She'd fed him apples in his retirement, but now he looked more than ready to fight. Reaper shrieked and more of his fellows poured from the crack in the earth with Loyalists on their backs.

She didn't see Victoria and Elizabeth, but she felt them. Somewhere Michael's mother sang and her sister played her cello. Their affinity wasn't as strong as Lily's but it was persistent. Their husbands rode with the army. She glimpsed them flanking Ezekiel on either side. They were buoyed by their wives' music. It strengthened the hint of Brimstone they both still had in their blood.

They were mortal. Coming to her aid was a horrible risk. Their courage sent a thrill of admiration through Lily's veins.

But it was a giant icy shadow that followed the army that finally stilled her song. This time the winged shadow had manifested as if it, too, rode a horse, one made of smoke instead of bone. Her warrior angel had responded to her call. Her stillness interrupted his charge. He "rode" over to her kneeling form and folded his shadow wings at his side. The giant bowed to her tiny form and she shivered beneath the press of his chilling presence.

But then she found her breath and began to play again. And Michael's father joined the fray. He leaped over her. The frigid air of his passing stiffened her fingers to the bone. There was only one who hadn't responded. It was too soon for her mother to return. When her ceremonies called ancestors, it was ancient ancestors who responded to guide her with their wisdom. Yet her frozen fingers warmed more quickly than they should have and she didn't feel alone. She suddenly had the sense that her mother had never left her.

His scars glowed with the light of a thousand suns and he allowed the fire to consume him. Once his body burned, every cell ignited and the flames channeled out through his father's sword to cut down every Rogue in its path. The Brimstone was his heritage as much as the sword and they were both tools he used to protect his loved ones. He harmed no one, but those that deserved it. His scars weren't a warning or a reminder of a time when he had no control. They were badges of honor. Crimson streaks on his skin that proclaimed him as the living embodiment of the flame that would protect the throne and the woman destined to sit upon it.

If he survived the conflagration.

The heat was agony as well as triumph and he was every bit as consumed as he'd been during his first Burn all those years ago. His battle cries were also cries of pain, but he didn't pause. He would face annihilation to save the ones he loved. He'd always known it. Now, he lived it. They fought all around him—Grim, Adam, Severne, Ezekiel—and Lily. He wasn't worried that his fire would harm them. He contained it except for the controlled bursts of power from his sword. He would die for them if he had to, turned to ash by the Brimstone he channeled to save them.

The carnage was complete.

The canyon floor was no longer sand and desert scrub. It was a field of ashes that shifted beneath the feet of the Loyalists in drifts they couldn't avoid. Eventually it would blow away or simply settle and become a part of the dirt that had absorbed millennia of detritus—from dinosaurs to daemons.

The fighting was over. Loyalists returned the way they'd come. Ezekiel led the way. She blinked back emotion when she noted that he had survived. She searched but didn't see Michael. The air was thick with ash and smoke. If he was hurt or worse, she was certain she'd feel the loss to her bones. She forced herself to kneel and pack her kachinas into her backpack. They had served her well. Her fingers shook when she placed her flute back into its velvet pouch.

"He's alive. He's alive. He's alive," she muttered the words aloud in a mantra of hopeful determination.

Grim had been by his side the last she'd seen. Severne and Turov would have risked their lives to help him. And the powerful spirit of his father would surely have prevented any harm coming to his son. Lily held her pack in front of her, curling her arms around it protectively, when she got back to her feet. Her shoulders were too tender to wear it the usual way even if the wings weren't in the way. She was surrounded by soldiers and their mounts. There was no way to see above or around the crowd to search for Michael. And there was no staying in place against the mass of movement. She had to move as well or risk being crushed beneath mighty hooves. Visibility was so poor that she would be nearly invisible if she stayed. She hissed when the first step jarred her back. But then she took another and another, ignoring the pain.

She would find Michael and Grim in the palace. One last look behind her was all she spared time for when she came to the crack in the earth. Ash and smoke. Smoke and ash. No Michael. No Grim.

Lily traveled between worlds, one second surrounded by an army and the next alone. She knew the way. Better than she had before. She saw the path although she had no eyes. It glowed in her consciousness in a way she'd never experienced before. Was this how Grim navigated? Had her fusion with Lucifer's wings given her this ability? If so, she could forgive the pain. She would heal in time and the gift of safe travel between worlds would be well worth whatever suffering she'd had to endure.

The palace welcomed her with a cacophony of confusion. The army channeled down hallways and corridors meant for much lighter traffic. Their passing stirred the denizens of the walls into a swirling torment of screeches and moans and grasping hands. In fact, when Lily materialized and saw the walls, she knew that much of the Rogue army they'd just defeated had found themselves trapped in stone.

Just as the wings had helped her see the pathway between the canyon and the palace, they helped her see that Michael had been right. She suddenly knew that the purgatory Ezekiel had caused to manifest in the palace walls was a reflection of his own loss and pain. He avenged Elizabeth's death, but the weight of all the tortured souls was wrapped around his own heart and soul like the chains of damnation.

Lucifer hadn't intended the hell dimension to be a place of darkness. He had wanted freedom. He had led others to seek the same. Allowing the imprisonment of Rogues and their human slaves to continue would make Lucifer's followers no better than those they fought.

Lily stepped to the nearest writhing wall. She ignored the painful groping of violent stone fingers. Lucifer's wings—her wings—spread out behind her so that she was protected from the press of the Loyalist army. She allowed her backpack to fall at her feet. Her hands trembled, but she pressed her palms against the wall. It—they—moved beneath her hands. She ignored the revulsion that tried to frighten her away from her task. She had given all she had to give during the canyon battle, but she searched deep within herself for more.

"Lily, no!" Michael shouted.

He was alive. He was alive. He was alive.

She didn't turn from the wall, but she felt a surge of renewed energy when Michael materialized behind her. His Brimstone blood was a bright, hot source of power he no longer tried to keep tamped down to prevent their connection. His heat amplified her affinity and it flowed through her hands.

"This is Ezekiel's pain. He's corrupted the palace with his grief and fury. I've got to set them free," Lily said. Her jaw was stiff and she spoke through tight lips. Her entire body had become as hard as the marble she forced her affinity to enter.

"It's not safe. Let go. Come away," Michael protested. He'd come as close as he could come to her without touching. He respected her choice and her interface with the wall even though his instinct was to warn her away from danger. His nearness bolstered her efforts. He supported even as he urged her to caution.

"It's not safe. You're right. They're trying to take me with them," Lily said.

When *they* became *he*, she sensed the change. Stone hands grasped hers with a punishing grip and a familiar face flowed into focus. Abaddon. The leader of the Rogues who had jumped off the skywalk when she used Lucifer's wings to ignite his Brimstone blood. She couldn't back away from the violent grimace on his marbled face, but even if he hadn't been holding her, she wouldn't give up. She tightened her own fingers and pressed her face closer. She met his stony gaze. She ignored the sudden lengthening of his clenched teeth as they became more like fangs. He had been a handsome daemon. But the carved representation of his soul revealed his predatory nature and the darkness that claimed him.

The other souls in the wall had drawn back, giving Abaddon deference. She immediately understood why. He wasn't only holding her. He was draining her. His darkness was a bottomless pit soaking up her soul like a hungry sponge.

The malevolent vacuum threatened to pull her apart. Her body had lightened as if she was completely hollowed out inside. She was a shell. Her physical form was still in the hell dimension, but the rest of her was drawn elsewhere by Abaddon and the other entities she tried to send away. The bag that rested on her feet interfered with the vacuum. The kachina dolls held her. They rooted her to this world where she belonged. But their hold was tenuous. Lily could feel herself slipping away. She watched in sinking dread as black marble began to seep from Abaddon's hands into her skin. It flowed like obsidian threads weaving into and replacing the flesh of her fingers and arms.

She cried out. Cold agony began to replace her human cells.

"No," Michael said. He pressed one hand between the wings on her back. Her world was with him. She knew it body and soul, and the emptiness inside her was suddenly filled with a rush of warmth and belonging.

"Oblivion calls. Or heaven. Damnation is a choice, not a sentence. Your time in limbo is over," Lily said.

Abaddon understood. His grimace turned to a silent scream. His grip loosened and his stone hands were absorbed back into the wall.

The threads of dark marble flowed out of her skin and back into the wall as well. But it didn't stop there. The inky color continued to flow. It moved away from where her fingers splayed against the marble, leaving alabaster stone in its wake. Abaddon and the rest of the stone carvings were swept along with the black, rushing away from Lily's hands and her braced figure. The former leader of the Rogues became one with the jumble of faces and figures as they turned into nothing but a mass of writhing, indistinct features and limbs. The hallway brightened as the walls lightened. Straggling soldiers stopped to stare.

Several bony destriers reared and shrieked in surprise. In the distance, greater reactions rang out, giving evidence that the change in the walls flowed outward throughout the palace.

"It's too much, Lily. You have to let go," Michael said. But he didn't try to force her away from the wall. She could feel him pouring more energy from his blood into her body.

"This won't just cleanse the palace of Rogue taint. This will save Ezekiel. It will help him to let go of his loss and move on," Lily ground between clenched teeth.

"I won't let you die to save him," Michael said. Both of his hands were spread on her back now. He was still giving her all he had to help rather than drag her away.

"I hope it won't come to that," Lily said. But she wasn't certain. Her body was human in spite of the affinity and in spite of her new wings. Michael was only half daemon. He gave her the power of his Brimstone heat, but although he was mighty he had a human half, too.

Grim had appeared with Michael. She only noticed him at the edge of her perception when he pressed his great ugly body up against his master's legs. From that contact, Lily felt a new surge of power, but it was much smaller than she needed to cleanse an entire palace. There were so many souls in the walls. She could sense each and every one as they flowed farther and farther away.

Michael's father showed in perfect gray contrast against the white wall when he suddenly appeared before them. He loomed as he spread his giant wings. Their tips stretched far to the left and right above them. Her warrior angel had arrived. Lily gasped. Grim howled. Michael jerked, but his fingers didn't lose contact with her body. She didn't pull her hands from the wall although she instinctively feared the touch of the frigid shadow. She'd seen him kill by absorbing daemons' Brimstone heat on the battlefield.

He was hungrier than the force she'd resisted moments before. And she wasn't free to cringe away from his touch.

"Don't hurt her," Michael ordered. Lily cried out again when Michael's hands grew hotter than her tender flesh could withstand without pain, but then his power entered her and strengthened her and the pain faded away.

"He won't. He won't hurt me. He's my warrior angel. He was always meant to save me," Lily said. The shadow had reached for her with enormous hands that suddenly became a normal size just before they met hers. Suddenly, she saw a version of Michael in her mind that she'd never seen. His father. As he'd been before he died. Beautiful. So beautiful and familiar he made tears well up in her eyes. But unlike his son, Michael's father had ancient eyes. He'd protected so many souls in his long life. And he'd died to protect the woman and the baby he'd loved more than any before. Somehow, Lily was a part of that love. He showed her that now. That he had always been meant to protect her because she would eventually love his son.

"Thank you," Lily said. Michael's touch kept her tears from falling. She could feel his hands shaking and she didn't want this to hurt him more than it had to. "He's going to help us, but it means we have to say goodbye."

"I'm sorry I resisted your legacy as long as I did. I was wrong. You'll always be a part of me. And I'm glad," Michael said.

The hands on hers seemed to solidify and warm. They still looked like shadow, but it was if a living person held her. The feeling passed in a flash as her warrior angel reared back and grew immense. He filled the entire corridor. Then he disintegrated in a thousand shadowy pieces that flowed outward to chase and complete the cleansing that Lily had begun.

He magnified the force of her affinity and Michael's

Brimstone by a thousandfold and the force of his clash with the remaining souls sent shock waves back through the connection. Lily was thrown from the wall. Michael was shoved by the blast of energy and his hands fell from her back. Grim left claw marks in the marble floor as his body was forced several feet against his iron will.

Silence filled the palace halls. Lily lay beside her backpack, drained, but breathing. She appreciated the slow, steady inhale and exhale before the silence was replaced by the noise of stunned soldiers getting back to their feet.

Michael came and found her collapsed near the newly emptied wall. She was completely depleted, but there was a smile curving her lips. He lifted her into his arms. He was covered in Brimstone blood and ash, but his jaw was soft. He was no longer pained by the wings now that they had become a part of her. The mantle of the hell dimension was where it had always belonged.

"My queen," he murmured against her ear. She wrapped her arms around his neck.

"Your father was a guardian angel, wasn't he? Before he chose to follow Lucifer to the hell dimension?" Lily asked. She already knew the answer. Her warrior angel had always been a guardian of sorts. Even before it manifested any power at all. And when Michael had first appeared to her with shadow wings, they had been his actual wings and not an illusion after all. They were with him like an aura, a gift from his real father that showed only when he was fully connected to his purpose.

"Yes. And he watched over us one last time," Michael said.

"Like father, like son," Lilly replied. Her wings, no longer Lucifer's wings, fluttered when he settled her closer against his chest. "Will you be the queen's Guardian, Michael D'Arcy Turov? Till death do us part?"

"I resisted the throne because somehow I knew it wasn't my destiny. I was always meant to follow in the footsteps of your warrior angel. But I'm no angel, Lily. I'm half daemon and I find my Brimstone blood drives me more than I ever knew it would. I burn for you. For the song we create together," Michael said. "So I have to reply till death do us part...and longer. Far, far longer."

"The queen of hell knows nothing of angels. I've spent my whole life in shadows, but Brimstone fire creates a light I can't resist. I was going to. I was going to run away to keep you from being tied to the throne. I didn't realize the throne was meant for me," Lily said. Something in the way her grip around his neck changed alerted him to a sudden shift in her mood, and Michael stopped to look down at her face. The remaining Loyalist army was returning to the hell dimension through the widened portal she'd made. They parted like a sea around Michael where he stood. It was still an intimate moment. With Michael, the whole world disappeared while they flew alone.

"You are free to go. I would never force you to stay in the hell dimension with me," Lily said. With the Rogue army defeated, she might be freer to come and go than she had ever been, but she was still determined to marry only for love. A tiny spark of hope in her heart reminded her that Ezekiel had always intended for her to assume the throne, but she'd loved him without being sure of a return of affection for too long not to be gun-shy. She hoped the empty walls would help him to heal and be able to give and receive the love he'd denied himself for so long.

"You'll be my queen and my wife for as long as it makes you happy," Michael replied. He leaned to kiss her and in spite of an entire army around them, Lily focused only on his wine-flavored lips until a very tired Grim bumped up against Michael's legs. Her soon-to-be husband lifted his mouth from hers and Lily reached to ruffle the top of Grim's smoky head.

"Ever after, then," she promised.

# *Epilogue*

Ezekiel groomed his bony destrier himself. After many months of retirement, he still enjoyed his time with the creature that shared his memories of the battle field. The great beast enjoyed the attention and after his eons of loyal service, he deserved it. The fading purple glow on the horizon indicated that night was falling. He led the horse-like creature back into the stables and into his worn stone stall. The destrier's plated leather armor was gathering dust on the wall.

Ezekiel had loved and lost. But he rarely lost otherwise. The Ancient One and former daemon king had been one of Lucifer's closest allies and friends. But he was rarely as impulsive and temperamental as the first king of the hell dimension had been. He was patient. He had spent centuries building a palace for a girl he hadn't met. One who would end up filling his life with song…and sorrow. Because he played a long game and it took precedence over his heart. That organ was scarred, but it had still been difficult to resist the beautiful, passionate Sophia and her persistent daughter.

They had been his dearest loved ones for many years, but he had kept his distance because it wouldn't do to coddle a future queen. It wouldn't have been safe to name her as his heir. Not until she was wise enough to fully embrace her affinity's power and accept her place. Not until Michael accepted the full burn of his Guardian legacy to stand by her side. He had channeled his love into the fight against the Rogues and the help he had given the D'Arcy family. All without knowing if his plans would fall into place. Autonomy was a tricky thing to manipulate. Lily and Michael had to be free to choose their places even if he'd been certain of what those places should be.

He had used the palace to slow time itself so that Lily and Michael would be peers. He hadn't done it lightly. It had been the greatest work of his long life, but it had also been his heart's desire.

He had long considered Lily the daughter of his heart.

Sophia had suspected. Especially when he had helped in the creation of the secret garden with his own two hands. She had visited the conservatory often to watch him dig in the dirt. He had kissed her once in a moment of weakness. Sweet, sweet Sophia. Nothing more than a kiss. He wasn't a monk, but she was human. And he'd already learned his lesson about loving mortal women.

He hadn't been able to save Elizabeth, but he had tried to be true to her memory by loving her family. They had become his even though he'd never been able to claim her as his bride.

Kissing Sophia had been a mistake, but no more so than the garden. She had loved him deeply ever after. Or at least as long as she'd lived. He'd tried his best to honor her even as he broke her heart.

He hoped she forgave him. Lily had been given a palace, the garden, a Guardian and ultimately the throne. He hadn't foreseen the wings. He'd thought she would assume the mantle and wear the bronze wings as he had worn them. Her affinity was greater than his plans. She had become a better leader than he could have foreseen even with his experience. And Michael was a formidable regent, a Brimstone prince by her side whom no one dared go through to harm her.

"You know she feeds him apples. I'm not at all sure they're good for him," Sybil said. The seamstress—among other things—came up behind him as he stood at the stables behind the palace. He had an entire wing for his retirement apartments, but he was often too restless to enjoy them.

His destrier whickered at the woman who threatened his treats as if he protested. Ezekiel turned to meet his oldest ally. She was as lovely as she'd always been. Daemons weren't immortal, only nearly so, but they did not age as mortals aged. If you knew where to look you could see their age in their eyes. Sybil's eyes were bottomless pits. Deep and dark and too knowing by far. He ignored the tingle of awareness she always caused when she appeared out of the shadows. He'd never had time to explore those depths or the feelings they inspired in him.

He had sacrificed much to fulfill his duties to the throne. And fate had seen fit to tempt him time and time again with strong, desirable women he was forced to admire from afar.

"It's time. Lily is asking for you," Sybil said. Did he imagine a softening in her tone toward him? Several centuries of experience with her speech patterns made him more aware than others would be of subtle changes. Then again, she was a beautiful and alluring creature and he was a former king with far too much time on his hands.

"All is well?" he asked. He acted as if he had expected her arm to slip into the crook of his as they walked back down the path from the stables to the palace. He prided himself on keen observation and an almost preternatural ability to manipulate the future, but Sybil was like time and tide—he'd never seen her wait for a man. Not since her heart had been broken by John Severne's father. When she took his arm and pressed close against his side, he was surprised…and warmed.

"There has been an interesting development. I'm to wait and let Lily share the news," Sybil said.

Ezekiel knew better than to challenge Sybil when she was wearing the slight curve of a Mona Lisa smile. Instead, he allowed her to lead him into and through the palace. He enjoyed the feminine feel of her body close to his. He had more time for such simple pleasures now. And no matter how long you lived, the beginning of a romance was something to be patiently savored. They walked by the alabaster walls that still startled him with their brightness. He noted that there were additions to the art collection his adopted children and grandchildren had begun to add on the perfect marble backdrop the walls now created. He appreciated the character and warmth the paintings added. He understood why they shied away from sculpture of any kind.

The walls had stayed white and smooth after Lily's transition. There was no way to know which of the prisoners had been redeemed or which ones wound up in Oblivion, but they were no longer trapped in the purgatory of the palace's walls. He hadn't intended to create a limbo out of anger and the need to avenge Elizabeth's death. He'd tapped into the power of Lucifer's wings in an unwholesome way and that's why they'd never really been his. He hadn't been truly worthy of the crown. He hoped he had rectified that by giving the wings a queen fit to wear them. So fit that they had become a part of her.

Finally, he and Sybil arrived at the new royal apartments he'd designed for Lily and Michael. They'd been built around the time he'd built her garden and had lain empty waiting for their queen and her prince. He hadn't only been focused on his loss. Deep down he'd had hope for the future.

He wasn't surprised to find the front living room filled with guests when he and Sybil stepped inside, unannounced. Even without a herald, everyone in the room turned to face him when he entered the room. His D'Arcys—Kat and John Severne and their gangly teen son, Sam, as well as a toddling daughter. The little girl cooed a French lullaby to a ferocious hellhound who could have eaten her in one bite, but instead, lay with his enormous head in her lap. Grim's puppy. Ezekiel had given him to Kat and John's son as a birthday present. Victoria and Adam Turov were also present, of course. They looked as striking as ever even with streaks of gray in their hair. He experienced a pang at the gray. One he'd felt before. When you loved humans, you inevitably lost. Sybil squeezed his arm as if she'd noticed his momentary distress. She was nearly as old as he was. She probably had.

"Lily's in the bedroom, glad to be home. Michael is with her. Then again, I don't think he's left her side since she conceived," Vic said.

"The hazard of being married to a man whose father was formerly a guardian angel," Adam joked.

"What's your excuse, love?" Victoria teased. They'd had two other children together after they married. Ezekiel didn't doubt that Adam Turov had been a fierce protector of his wife when she'd been pregnant. He was a bonafide hero with a following of hundreds if not thousands of people who owed him their lives.

"Elizabeth and Charles?" Ezekiel asked.

"They had to return to school, but they promise to visit during summer break," Vic said. The palace was no longer a place that her children avoided at all costs. In fact, Ezekiel had noticed the younger the child, the less fear they had for different worlds and different beings.

Yet he still stalled rather than go to Lily's room. He

wanted to see her baby. He wanted to see her and reassure himself that she was fine. But he was experiencing an unusual amount of uncertainty. Of all his adopted offspring, Lily was his greatest treasure. He'd loved her before she'd been born. He'd loved her long and risked everything to give her the throne she deserved.

"Come on. She has a surprise for you," Sybil said. Kat came over to take Ezekiel's other arm and the two women flanked him on the way back to the queen's bedroom. The royal suite was warm and filled with Southwestern touches that made Ezekiel think of Sophia. When they entered the open door of Lily's bedroom, the first thing that drew the eyes was a mantel filled with kachina dolls above a cheery fireplace. In the very center of the display was the smallest doll. Unlike the others, it was finely carved in the manner of a Renaissance sculpture. It looked very like Michael Turov, but it had actually been a carving of his daemon father. One of Lily's Aztec ancestors had seen the fallen warrior angel in a prophetic dream. Ezekiel wasn't surprised to see the tiny kachina Lily had always treasured in a place of prominence among her belongings.

"It's about time you came to welcome them home," Lily said.

Ezekiel turned from the mantel to a large chaise where his adopted daughter and heir reclined. He was ancient. He was always. He was the Great Manipulator who had saved the hell dimension from Rogues and the evil intentions of their human slaves, but he was speechless when he saw that Lily Santiago Turov held two bundles in her arms, one on each side.

"Allow me to introduce Sophia and Samuel," Michael said with a bow and a gesture toward the babies Lily held. He was dressed in worn jeans and a black T-shirt. It didn't matter. His bearing was every inch his father's in that mo-

ment—a warrior angel—with the impression of his con-
stantly carried guitar faded onto the back of his shirt. "His
cousin Sam gave us permission to use the name again as
long as we promised never to shorten it."

Ezekiel stepped forward. Kat and Sybil let him go, but
when he glanced at them their hands joined to clasp and
they drew together as the dear old friends that they'd become in spite of some rocky times they'd experienced in
the past.

Time flowed in unusual ways in the hell dimension and
there were pathways between worlds that whispered the
secrets of future events, but Ezekiel had been so focused
on his plans for Lily that he'd never looked beyond her to
a bright alabaster palace and the joyous, growing family
that would fill it for generations to come.

"I've succeeded in surprising you. That's one to record
for posterity," Lily teased. She looked tired, but lovely. Her
navy silk gown was covered in stars that had been pains-
takingly embroidered with silver thread by Sybil's loving hands. The twins, a boy and a girl, were wrapped in
patchwork blankets that looked too fine to have been created by anyone other than the daemon seamstress herself.

Ezekiel moved to Lily's side. He didn't bother to wipe
the tears that tried to stream down his face. They turned
to steam and evaporated before all but the most astute of
observers could notice them. When he reached his adopted
daughter, he looked down at the babies and saw hints of
both Michael and Lily in their tiny faces. When he touched
their cheeks, one was hot and one was cold. There would
be interesting days and years ahead as they learned what
parts of their fantastic heritage would pass to them.

"You have given me a great gift this day," Ezekiel said.

Michael stood beside him beaming, but also watchful.
The former daemon king imagined it might take a Guard-

ian to keep up with two growing children who might manifest interesting abilities.

"They *are* the greatest gift," Lily said. She looked down at her sleeping newborns and then up into Ezekiel's moist eyes. Hers widened. Perhaps she had seen the tears.

"No. You are the greatest gift. You saved this world. You gave us light and song," Ezekiel said. "I love you."

The whole room seemed to gasp at his declaration. Which was ridiculous. No one loved as a daemon could love and he had loved more than most. He just didn't make a habit of saying it. Words didn't do the depth of his feeling justice. They never had.

"I know," Lily said. Her dark eyes shimmered with the reflected light of a thousand embroidered stars before he leaned to wrap her and her two babies in his gentlest embrace.

The babies were sleeping. Lily was glad to have a babysitter with Victoria's ability to sing the perfect lullaby. No challenge she'd ever faced had prepared her for the birth of her twins. After several weeks of motherhood, she was happy to escape the palace for a little while. She followed the pathway Michael and Grim had taken before her. Her wings weren't capable of flight, but they stretched out behind her and the feeling of flight claimed her as it always did when she thought of her husband.

She leaped from the pathway onto the desert sand and gloried at the broad expanse of midnight-blue sky and stars that twinkled above her. She and Michael often visited this particular place at night.

He was waiting where she'd expected him to be with Grim by his side. They were silhouetted against the sky on a small rise over the earth-bermed hideout where she'd first seen his scars.

"Your mother is brilliant with the babies, you know. I'll never be able to get them both down and out at the same time," Lily said. She took her place on the other side of her husband. He reached to welcome her with a strong arm, pulling her against him so the night air wouldn't chill her.

"Never is a long time for a daemon queen," Michael teased. He turned toward her and leaned in silent invitation. She wrapped her arms around his neck. He lifted her when he straightened until he held her above him. She dipped down to kiss his upturned lips. More perfect than any statue. More hers than she'd ever imagined they could be.

"This night is ours," Lily said.

"Ezekiel gave you the sun. I like giving you the stars as often as possible," Michael said. He placed her feet back on the ground and nudged her toward a plush quilt he'd spread while he waited for her to join him.

Anticipation tingled along her skin. It joined the lightness in her stomach and the flush from Michael's Brimstone and the vast sky all around them to make her dizzy. She gladly tumbled to the ground, pulling Michael with her. Tonight they would sleep under the stars, protected by the sword that Michael had stabbed into the ground beside the quilt, their hellhound who stayed silhouetted on the hill and the power of her wings.

"Ezekiel gave me wings, but you're the one who taught me to fly," Lily said.

Michael's wicked laughter drifted out into the night to echo down all the pathways from heaven to hell and all worlds in between.

\* \* \* \* \*

# MILLS & BOON®

## n o c t u r n e™

**AN EXHILARATING UNDERWORLD OF DARK DESIRES**

---

## A sneak peek at next month's titles...

**In stores from 19th October 2017:**

- **The Witch and the Werewolf** – Michele Hauf
- **Vampire Undone** – Shannon Curtis

---

*Just can't wait?*
Buy our books online before they hit the shops!
**www.millsandboon.co.uk**

**Also available as eBooks.**

# MILLS & BOON®

## Why shop at millsandboon.co.uk?

Each year, thousands of romance readers find their perfect read at millsandboon.co.uk. That's because we're passionate about bringing you the very best romantic fiction. Here are some of the advantages of shopping at www.millsandboon.co.uk:

* **Get new books first**—you'll be able to buy your favourite books one month before they hit the shops

* **Get exclusive discounts**—you'll also be able to buy our specially created monthly collections, with up to 50% off the RRP

* **Find your favourite authors**—latest news, interviews and new releases for all your favourite authors and series on our website, plus ideas for what to try next

* **Join in**—once you've bought your favourite books, don't forget to register with us to rate, review and join in the discussions

Visit **www.millsandboon.co.uk**
for all this and more today!